Praise for
Ruby Among Us

"Ms. Forkner has given us a gift
spiraling pace. Neither rushed nor
fying journey I will long remembe
—JANE KIRKPATRICK, award-wi

"Highly recommended. If you're a mother or daughter, you're going to love *Ruby Among Us*. Forkner does an extraordinary job.... I look forward to more from this author."
—ANE MULLIGAN, Novel Journey

"A multigenerational saga of hope, regret, and the grace that brings us home, *Ruby Among Us* evokes an invitational sense of place, a cache of characters you enjoy knowing, and a story that rips and mends your heart all at once."
—MARY E. DEMUTH, author of the Maranatha Series

"So engaging from the first sentence. I found myself holding my breath as I read. Tina has painted the pictures so real. I love the honesty and innocence. Mothers and daughters alike will feel very connected with this book."
—CINDY MORGAN BROUWER, singer/songwriter

"Don't miss this one! Tina Ann Forkner is a strong new voice in fiction and *Ruby Among Us* is an amazing story of trials, regrets, and, ultimately, redemption. Lucy and her family history in the historic wine country of Sonoma bring to life the Scriptures about the Vine and his branches."
— KRISTIN BILLERBECK, author of *The Trophy Wives Club*

"*Ruby Among Us* is a haunting, beautifully told novel of past secrets and present pain. Lovely, lovely voice and story. A remarkable debut by Tina Ann Forkner, an author to watch."
—COLLEEN COBLE, author of *Anathema*

"A subtle, intimate story of grace and redemption that touches the heart!"
—PAMELA NOWAK, author of *Chances*

"Forkner writes from a place of intimate transparency, allowing the reader to discover priceless treasures found in the pursuit of truth. Ruby's story unfolds in fascinating layers, revealing at its core the universal power of a mother-daughter relationship."

—BONNIE KEEN, speaker, vocalist, and author

"Reading is a passion of mine, and when I find myself identifying with the characters, anxious to get to the next page to find answers to my questions, I know I'm into a good book! The daughter-mother-grandmother theme in *Ruby Among Us* pulled me in. Wonderful storytelling."

—JORDIN SPARKS, 2007 winner of *American Idol*

"If you're a fan of fiction that inflames your heart and your spirit, Tina Ann Forkner has a debut novel you should read. *Ruby Among Us* is filled with powerful emotions of secrets, joy, grief, the freedom that is found in the truth, and, ultimately, in redeeming love."

—KIM HILL, worship leader and recording artist

"What an incredible story. As both mothers and daughters, *Ruby Among Us* struck a special chord in each of the four of us. Tina writes in a way that makes us feel like we're there; from the first line, we were captivated and drawn into an intricate weaving of the precious and fragile relationships that define us."

—POINT OF GRACE

"A skillfully written, moving tale of women (and their men) who find that love covers a multitude of sins. Tina Ann Forkner weaves this story together with great detail and, like the quilts that are such an integral part of the novel, pieces it together with beautiful results."

—DEBBIE SMITH, songwriter with and wife of Michael W. Smith, and mother of their five children

"From the first page of this emotionally gripping novel, I was absorbed in Lucy's story. The author weaves a beautiful tapestry of meaning and grace, with an underlying truth: every heart needs a place to call 'home.' Lucy's journey toward her place of belonging is poignantly told."

—KIM VOGEL SAWYER, author of *Blessings* and *My Heart Remembers*

Ruby
AMONG US

A NOVEL

TINA ANN FORKNER

WaterBrook
PRESS

RUBY AMONG US
PUBLISHED BY WATERBROOK PRESS
12265 Oracle Boulevard, Suite 200
Colorado Springs, Colorado 80921
A division of Random House Inc.

ISBN 978-1-4000-7358-0

Emily Dickinson poem #561 is taken from *The Complete Poems of Emily Dickinson,* ed. Thomas H. Johnson. Boston, MA: Little Brown and Co.

Ruby Among Us is a work of fiction. Names, characters, places, and incidents are the products of the author's imagination or are used fictionally. Any resemblance to actual events, locales, or persons, living or dead, is entirely coincidental.

Published in the United States by WaterBrook Multnomah, an imprint of The Doubleday Publishing Group, a division of Random House Inc., New York.

WATERBROOK and its deer design logo are registered trademarks of WaterBrook Press.

Library of Congress Cataloging-in-Publication Data
Forkner, Tina Ann.
    Ruby among us : a novel / Tina Ann Forkner. — 1st ed.
        p. cm.
    ISBN 978-1-4000-7358-0
    1. Mothers and daughters—Fiction. 2. Intergenerational relations—Fiction. 3. Domestic fiction. I. Title.
    PS3606.O7476R83 2008
    813'.6—dc22

                                                            2008001777

Printed in the United States of America
2008—First Edition
10 9 8 7 6 5 4 3 2 1

*For my light, Hannah, who made
my time as a single mom brighter.
Having you makes everything happier,
sweeter, and lovelier. May your talent
and determined spirit brighten the lives
of others when you grow up.*

I love you.

ACKNOWLEDGMENTS

To my buddies, Jake and Dawson, who brought SpongeBob and *Star Wars* into my life. I could not have found a better pair of brothers for Hannah anywhere. I love you both.

Albert, thank you for encouraging me to get out of bed every morning and finish this novel. Your belief in my writing is a gift that I will always feel undeserving of, but my love and gratitude will always be yours. Your commitment to me, the boys, Hannah, and this family has changed my life for the better. Thanks for giving me the opportunity to soar.

Thank you to my parents, Dennis and Barbara Ann Gray, for never doubting that I would someday get published. I am forever grateful for your encouragement and belief in my dreams. I would never have been a writer if not for the both of you. And to my brother, Troy, and my sister by marriage, Laura, for supporting me through the tough times of single motherhood, when much of this book was truly conceived.

A heartfelt thanks goes to my manager, Cheri Kaufman, who put herself on the line by placing this manuscript on my agent's desk. Sister, this book might never have seen the light of day without you. Many thanks to my agent, Chaz Corzine, for his unwavering belief in my abilities and to the folks at BHCC Management. I hope I live up to the wonderful expectations you have for my writing.

Thank you to my late grandma Carrie Mae Gray; Clara Mae Brewer, the grandmother I learned about through stories; and Wyvonne Guthrie, who was taken entirely too young. Their stories still inspire.

Thanks to the WaterBrook team for believing in a first-time novelist and for working so hard to get *Ruby Among Us* to readers and to Kelly

Santee for my first amazing cover. Special thanks to my editor, Jeanette Thomason, for believing in this book from day one.

To the CSU Sacramento English Department for introducing me to great writing and particularly to poet Dennis Schmitz, who helped me find my voice, and to author Mary Mackey for her course about writing maternal biographies. Thanks for letting a fledgling undergraduate into your grad courses. My writing is better because of it. And to my poet friend Lisl Swinehart for telling me to keep writing after graduation.

There are many who did things big and small during the writing and publication of *Ruby:* the Laramie County Library Foundation in Cheyenne, Wyoming; the Laramie County Library; Dardi Roy; Kim Giffin; Marjorie Smith; Victor Simental, for helping me name Lucy; Nancy Forkner; Art Brewer; Marcia Linde; Jami Kirkbride; Veronica Linde; Phyllis Guthrie and Rosalie Forkner for being grandmothers through love if not blood; my RMFW (Rocky Mountain Fiction Writers) coffee group (Mary, Amanda, Liz, Marjie, and Pam); and friends from ACFW (American Christian Fiction Writers).

And to my friends: I can't name you all because I might leave one out. Thank you for being there. If I canceled on you, thanks for being patient every time I said, "I have a deadline…"

And to the One who brought me through my darkest times. Thank you, Jesus.

CONTENTS

PROLOGUE

I've seen it in winter, a mangled-looking structure even when cut back, the house itself faded and worn beneath the blossomless, dormant branches. Always in spring it rejuvenates itself, its stunning softness covering bare thorns, redeeming itself after only a few weeks of redressing its vines. We call it the Rose House, and I can only describe it as it stands before me, abundant roses in various shades of scarlet and burgundy climbing up its sides and rambling across the rooftop.

It has become a symbol of our homecoming, and the grapevines themselves cannot counter the beauty of that cottage in full bloom, but they come close as their leaves flesh out along the branches of the vine. Around me, the mission-style main house sits among the working buildings and gardens, parading more heirloom roses, herbs, and cascades of flowering vines that I know Ruby has touched. The vineyards of Frances-DiCamillo roll away and swell out over the hills and across a good part of the Sonoma Valley, where the town of La Rosaleda sits almost in the center.

Tourists come here too, and most can't resist snapping photographs of the Rose House. I think for them the Rose House symbolizes the possibility of a great romance that once surpassed time and place. They need to be reminded, in the midst of their personal sorrows and failings, that love does still exist somewhere in this place between us and heaven.

I like to think all those photographs of the Rose House are hanging on the refrigerators of housewives, pushed into the visors of taxicabs, framed and hanging on the walls of busy offices, or maybe even tucked into the wallets or purses of those who dare to dream that something as astonishingly beautiful might await them somewhere over the next hill.

For me the Rose House, like Frances-DiCamillo, means a lot of things, but remarkably it signifies one important event in my life that I only dreamed could happen and that I will never let myself forget—this is where I found Ruby again, even though I know now she was never really gone, only in flesh.

Ruby's life left an imprint among these vines and roses, and these days I find myself spending more time at Frances-DiCamillo than anywhere else, always seeking that embrace from the one who loves me unconditionally. I go home to be encircled by the vines, the Rose House, to be reminded of who I really am, and to revel in the inheritance Ruby sought out for me before it was lost again, for a time, with her death.

HOW TO MEASURE GRIEF

Lucy

The first person to hold Ruby was the last person to let her go. That was her mother, Kitty. I watched her kiss Ruby gently on the forehead while she was still connected to that big, noisy machine, though I already felt that Ruby wasn't really there. She'd been asleep so long that day. They said it was a coma. I was on the other side of the window but could tell the moment her heart stopped. I saw a doctor turn off the machines I knew had kept her body breathing. I knew; Ruby was gone.

I watched through the glass as Kitty fixed her gaze on the monitor, a frightened look in her eyes, as if she hadn't been aware her only daughter was dying. Her face contorted with pain, and she crumpled over Ruby's body. Her shuddering seemed to shake the walls around me.

I wrenched away from the white-collared preacher and his wife and ran and ran toward that gleaming silver room. People called to me.

"Lucy. Stop. You can't go in there. Children aren't allowed."

Big hands tried to grab me.

But no one could stop me. Ruby was gone, her breath taken away when the respirator had been removed, and Kitty was alive and alone. She needed me.

I burst through the heavy door and threw myself toward Kitty's slumped body. She turned to me in time to spread her arms wide. I fell into them, and she caught me and held me so tightly I thought I might stop breathing. I kind of hoped I would; I could have died at that moment, snug in Kitty's arms. But after a little while she loosened her embrace, and I reflexively inhaled, an involuntary instinct of survival my eight-year-old body performed against my will. My lungs, now filled to near bursting, could no longer contain the sob that had been crawling from the well in my chest since earlier that day when I'd found Ruby lying on the back porch.

Ruby had been watering our flowers—a wild mix of cosmos, daisies, and tall wild varieties of blooms that attracted butterflies and hummingbirds to taste their sweetness. That afternoon she'd called for me to look at a hummingbird drinking from the hanging feeder beside the back door.

"Lucy! Come see! The hummingbirds are like little bees!"

She always told me when they came so we could watch and count them. The weekend before we'd seen ten at the feeder.

"And *mija?* Please grab my inhaler too."

She said the part about the inhaler casually, almost like an afterthought.

"Coming, Ruby! I'm pouring the lemonade!"

I'd always called my mother and grandmother by their given names. I don't know why Ruby or Kitty allowed it, but they did.

I knew other children who had mothers and grandmothers with boring names, but not mine. Even my own name was picked by Ruby because she thought it was special: *Maria Lucero.*

"Oh, my Lucy," she explained. "*Lucero* means *light.*" And where a ruby is loud, red, and hard, she said, *Lucero* meant all that was bright and the very air I was to her. "You are my breath, my very life," she would whisper in my ear, kissing the top of my head. I never imagined Ruby as hard and loud—the things she said her name meant—but instead as smooth and vibrant. Though I didn't know how to tell her at the time, she was my light, and I wanted to be just like her.

Ruby. Kitty. The names rolled off my tongue like crayons on paper; I liked that. The day before, my red crayon had rolled off the table as I drew a picture of Ruby, my hand in hers, each of us with a blue flower tucked behind our ear. We dove to catch the crayon as it dropped to the floor and giggled at how it seemed late for some appointment under the couch where we couldn't reach it.

"We will need helping getting out that one, Lucy." Ruby smiled, and I knew someone would be over to help, a friend whose name I could never remember...

"Lucy!" Ruby called again from outside. "The hummingbirds are going away!" I heard a cough. "Do I need to come help you, mija?"

"No, Mommy! I'll hurry!"

During special times, like before bed, I'd call her Mommy. Sometimes I called her Mommy Ruby, even if it sounded silly, because it was our secret name. She was Mommy *and* Ruby to me, and I could call her both.

I'd carried the glass pitcher toward the fridge, sloshing lemon-ade all over the floor, when I heard Ruby call me a third time.

"Lucy, hurry!" she coughed, hard. "There are two now!" Ruby coughed again, more violently.

Hurry, I told myself. I grabbed our glasses and scrambled to the coffee table in search of Ruby's inhaler. She usually left it there, but not this day. I thrust the glasses on the coffee table and rushed to look in the bathroom. Kitty was always nagging Ruby to keep her inhaler in the same place all the time, but Ruby was too busy.

Running from room to room, I searched until I finally found the inhaler on the nightstand beside Ruby's bed. My breath came out in deep, short gasps as I rushed back to the coffee table for the lemonade glasses, this time careful not to spill the drinks.

When I reached the door, the hummingbirds were gone and the heavy glasses of lemonade crashed to the deck, covering the porch with sticky glass shards. Slivers of glass surrounded Ruby, glistening like jewels as she lay on the porch where she'd fallen.

My hands flew to my mouth to stop my scream. I needed to help Mommy Ruby. I knelt to wipe away the glass, but it cut both of us, spotting my hands and her arms with little dots of blood. I shook Ruby and she moaned.

"Wake up!"

I remembered the inhaler and frantically pawed to the edge of the porch where it had been flung, cutting my hands more on the glass shards.

"Breathe, Mommy Ruby! Breathe!"

But she couldn't. I saw the panic in her widening eyes and tried to spray the inhalant in her mouth and nose. Her flailing began to stop as I tried to breathe into her with my mouth like I'd seen on TV, my own breath a weak whisper.

"Ruby..." I cried as loud as my cracking voice would allow. "Help! Please, help!"

Nobody came.

So I screamed, loud and piercing.

Neighbors appeared. Someone pulled me off Ruby and handed me to someone else with a hard chest—someone who held me while my small fist bounced off him. I tried frantically to force myself down. Neighbors had circled round Ruby, and I was pulled away to the scream of an arriving ambulance.

In the emergency room the flat red line on the machine blared in my ears, and Kitty pressed her wet face against me as her tears mixed with mine. The nurses wheeled Ruby out, leaving Kitty and me standing in the hallway, very still. It was that quiet moment of death, when things move in slow motion, when strangers turn sadly away as they pass your family in the halls and the medical staff stares with hopeless expression at the floor.

I felt poised, panicky, and completely frozen in time all at once. I searched the hall. Cold floors, shiny metal, too-bright light hurting my eyes. Then it rose like an earthquake and rumbled out of me: a quiet broken noise followed by a clear, piercing cry.

"Ruby! Mommy Ruby!"

I tore down the hall.

The nurses who were rolling away her bed froze on the spot, staring as if I'd turned into a monster. One nurse tried to keep me from tearing the sheet from Ruby's face until a doctor stopped and silenced her with a look.

"Let her say good-bye to her mommy," he said quietly.

The other nurse turned to me with tears and helped me fold back the sheet.

I put my hands on each side of her face. "Mommy Ruby, I love you." I leaned over to kiss her lifeless lips and gave her a gentle hug, like I would have done when she was napping or when I was the first to wake up in the morning. Then I smoothed her hair and put my hands on her face like I'd done a million times when I tried to sweet-talk her.

"I'm sorry for not coming sooner with your medicine," I whispered.

The nurse gently helped me cover Ruby's face, and she was gone.

I turned back slowly to find every person in the hallway sobbing and not one grownup to hold me. The abandonment terrified me. Where would I go without Ruby? Who would take care of me? Would I be sent to an orphanage like in that movie *Annie*?

"Lucy!"

Kitty moved from the back of the small crowd where she'd been standing, stunned by her own grief. "Lucy! Come here, baby. Come to Grandma Kitty."

I ran. Grandma Kitty wanted me, and I knew in her arms I would be safe.

No one questioned Kitty as she carried me out of the hospital, put me in her car, and drove me home—to Ruby's house.

How strange it was to come home without Ruby. Only the buzz of the fridge greeted us; immediately I had the urge to find Mommy Ruby even though I'd just felt her cooling skin on my lips back at the hospital. I ran around the house, calling her name, looking under the kitchen table where she used to take cover during games of hide-and-seek. Kitty hadn't stopped me in my mission to find Ruby alive until I stood in the center of the living room crying, reaching out to touch the roses in the middle of the coffee table, as if they were Ruby herself, not loud and vibrant but soft and delicate.

Wordlessly Kitty reached for me, hugged me to her, and took me for a bath.

I screamed when she doused my shampooed head with water. Ruby had always warned me before rinsing so I could hold my nose. Kitty didn't even tell me the water was coming. I coughed and sputtered, lashing out at her for being so mean, half expecting to be given choice words of punishment.

Instead Kitty pulled me out of the tub and wrapped my goose-bumped limbs in a fluffy pink princess towel. I slipped into the Barbie gown she held up, and she tucked me into bed, saying it wasn't my fault Ruby died. In my heart I didn't really believe her.

Kitty had a way of looking at things that most people found strange. Ruby had always said so. Now Kitty said that since she was my Ruby's mommy, I could be her daughter too.

"A granddaughter is a kind of daughter." She leaned down and kissed my nose, just as Ruby would have done, and turned out the light.

I felt only a short moment of panic that Kitty wanted to replace my Ruby, but I was too tired to argue about it.

Kitty said good night; it was so much like Ruby that I knew Ruby had learned it from her—except for the prayer. I wanted our prayer that night, but Kitty didn't know how to say it. With her eyes cast to the side of my pillow, she quietly offered to learn if I'd teach it to her, but I said no. It was my prayer and Mommy Ruby's prayer anyway, I'd decided. I would never say it with anyone ever again. Not even Kitty.

The morning before Ruby's funeral, Kitty found me in a big, old white chair on the back deck staring at the sunrise. There were no hummingbirds, just bright, empty sky.

I pretended Ruby sat with me in the chair the way we'd sit together in the mornings before school. I imagined that my hands resting on the arms of the chair were interlaced with hers; if I closed my eyes long enough, I could feel her breath on my neck and her kisses—unending kisses—behind my ear, through my hair, at the nape of my neck as she whispered how much she loved me.

I had dressed in the yellow and orange floral print sundress Ruby had bought for my first day of school. I hadn't worn it yet and wished Ruby was there to iron out the wrinkles still creasing it from the store racks. I knew grownups wore black to funerals, but I didn't have anything black. Besides, Ruby had always said I looked pretty in bright colors. I smoothed the soft cotton dress over my knees and waited for Kitty to chide me.

"I should have known I'd find you here." Kitty stepped onto the deck. "Ruby told me about your little morning teatimes together."

I said nothing. It was true, but I didn't want to share it with Kitty right then. I only wanted Ruby.

Kitty extended a red floral teacup. I stared hard at the steaming cup for a few moments, trying to imagine Ruby's hand giving it to me. But I couldn't summon the vision. I took the cup without a word and sipped deeply. The tea tasted good, just how I liked it— not very hot, not very strong, with cream and sugar.

"You look beautiful, Lucy, just like Ruby."

I looked up at Kitty and admired her long black muumuu dress with the rich red rose print. The roses blossomed over her heavy chest, down her trunk to the hem, enfolding in the seams and opening back up, the fabric flowing with her steps as she walked toward me. I couldn't articulate the idea at eight years old but grasped clearly that this was Grandma Kitty's way of rebelling against dreary mourning garb at her daughter's funeral.

"Look at me, Lucy."

I stared at the roses on the muumuu, unable to look in her eyes because then I'd see Ruby and the big hole in my chest would deepen and hurt even more.

Kitty cupped my chin with her hands and turned my face to hers. I saw her red-rimmed eyes, teary pools in the center.

What happened to my strong, bossy Kitty? I wondered. This face was so forlorn and weak.

I was happy when Kitty barked again for me to look at her. The sternness in her voice made me feel more secure, like she was in control, taking care of me. She took me firmly by the shoulders. "It's terrible, a terrible thing, you losing Ruby. I-I don't know why." She fumbled with words between sobs. "I don't know why God did this to you—to us. I don't." She took a breath and fell silent, her carefully applied makeup now tear-streaked.

Tears streamed down my face too.

Once, Ruby had said God was a friend to children. I wasn't sure when she'd said it—so many memories had already begun to fade the day after her death—but if it were true, then why did he take her from me?

"Your mom," Kitty was saying, "would defend God and say he always has a purpose." She shook her head and stared at her hands, then away at the sky, as if she wasn't really talking to me. "I don't know what God was thinking." Her eyes followed the sunrise as we sat quietly. "How could you do this?" she asked the sky.

Something brought her attention back to me. "Oh, Lucy, you're shaking."

"I'm sorry, Kitty."

"You haven't done anything to be sorry for, dear." She reached to me with a lace-edged embroidered handkerchief. I worried about soiling the pretty fabric with my tears, but Kitty dabbed at my face like she didn't care. "You're just a little girl and can't understand such things. All this talk about God and his not being here for us must be confusing."

But I understood more than Kitty knew. I'd already begun tucking away most of the memories of my mother; I felt my faith being hidden away too. Later I'd wonder if I was tucking away my faith to protect it or to get rid of it.

But then all I knew was that Kitty didn't think God was there for us, and I felt the heaviness of that drop over me, a blanket of fear and confusion.

Even as I followed Kitty's emotional leading, I thought of Ruby, and at that very moment I felt like a bad girl doing something I was sure my mom told me to never do…because secretly I still believed in heaven. Ruby was there. And if there was heaven, wasn't there God? Ruby had told me so, hadn't she?

I reached from my confusion toward Kitty, wanting to make her feel better and hoping she could make me feel okay too. She was so sad for Ruby; I was so sorrowful for Kitty. We both loved Ruby and we'd both lost her. And then Kitty told me a granddaughter is a kind of daughter, and I was hers.

I looked over at Kitty, who was staring up at the hummingbird feeder. A jeweled green bird had appeared, flitting around us like a bumblebee. I wondered if it noticed that Ruby was gone, if it had watched the whole thing, witnessing how slow I had been that day.

I balanced my teacup on my knees and watched the hummingbird dart around us. It paused near my shoulder, its wings buzzing, as if studying the splashes of color on my dress. Was he accusing me? I glanced at Kitty again, but she said nothing, as if it was an expected thing to have a hummingbird fly right up to me on the day of my Ruby's funeral. Her eyes followed the hummingbird as it darted away, staring long after it had disappeared.

My cup rattled, causing Kitty to finally turn her head slowly toward me, and the hollowness of her eyes, so lost and sad, engulfed me. I knew that I somehow should have found Ruby's inhaler faster, but I didn't know Ruby could die. Now I had not only hurt my Ruby, but I'd hurt my Kitty too. The doubt seeded in my mind started to grow, its roots already reaching deep. What if God was mad at me for not getting help to Ruby in time? What if he had already forgotten about us?

What if Kitty didn't have anyone but me?

Kitty leaned toward me then and took one of my small hands in hers, careful not to upset the teacup in my lap, her red wooden bracelets softly clunking with the movement. We didn't talk anymore before the funeral, just sat holding hands and looking out over Ruby's garden. I knew one thing only then. Kitty wasn't Ruby, but she would take care of me.

A grandmother was a kind of mother too.

2

M y home, Ruby's home, became Kitty's too, and she moved in all of her things.

"You will always be close to Ruby this way," she said. Secretly I wondered if this was really for my sake or more for Kitty's because, as she moved in, we moved out none of Ruby's things. Her antique piano still sat in the corner. Her blue velvet wingback chair stood nearby. Her bent tubes of oil paint lay heaped on a small table surrounded by canvases, some empty and others half-finished, waiting for details to be filled in. Finished paintings filled the house too. Fifteen self-portraits by Ruby lined the walls of my bedroom. The twelve-by-twelve blocked canvases hung side by side, a sort of border that I loved and studied every day as a soldier does a photo of his children and wife, hoping to be reunited when the war is over.

Only I knew I didn't have the hope of seeing Ruby again. At least not in the waking hours.

In dreams Ruby came to me. Sometimes in nightmares I would see her moving desperately through the house, looking for an inhaler. When she found it, she'd clasp it to her lips, sucking deeply, like getting a fix from a cigarette. I could only watch, paralyzed, all the fear and sadness coming over me. Then Ruby would sit down, breathe deep, and when she had her breath back, she'd smile at me like this had been no big deal.

I would wake relieved. But only for a moment before remembering that Ruby was gone.

In more pleasant dreams, I relived our last day, remembering how she woke me with a glass of orange juice. I'd been parched from the heat of the evening before and gulped down the juice so fast Ruby laughed—clear, happy. She handed me a pair of scissors then; together, on my bed, we cut out paper dolls as we had so often when she was alive.

My favorite, even to this day, was the woman in a full, green taffeta gown. Ruby said she looked like Scarlett O'Hara, a brave lady from a book she'd read once. Scarlett had yanked her curtains off the wall and sewn a new dress when she had no more fabric.

I laughed and told Ruby the curtain trick sounded like something she or Kitty would do. Ruby nodded in agreement and fluttered at me her favorite paper doll, a skinny woman wearing a water-blue straight gown and a tiara.

"Curtains fit for a queen." She winked. "Or Diana, a real, true princess."

Ruby told me a long story about Diana, how nice she was, how she liked to help people, how everybody in the world loved her because of her kindness and grace.

"Like you, Mommy Ruby!"

Her lips, red and shiny, broke into a smile, and the tear that slid down her cheek surprised me. "Mommy!" I whispered, touching the wet spot.

She smiled reassuringly at me. "Mija, thank you for thinking I could be a princess. You are the real princess. My breath, my…"

I giggled then. "I know. I am your light."

She'd kissed the tip of her finger and placed it on my forehead. "Yes, you are!"

The irony that she and Diana both died young in their lives and that Ruby told me about Diana on the same day she herself would die was never lost on me.

I always wondered if Prince William and Prince Harry missed Diana as deeply every living day as I did Ruby. I watched them during Diana's funeral on television, recognizing the grief on Harry's small face because it so perfectly mirrored my own. I'd bawled throughout the coverage, my own sorrow for Ruby pouring out as compassion for Harry. Watching the scenes from the funeral over and over, looking for Harry, I relived my own mother's funeral. The feelings were the same ones I would have later, in junior high too, when I discovered Emily Dickinson's poem, which begins:

> I measure every Grief I meet
>   With narrow, probing, Eyes—
> I wonder if It weighs like Mine—
>   Or has an Easier size.

I'd found the poem in the center of a book at the library—a large leather-bound volume creased open to poem #561, as if it had been read repeatedly by some other library patron. Instinctively I knew the other reader, like me, had grieved terribly, and after that I began searching the faces around me.

For years I treasured the Emily Dickinson poem in my heart. Only later would I understand why: that grief, though universal, can only truly be recognized in its purity when active and present and by others trudging through the same dreadful bog.

There is a picture of Ruby and me on the lamp table in our living room; in the picture I'm astride a shiny red tricycle with my light brown curly hair in pigtails and a huge grin on my face. Ruby, curly brown hair hanging forward over her shoulders, smiles too with rosy lips. Her whole face is lit up as she leans over me like she's pushing me along. We both look happy, but I can never recall the moment.

I couldn't recall much of life with Ruby, though her things surrounded me every day: the linen curtains on the patio doors that allowed the sun to pour through, the pictures of antique roses adorning the walls in frames of gilded gold or ornate, cream-colored frames, the painting of me in watercolors hanging in the center of the small living room above the antique piano. In the painting I have a small smile, and I'm holding roses tied with a bit of lace. Light pours out of the roses, shooting out an open window; next to the window is a ladder like I've seen on television in Spanish movies, the same kind women tossed handmade rugs over and tourists bought in gift shops. The ladder is knotty and almost red, with two clusters of dried yellow roses hanging upside down from one rung. Light from my roses shoots past them. The portrait is called "Ruby's Light," but I couldn't remember Ruby painting it.

Kitty said Ruby had been interested in her roots, and that's why she'd included the ladder.

"What roots?" I'd asked.

"Oh, Ruby was always enamored by the idea that we had some kind of Latino roots—even though she obviously wasn't full-blooded Mexican."

"Are we Spanish?"

"Oh, Maria Lucero. My Lucy. You sound like Ruby." Kitty reached out and smoothed back my hair before turning and busying herself with making tea.

While the painting intrigued me, the blue velvet chair held more mystery. I had a fuzzy memory of it, something never clear but seemingly important about Ruby and me in that chair. Kitty always dismissed my questions.

"It is just a chair, dear."

These were times I didn't really understand Kitty. I was confused that she seemed sad about my lack of memory of Ruby, but she seemed to always avoid my mounting questions or at least redirect my attention to something else, especially when I probed about the many quilts she'd made and placed over the couch, on the arm of a chair, and on the wall behind the desk. That last one was the masterpiece. Made of rich gold, red, and green patterned squares, this was the quilt Kitty said she'd hand-stitched for Ruby's high school graduation.

I asked Kitty if I could have it to lay across the edge of my bed with my other quilt of Ruby's.

"No," she said without explanation. It was rare for Kitty to ever outright tell me no, so I assumed the quilt was one thing in the house she'd claimed as her own—that is, besides me. She'd claimed me as her own the day Ruby died.

Sometimes I would test Kitty, asking her about things I knew were Ruby's, looking for something to hang on to—stories about the mother I was losing more in memory every day.

"Where did this come from?" I'd run my hand across the top of a heavy cherry chest or the mahogany table. I was getting older and becoming more aware that most single mothers—or grandmothers—in an apartment the size of ours couldn't afford such things. Ruby was never wealthy, according to Kitty, and these pieces were expensive. They didn't really seem like the Ruby in my mind. I'd always imagined that she would have picked out wicker or something else simpler.

"We found this at the flea market," Kitty explained once. "Other things were gifts from people who wanted to help your mother."

"Who would give such expensive furniture to us? Wouldn't Ruby have been happy with something not as expensive?"

"Yes, of course she would have settled for less, and she did settle in many ways." Kitty paused a long moment. "But some people like to give more than simply what is needed, dear. Ruby brought out that quality in people. And besides, she never would have refused their gift. She was too nice, a lot like you, Lucy."

"Who were they?"

"The people who gave the furniture to her? We don't know them anymore."

And that had been that.

Intuitively I knew I wasn't supposed to question Kitty, and so I didn't repeat my questions often. I'd always trusted Kitty because she had been the most steadfast person, if not the only person, in my life, but her secretive silence bothered me.

Even if I never quite understood how we had so many nice things in our tiny apartment, I loved our home and its furnishings. The roses, lace accents, quilts, and furniture had always represented Ruby's personality to me, giving me a taste of who she was and what she liked. I clung to certain things, willing them to bring back faint memories of Ruby. In particular I loved the round, amber-colored glass bowl that still sat in the center of the mahogany coffee table. Ruby had placed deep red roses in that bowl her last day; I always tried to keep it filled with flowers in her memory.

I did remember how she'd leaned over from her seat on the couch to inhale the roses' sweet fragrance in the morning, a cup of tea in one hand. The memory emerged on canvas when I was only twelve, and even though my strokes weren't as good back then, it became Kitty's favorite. She'd set it on a small tabletop easel on a side table in the living room.

That was when I threw out my crayons and started painting my memories on canvas. I couldn't photograph them, but on canvas I could refine them over time as things came to me in dribs and drabs. Most of my memories were as incomplete, hazy images emerging, broken and faded, like a photograph that doesn't develop all the way. But the memory of the rose bowl was complete, and my dream was to fill in all of the half paintings in my life with the truth.

"Your mom was good at painting and piano," Kitty had told me. "You will be too. You have Ruby's gift. If you keep practicing, you will no doubt surpass her." I took that to mean I had a long way to go to live up to the beautiful paintings by Ruby that were left to me.

My room was decorated with Ruby's stunning self-portraits and portraits she'd painted of Kitty and my great-grandmother Freda.

I tried my own painting of Freda from the only photograph Kitty had of her. I found the black-and-white photo in a dresser drawer. It had taken a week to paint, but it was worth it when Kitty saw the portrait propped on an easel in the living room. Tears had pooled in the dark circles under her eyes.

"Oh, Mama," she'd whispered as her hands found her damp cheeks. I'd known then that the likeness, even though it was painted in color, was accurate.

My paintings of Kitty, who was the one DiCamillo woman I knew well, were of her full figure, head to toe: voluptuous but trim and healthy, dressed in her favorite kimono-style dresses from old photographs when she was in her twenties and thirties. I painted her reading books, sewing quilts, and once, to her chagrin, I even painted her nude. I'd almost destroyed the painting when I saw her mortification. But when she calmed down, she asked why I'd do such a thing.

"It's a study of the human body, and yours is the only one I've ever really seen."

Kitty laughed and thanked me for shadowing various areas of the painting so that it really was modest. She said I'd been very complimentary by covering most of her generous derrière with her long, graying hair when she didn't even have long hair anymore. She'd loved the red scarf, which was the only color, though muted, that arose from the soft sepia tones.

After being assured I was simply experimenting with the human form, she made me promise I wouldn't study nudes anymore.

I did promise and continued to paint Ruby more than anyone else. Sometimes she looked a lot like me in the paintings, but I also painted her as she might have been at ages she never reached, like thirty or thirty-five, based on comparisons of her pictures and Kitty.

I lined these portraits above the self-portraits in my room painted by Ruby. I thought they were a nice comparison study of the way Ruby saw herself at times and the way I saw her or imagined her to be.

As well done as most of my paintings of Ruby were, they never seemed as good as Ruby's. Even Kitty hinted that Ruby was the more gifted painter of the two of us.

"But you, Lucy, are the most gifted piano player of the whole family."

Kitty did that a lot, compared Ruby and me like we were sisters and not mother and daughter. Of course, she might have gotten confused because I wasn't too much younger than my mother was when she'd died.

Often I sat at Ruby's piano and thought how someday I'd out-live the age of my mother. Would Kitty think then that Ruby was the younger of two daughters? I'd reach for the sheet music Ruby had left on the piano, imagining in my mind that my fingers were hers, dancing over keys she had touched. I wished I could play the music with her, that she would be sitting beside me on the piano bench, teaching me like I knew she had before she died.

I would have given anything to play one song with her, to feel her beside me, to ask her any question I wanted. So many times I wished I could just talk to Ruby.

As I grew, I longed for letters from Ruby to me, for friends of hers to dig information from, for a scrap of history beyond what was in our house. Sometimes I'd lie on my bed on top of the Wedding Ring quilt Kitty had made for Ruby and dream of her.

The quilt was made with green, purple, and gold fabrics, and

I wondered if Ruby had helped stitch it. Had she lain on this quilt before, dreaming of who she would be one day? Did she dream of me? Had we snuggled beneath the colors together?

I asked Kitty things like this because Kitty had kept Ruby's memory alive for me. But as Kitty became more reticent, I became more certain that the picture Kitty painted of Ruby's life wasn't totally accurate—like one of the unfinished paintings that had been left behind.

What could I do though? I was just a kid and owed everything to Kitty, who juggled a part-time job at the university museum with raising me, homeschooling me, and sewing quilts for extra money. It was an amazing feat really, sometimes requiring me to do my homework during the day while she worked, and then we'd have school when she got home at night. I liked the solitude we had because it allowed me to read, paint, or play my piano all day long. This encouraged Kitty, who always kept a close eye on me, constantly pushing me to work harder.

"I have plans for you, Lucy. I want you to do better than I have."

I took her meaning to be that, at some point in her life, she felt she'd stopped trying. I didn't want to disappoint her. So I studied and tried and pushed myself. Every day.

Later, when I walked to the museum after my college classes, Kitty would tell the museum curator, Louise Roy, that when I graduated with my humanities degree, I'd go straight into the master's program.

Louise, who had given Kitty a flexible schedule for the past several years so she could raise me, would always say, "I believe it. Lucy can do anything she puts her mind to."

While I hated for Kitty to brag about me to her boss, I had been admitted to graduate school and hoped it might make me more acceptable in the eyes of the older students. It's not that I really wanted to impress them, but I think they thought I was even younger than I actually was. I was young, but I hoped maybe by the time I started graduate school, I would be a more mature age—twenty—and I would get on better with the older students. Of course, I hardly had time to think that far ahead since I needed to get through my final undergraduate semester first.

The only thing that seemed to take away my joy of going to graduate school was the fact Ruby wouldn't be there.

I still wasn't over her death. Inside time had stopped—stopped the moment I watched Ruby's cherry wood casket lowered into the dirt. I'd sent a part of myself into the soil, and I felt an invisible pull toward that pit. Maybe that's why I had such a hard time remembering so many things about Ruby; a part of me had disappeared with her.

I wanted to remember all of my years with Ruby though. I'd been eight, almost nine, when she died, so I always thought I should have at least been able to recall back to age four or five. It wasn't so. My mind refused to hang on to hardly any of my memories.

Often I would pick up the picture of me on the tricycle, wishing for the millionth time that I could remember that moment. I stared into the image, imagining what Ruby's laugh sounded like.

Hadn't she laughed many times on the day she died?

I remembered one instance when I'd walked out of her bedroom in my Barbie nightgown, wearing her high shiny black heels and big, floppy straw garden hat. Her favorite red beads were draped around my neck, and I'd borrowed her lipstick. I could still hear her laugh, and for a moment I imagined it all around me. That was one memory I knew I must hang on to. I knew I mustn't let myself forget her laugh. It was the one thing I was never able to paint.

Mostly I worried that what I remembered weren't my memories, but stories Kitty told me that had become my own.

Was I like the woman who was so into her work as an archaeologist that when she was old she thought herself to be an Egyptian princess? I cannot remember which book I read that in, but the woman had heard so much about the princess, she'd simply adopted the facts she'd learned as her own reality. Maybe that was me. Maybe the few things I recalled were just stories I'd heard told to me or pictures I'd seen.

At some point I decided I would never be able to remember Ruby on my own, no matter how desperately my heart wanted a mother—not that I ever stopped wanting to know the truth of her every day. If I could only remember her and know who she was, maybe I could figure out who I was; maybe if I knew myself, I'd be able to paint a self-portrait to hang on my wall beside Ruby's. I imagined the completed paintings hanging side by side, but in reality Ruby had finished her canvas and I could not.

In fact, my self-portrait seemed ridiculous. I had no mother, no father, no other grandparents except Kitty. I could never get out of her why she wouldn't share about my grandfather with me, but she always said I didn't need to know everything.

She was wrong. I did. And so I replayed several times a day the rare memories I had.

Sometimes Ruby seemed so near that I could feel her arms wrap around my shoulders in a morning hug, pulling me against the warmth of the red lacy shirt she was wearing in her self-portrait. But constantly revisiting the day of her death became exhausting.

I went through a phase where it hurt to know—to literally feel—that Ruby had loved me and yet not be able to remember anything about her except the day I let her die. That part of me was still the little girl who wanted to know her mommy.

Nothing Kitty could say then comforted me as I turned to my dreams, trying to remember Ruby on my own.

In fact, Kitty would have to wait until I started to ask real questions, and by then she might've wished the questions had never started.

3

Kitty used to say that working hard is next to godliness, which surprised me because she claimed she didn't even believe in God. But I understood what she meant. Working hard was always a matter of self-respect for her, and it always had been for me too. She claimed that our family was filled with hard-working people.

"Our family?" I pressed.

She was quickly dismissive. "Let's just let bygones be bygones, dear."

Most of the time I did.

This night Kitty had worked extra hours at the museum, and I worried about how heavily she leaned now on the cane she tried to avoid using but needed on days when her arthritis flared up. She was too young to be afflicted by such pain, but she often joked it was her punishment for not leading the best life.

Louise, her supervisor, was a fortyish single mom who had always been able to afford day care and a housekeeper on her single salary. Kitty said Louise tried to pass her good fortune on to someone else, and the "someone else" just happened to be Kitty. I believed our lives might have been much different had it not been for Louise's compassion and the small amount of Ruby's life insurance. I appreciated Louise, but on nights like this one I couldn't help but wonder if Kitty should be working less.

I glanced up at Kitty from my chair.

"Why don't you sit?"

"You look busy," she said, sitting down in the blue velvet wing-back chair. She looked past me out the window and asked casually what was bothering me.

I swiveled my desk chair around to gaze out through the back patio doors with her and explained how I hadn't been able to concentrate because of thinking about Ruby.

Kitty patted my leg and gazed out the window at the sunflowers leaning in the breeze, their heads bowed toward the sun in the backyard of our Sacramento home. The sun was low in the sky now, with just a slant of light at the edge of the garden, giving the roses an old-fashioned daguerreotype appearance.

We both still loved Ruby's garden. Kitty usually came out on the back deck at about seven every morning with a much-appreciated cup of Earl Grey, cream, and sugar. We'd spend a few moments, comfortable in the silence, until someone eventually, regrettably shattered the silence with thoughts about the day. We'd share our plans with each other—little updates that kept us in tune. Sometimes it seemed it was the garden itself that kept us in tune. Often, we ended our evenings, like this one, gazing out at the garden again.

"What have you been thinking?" asked Kitty. "Is there some question I can answer?"

I watched her face, compassionate but guarded. I had been asking her many questions lately, and I wondered what she was reluctant to share. I knew she wouldn't tell me all I needed to know, and I guessed it was her right. In the end I had more respect for her than to pry too much.

As I sat with Kitty, I thought of the secret photograph I'd been hiding of Ruby, pregnant, with a man who looked to be in his thirties. Before I'd always thought the man my father. I'd wanted to ask Kitty about it, but the time I decided to ask, I looked at her eyes, so devoted to me and concerned, and decided it wasn't right. Maybe this night would be different. Perhaps it would be a good time to see if Kitty would explain some things about the photograph.

Afraid Kitty would say no, I took a deep breath and turned my now streaming eyes away from hers. I really did want to remember Ruby, my amazing mom born on the heels of an earthquake, but it seemed like I could never get the memories on my own. If I could do that, I wouldn't have had to rely on tugging difficult answers out of Kitty.

"Don't look so sad, dear." She leaned toward me, kissed my forehead, and gestured toward the cup of tea still sitting beside me on the desk. "Maria," she said, reverting to my first name. "I'm not that old, but my health is already failing"—she motioned toward the cane. "I might be alive until I'm ninety-nine, but I could die tomorrow. And I don't want to take your mother's memories to the grave with me. I will try to answer your questions, dear. Just ask them."

But not all of them, I thought to myself. I was feeling so conflicted about Kitty's selective sharing that I was almost ashamed of myself. My doubt about her honesty had been building over the last few weeks, and for the first time in my life, I considered sleuthing on my own for details about my mother and our family.

The idea haunted me like Ruby's face hovering in one of her self-portraits.

Every time I walked across the campus, I thought about her short tenure as a student at the small private university I attended. I wanted to know more about her. My anxiety had been building up, and nothing seemed to help. Even my more relaxing pursuits did only a little to help me escape from the thoughts that tormented me. The hole my mother had left grew as deep as the lake in which Kitty had once tried to teach me to swim. I'd felt myself sinking into the dark water and was sure I was drowning when what must have been a current swelled and lifted me up. I'd sputtered and cried, making Kitty promise I never had to go back in again.

Lately my paintings remained as incomplete as the emptiness of my heart. I could barely compose the piano sheet music I'd been working on, and sometimes I didn't even feel like eating. My desire to remember Ruby tormented me, and each time I asked Kitty questions about Ruby or our past, she responded but wouldn't say what I really needed to know. And I wasn't sure what that even was, but I knew she wasn't willing to tell me everything. I was convinced there was more.

Sometimes I would lie on my bed and let my eyes sweep the room, resting finally on the unfinished paintings, knowing that some of the details were on the canvas of my brain but cloaked by something darker that kept me from remembering. I realized it was partly a protective covering I'd draped over my memories as a child, but now I wanted to rip it away. If Kitty could help, I wasn't sure she would. I considered telling her I needed more than what she seemed willing to tell me, but every time I tried, I felt guilty. I needed facts too, not just her stories. I wanted to demand all of it, but I was afraid of hurting her feelings. After all, she was my grandmother and mother combined in one form.

"I don't mean to upset you, dear," she said, "but I've tried not to push. I admit I pressed too much when you were younger, but talking about it now might help." These were the times I was the most confused by Kitty. She wanted to talk, just not about everything—I knew.

She laughed quietly, oblivious to my inner turmoil. "Of course, you might not be a little girl, but you are still stubborn. You get that from me."

I had to smile then because she was right.

"Dear, even if you can't remember everything about Ruby, it all really happened. Wouldn't you at least rather hear about it from someone else than never know about her?"

Yes! I thought. *I would!*

If only she knew how much I really wanted to hear about everything, I wondered if she would tell me. I wanted to know the answers to things Kitty had not talked about for years. I wanted to know: Who was Ruby? Who loved her? Who was her father? And, of course, who was mine?

Kitty took a sip of her tea, allowing a moment for her words to register with me. I stared at my own cup, the steam now gone. I wrestled with the stubborn idea of remembering on my own.

"I will share my memories with you, dear," said Kitty. "They can be your memories too. And who knows? Maybe someday your own will open back up."

Yes, please, Kitty. Please share them with me, I thought. Share more than Ruby's talents and her day-to-day activities. Tell me where she came from. Tell me where you came from. Why do we look Latino, especially you, the darkest of the three? Why doesn't this matter? Who are the men in our lives? I wanted to know. All these thoughts circulated through my mind, but as usual I didn't say anything.

My heart thundered in my chest as I reached for the inhaler on the coffee table, but Kitty was already handing it to me. I breathed in deep before erupting into a mess of coughs. Kitty leaned over and gave me a small hug.

There was nothing else she was able to say that hadn't been said a million times, so she stayed silent and gently rubbed the back of my head until I could breathe normally—the same way Ruby had on her last day when I'd banged my knee on the coffee table. I recalled how she'd kissed my knee, rubbed the pain away, and then rocked me, rubbing the back of my head until I must have fallen asleep.

How I wished I hadn't taken that nap. I could never stop thinking about how I'd wasted all that time sleeping when I should have been spending time with Ruby. I was so slow at everything that day, especially at taking her the inhaler.

Taking a deep breath, I gave the inhaler back to Kitty. I inherited my asthma from Ruby—a bitter and cruel constant reminder of how she'd died. I sometimes thought the inhaler was a curse, maybe a punishment by an angry god that I wished I could throw away but couldn't live without. Just like Ruby couldn't.

Once, a long time ago, I tried to throw out my inhaler. When Kitty wasn't looking, I'd secretly walked out to the alleyway and quietly dumped every bit of apparatus and the refill cartridge into the garbage can. A neighbor, also taking out his trash, had looked curiously at me as if trying to see what I was up to. I remembered him as being the man who held on to me the day Ruby died.

I made eye contact with him as I stood beside the garbage can, and he looked straight at me. He didn't say anything but stared at me with a question in his eyes. And pity, of course. Everyone in the neighborhood would stare at me with pity every time I walked outside. The ones who still lived in the neighborhood knew about Ruby, and they all knew about my inhaler.

As I held the lid of the trash can up, the man who wouldn't let me go when the ambulance took Ruby away cocked his head, as if to ask what I was doing. We'd never actually spoken, me and this man, except for the look we shared sometimes when I would walk to the mailbox. We'd share a look that said he knew and that I knew he knew. We weren't friends, but I couldn't say we were strangers either.

On that day when I threw my inhalers away, I'd avoided the question in his eyes and knew he understood I was telling him to stay out of it. Then I simply shut the lid and walked back into the house.

I regretted all of this later when I had a particularly overpowering asthma attack. I recall I tried to hide out for a while in my room to conceal what was happening until finally I stumbled out to find Kitty. Surprised, she sprang into action but couldn't find an inhaler anywhere in the house. She'd rushed me to the hospital in a whirl, barely making it before I suffocated. I remember how the white-coated medical personnel met us in the parking lot as Kitty half dragged and half carried my twelve-year-old body toward the emergency room.

Of course everyone chastised me harshly, and Dr. Larimer grasped me tightly by the shoulders. He had treated Ruby for her asthma too and felt justified to give me a speech every time I did something an asthmatic wasn't supposed to do, which he said was far too often.

His hands actually hurt my shoulders that day as he squeezed, but I didn't care. I liked how the pressure felt. It brought me back to the present.

"I'm sorry, Doctor."

He surprised me then by pulling me close, like I was his family. At first I'd wanted to push him away, but when I felt his strong arms around my back, I was amazed at the firmness of his arms compared to Kitty's and decided to allow him to hug me. I remember thinking this was what it might feel like to have a dad.

I felt the need to ease my embarrassment. "Does this mean I'm your favorite patient, Doctor, or do you just feel sorry for me?"

As he consulted a chart, he winked and said, "You and Miss Kitty are my favorites, but don't tell anybody. I'm supposed to treat all my patients equally."

He then looked in my direction and said sternly, "Don't ever do something like that again, kid. We need you around."

I nodded soberly as he shook a new inhaler at me. "You have to use this, Lucy."

His face softened, and I noticed the tiny lines at the corners of his eyes.

"I know it's hard because of your mom, but if she were here today, I bet she'd make you use your medicine." He handed me a sucker then from a drawer and ruffled my hair. "You sure do look like her."

The thought of me looking like Ruby made me smile. I glanced at Kitty, who was watching the interaction from her chair. I think she agreed because the corners of her eyes looked moist.

Did I really look like Ruby? I felt proud as I thought of my curly brownish-blond hair, always in the way. Ruby's was the same but darker, and I wondered if she liked hers or if she ever wanted to cut and straighten it like I'd thought of doing.

Kitty seemed lost in thought when the doctor reached over and offered a hand to help her out of the chair. I recall how he put an arm around her and pulled her as close to his side as she would allow.

"Thank you, Matt." She used the sort of tone as if he were a son. "You're such a great doctor. It's good you're here helping so many people."

"Thank you." He looked at me. "Don't give Miss Kitty a hard time, you hear?"

I nodded my consent as I opened the sucker.

"Deal."

When we'd returned home, we found a bag on our front porch that, when Kitty opened it, revealed the inhalers and refills I'd thrown in the trash. Kitty had looked confused, but as she huffed at me and walked into the house, I turned to spot the neighbor man across the road sitting in his rocking chair.

He nodded at me. I flashed him a sheepish smile and, as I turned away, the hint of a wave.

I caught the slight wave of his hand out of the corner of my eye, and after that our interaction went from a look to a wave. We didn't really need more than that. We'd already shared the most important moment of my life so far. That was all we needed.

To tell the truth, I was embarrassed, and when I saw Kitty crying that night, I understood what I'd done. She'd been terrified she would lose another daughter, the same as before.

Looking at Kitty now, sitting beside me in the old, blue velvet chair, I started to think maybe she needed to revisit Ruby's memories for her own benefit, not just mine. Then again, how could I know what Kitty needed? Maybe it wasn't my business… but wasn't it? It was my history, not just hers.

I had a father, even if Kitty refused to talk about him. I had a grandfather whom she rarely mentioned and, when she did, never in any detail. Who was Ruby really, besides the collage of pictures and broken memory? Maybe the key lay with Kitty. Who was Kitty before I knew her?

4

H ow about in the Union?" A young woman from one of my courses suggested heading to the student building for lunch together. I still hadn't figured out why she was inviting me, even as I mumbled an acceptance. I suppose it could have been because of the day I'd embarrassed myself by having an asthma attack. I couldn't remember what brought it on that day, but I'd been trying to ignore it. Eventually I'd fumbled through my backpack looking for my inhaler as the teacher and other students glared.

Only Susannah, sitting at the desk beside me, had leaned in to help.

"Do you have asthma?"

Yes, I'd nodded, knowing I had the eyes of a wild woman as I dug through my pack, trying to pretend the other people and the hawk-eyed instructor weren't there.

Susannah dumped the contents of my backpack in search for what she must have known was an inhaler. I tried to mask my gasps for air, but the desperation grew as we saw the inhaler at the same time. We both reached for it, sending it skidding across the floor and at the feet of a man about the same age as Susannah, early- to midtwenties. He scooped up the inhaler and hurried over to me, not bothering to hold it out but putting it straight to my mouth. As I'd sucked in the medicated air that would clear my lungs, I felt Susannah's warm hand on my arm and the pressure of the man's hand on the back of my neck, his fingers gently propping up my head. *Humiliating,* I thought.

This is how the three of us first met, Susannah, Max, and me. Later there would be Susannah's husband, but at the time I didn't know she was married or that he was not. In fact, I was hardly able to think about either question as I gulped air.

The teacher's gaze fell to her shoes as she said softly, "Lucy, you may be excused for today."

I felt my face redden as Susannah packed my backpack; the young man even gathered my notebooks and placed them inside.

"Are you okay?" he'd asked gently, staring intently into my eyes, his green and deep.

I nodded, my eyes wide not only from the asthma attack, but also from the sudden closeup view of this man's face. I'd seen him before and had noticed instantly how handsome he was, the easy way he would walk to the front row desks and sit down each week, his long legs stretching before him. I'd never imagined seeing his face so near.

"I'll go outside with her," said Susannah.

He said something to her I couldn't understand and patted my arm before he returned to his seat.

I avoided him at every turn after that, embarrassed about the situation, but Susannah and I had continued to talk some after each class. We didn't know each other well, but I enjoyed our hellos and good-byes. It was almost like having a friend; until then my friends had been my instructors. Or worked at the museum with Kitty. They were quite a bit older than me, to say the least, and didn't really understand why some things made me giggle, cry, or hide.

"Sure—eleven thirty?"

"Perfect." She slung her backpack over her shoulder.

Susannah leaned over and squeezed my shoulder. The touch surprised and warmed me.

I thought I'd never had a real friend, and the realization nearly crushed me. It took a moment to get my bearings before looking up at Susannah.

"I'll see you tomorrow!" she said brightly.

I watched her ponytail bounce away and remembered all the times Kitty had told me I wouldn't have liked public school. I wondered, though, would I have made friends like Susannah?

Hiding the warmth rising in my cheeks, I turned to leave the classroom that day only to be ploughed into by a fairly good-sized backpack. Not a particularly petite person but still less than five foot eight, I bounced heavily off the obstruction and fell straight to the floor. The blood rushed to my face, and I felt incredibly embarrassed for someone else to have witnessed my natural klutziness.

"I'm sorry!" said the guy from class.

It was him. Of course I recognized him immediately. I'd been secretly admiring him all semester, even if I'd avoided him of late.

I accepted his offered hand and stood.

"Oh," I said quietly. "It's okay, I'm not exactly full of grace."

"Sure you are." He picked up my backpack and handed it to me.

Able to concentrate more than on the day I'd made a fool of myself with the inhaler, I noticed how deep green his eyes really were. His dark brown hair was combed over to the side but a bit unruly. He gave me a wide, crooked smile, and I suddenly felt paralyzed. Even though my complexion was more olive, I could feel myself blushing. I hoped he didn't notice my adolescent response.

I accepted the bag. "Thank you."

"For what, knocking you over? You should be perturbed and walk out of here in a huff."

I stared up at him, perplexed, but he wasn't chuckling.

"I would if you did that to me." He smiled. "And I really am sorry, Miss…"

"DiCamillo," I said, happy at the moment that Kitty had decided to give Ruby her beautiful surname instead of whatever Ruby's father's had been. For a second I thought about the strangeness of it. I really wished I knew what my paternal ancestors' names were, but at that moment DiCamillo was a good name to have.

As I expected, he said, "DiCamillo is a great last name."

"My full name," I said proudly, "is Maria Lucero DiCamillo, but you can call me Lucy."

"Wow," he said, seemingly amused at that point about how proud I actually was of my name.

Embarrassed, I lowered my chin. Now there was this uncomfortable silence similar to what I remembered reading about in some novel, where nobody says anything and you stand there feeling stupid.

"Well, Maria Lucero *Lucy* DiCamillo," he said, bowing slightly, "it's a pleasure to bump into you—this time it's more pleasant, right? How about I buy you lunch?"

My eyes widened, and I stammered but couldn't get any sound to come out. I'd never been asked to lunch by a man. In fact, I didn't know if I'd ever said more than a few words to any young man. I just wasn't used to men at all. Having been homeschooled, I'd always spent afternoons working on schoolwork at the museum or library and all my free evenings with Kitty. I found men completely foreign and avoided them just as Kitty seemed to do.

Apparently mistaking my confusion for disinterest, he quickly apologized. "I'm sorry. You don't even know me, and I'm already asking you to lunch. Maybe another time." He smiled tentatively as if he suddenly wasn't too sure of himself either.

His uncertainty gave me confidence. "Maybe another time, Mr...."

Now it was his turn. He bowed. "Maxwell Crawford Sheffield." I smiled. His name was a mouthful too.

"Call me Max," he said and with that walked away.

I stared after him. He was wearing Dockers, and his polo shirt, wrinkled at the bottom, looked just untucked. He was quite a bit taller than I was, broad shouldered, and I had to admit that I liked what I saw, which caused me to turn even redder. *Kitty would love that he looks a lot like Harry Connick Jr.,* I mused.

One thing I was pretty sure of was that Kitty wouldn't even meet him. He'd only asked me to lunch, and I'd turned him down without even saying a word. That was all.

I headed home, happy we didn't live too far away and wishing I'd accepted Max's lunch offer. I suddenly felt even more stupid. Obviously I had no idea how to talk to men. Was there a right way? I had no idea, but I did know my face was still warm and pink. I rubbed one side of it, admitting to myself that I rather enjoyed the tingling feeling in my chest and the sound of my heart pounding in my ears. The best part was, my inhaler was safely stowed away in my backpack unneeded, so there was no way I could blame Ruby's asthma on my shortness of breath.

No, this was something different, something Emily Dickinson knew about even in the midst of all her grief-themed poems. She might never have ventured out of her house after she graduated from school, but she must have experienced such feelings before she decided to become a recluse. I decided she must have had a Maxwell in her life.

Like grief, this feeling was universal, and I found myself wishing once again that I could ask Ruby about it. Ruby would have given me some enlightenment—don't mothers explain all these feelings to their daughters?

Suddenly I wanted to know more about Max, more about men, more of my mother's love life. Again I thought about the photograph hidden in my drawer. I wanted Kitty to tell me why I didn't have a father, an uncle, or a grandfather. Was my father really a snake? Were all men horrible? Wasn't there one father out there who was good and decent? One man worth a date?

Maybe I'd been reading too many Jane Austen books, but after my recent crash with Maxwell Crawford Sheffield, I could no longer deny the existence of men or keep from pondering what I was supposed to do with their presence. I found myself dreaming that Max would truly ask me to lunch again, but even as I thought it, I decided he wouldn't. I was probably too young. He had to be at least twenty-three or twenty-four. At least, that's how old he looked.

I was barely nineteen, and as I thought about it, Kitty probably wouldn't like him for his age. Or simply because he was a man. I figured she would probably tell me not to trust him and then remind me of how men hurt women like me and her. And they in fact had, or they would be here for me during my college years, right?

The logic of Kitty's possible arguments aside, as I pictured Max's green eyes twinkling down at me, he certainly didn't seem that bad.

As I walked into the house a few minutes later, I nearly knocked Kitty off her cane.

"Oh! I'm sorry!" I reached out to steady her.

"What's the rush, dear?"

"Nothing," I said, trying to brush off any concerns she might have had. "I'm just more of a klutz than usual today."

She patted my arm. "Come sit with me in the kitchen and have some tea. I want to hear about your day."

I smiled and gave her a quick hug, reminded of how lucky I was to have her. I'd never lacked love from Kitty in my life. Love for me overflowed, even if in the form of overprotection.

I'd been at the university for almost four years, but since I was so young Kitty made sure I only went to and from class. I really hadn't minded up until now. I didn't want to worry her any more than necessary, so as much as I wanted to, I didn't dare mention Max.

"Let's have tea, dear."

She handed over my favorite rose-patterned cup. "Kitty, when did my mother go on her first date?"

Kitty hesitated, stirring sugar into her tea and taking a very slow sip. When she set the teacup down, she looked up at me. "Too young, that's for certain."

"Younger than I am?"

"Oh my. Much, much younger. She was about fourteen."

"You let her date at fourteen?" I was shocked.

"I did—and it was a mistake. I wish I hadn't. I suppose I was trying to be the opposite of my parents. They didn't let me date until I was almost out of school, and I ended up pregnant."

I was silent, thinking about Ruby, but Kitty read my mind.

"And I tried not to smother Ruby, but by the time she was out on her own, she ended up pregnant and unmarried anyway."

I said nothing, thinking about the photograph. Maybe now was a good time to ask her. I walked quickly to my room and back, avoiding Kitty's eyes as I sat down at the table. She glanced down at the photo album I placed in the center of the table. She looked scared but resolute.

"Who is he?" I pointed to the picture I'd found of Ruby.

"That man is who Ruby claimed was your biological father, but he is no father."

Not surprised at the disgust in her voice, I asked, "Do you mean he doesn't deserve to be my father or he really isn't?"

"That," Kitty said, "is part of your mom's story, and I have a few things to explain before you can understand, so you're going to have to be a little bit patient."

I leaned toward her and smiled so she'd know I wasn't upset at her. And I wasn't, at least not really. I just wanted to know the truth. I had never even asked about him before now. Kitty had once said he was supposedly my father, but it's all she'd said. Her tone had let me know not to ask more.

"He never married Ruby. His name was George T. Fields, and he was more of a fling."

"That's what I thought." I was surprised at my disappointment.

"I'm sorry, Lucy." She squeezed my hand.

I looked up and tried to laugh as I told her, "I didn't even know it mattered to me."

"Well, of course it matters. You are a daughter who was abandoned by your father, maybe even before you were born, and God took away your mom before you even got to spend very much time with her."

"How did they meet?"

Kitty thought for a moment. "It's important for you to know, but remember that it has very little to do with who Ruby really was."

"Sure."

She reached over and patted my hand. "I had been living just outside of San Francisco for quite a while by the time she met George Fields. She wanted to live in the city with some girlfriends of hers. They were just trying to spread their wings a little and get away from their mothers, so they spent most of their time waiting tables and partying. I didn't approve, and neither did the mothers of those other girls. We all knew the dangers waiting out there, but daughters never listen to their mothers."

I bit my lip. The idea that I would not listen to my mother, or grandmother, was a new one to me. But then again maybe that's why I'd grown increasingly frustrated with Kitty's way of selectively sharing details about my mother.

"It's true," she assured me. "It's true from the beginning of time, Lucy. You are a good girl, and so was Ruby, but a time will come when you won't listen to me anymore."

Guiltily, I thought of Maxwell Sheffield and realized I already had a secret of my own. Was this just part of stretching my wings? I was torn and decided I'd better tell her soon, or the guilt would start to smother me.

"She met George at a literary reading and was sure he was an intelligent-minded man I would like."

"Did you?"

"No," she said emphatically. "It was obvious to me that he was all about himself and lazy as heck." She shook her head. "I know poetry, and this man was no writer. He was just some rich boy still living off of his parents and using writing as an excuse not to work."

The man who was supposedly my father was a huge failure. I felt like a shot of lead had hit my stomach.

"He broke her heart and disappeared when Ruby was seven months pregnant with you. She never heard from him again as far as I know." Kitty's tone was biting, and it sharpened my disappointment.

I sat still a long while, trying to process this new information. I wanted to know more and yet didn't. I felt emptier now than before I knew anything about him. The warm fuzzy feelings I had after talking to Max were gone.

"He was a loser, wasn't he?"

"Oh yes. More than you know. But Ruby was not." She smiled. "You should also know that Ruby really wanted you, Lucy."

I gave her a rueful look. "I do know that much, Kitty."

She shook her head. "I mean she *really* wanted you even though many of her friends urged her not to have the baby after George left her—but she said no, that she wanted you. It was a terrible time in her life to be pregnant, and her friends were worried about her, but she had you anyway."

I smiled to myself, thinking it was ironic since she wasn't here with me now. But the connection I felt with her deepened knowing I was wanted.

5

W here have you been?" Kitty stood beside Louise, both of them with hands planted on their hips. I didn't want to disrespect either of these women this day. I'd stayed after class at the request of an instructor, and right in the middle of a discussion we were having, I'd jumped up, grabbed my backpack, and practically ran out of his office with barely a good-bye. I ran halfway across campus before stopping and nearly choking from lack of oxygen. After a puff of my inhaler and a brief sit-down on a bench, I quickly walked the rest of the way to the museum.

Today Louise was having a display of early American art types by women, and Kitty's quilts were the center attraction.

"I'm so sorry. So sorry, Louise. I'm sorry, Kitty." I leaned in and kissed both of them. Both held their grumpy stances, but I could tell from the pats they give me on each arm that they weren't mad, just nervous. Not only had the invitations been sent to everyone in the fine arts and humanities departments, but the governor's wife was stopping in as well.

My job was easiest, so I wasn't nervous. All I had to do was play the beautiful grand piano that had been donated by a benefactor of the art museum. I'd played it on other occasions for Louise and loved it. The piano was turned away from the center of the room, facing a corner filled with colorful abstract sculpture. Even though I loved the piano in our living room because it was Ruby's, this piano was something amazing. I considered it a privilege to be able to play on both of them.

Apologizing quickly for my jeans, sandaled feet, and white peasant top, I parked myself on the bench and Beethoven's Fifth poured out. As the sounds carried throughout the gallery, I wasn't even aware of those who browsed around me, studying quilts and other art.

I didn't need to see the visitors to know that Kitty's quilts were a hit. Her artistry in quilting wasn't unknown in the area. In fact, it was famous among quilters all the way over to Colorado. She'd even won numerous awards in the arts and often had quilts commissioned, which is why the governor's wife had been invited to the show. She had already commissioned quilts for each of her children, and Louise was hoping she would be in the market to buy more.

Kitty's quilts were loved because they told stories. They were maps of a life that people speculated about, but Kitty always said their guesses were all wrong. There wasn't anything special about her life. When she said that, I always got a feeling she wasn't telling the truth—not really lying but withholding. This is another reason I was late.

The instructor I'd been meeting with was an excellent researcher, and I'd been asking for advice on how to reconstruct my past through research. He had been giving me some excellent advice, and now I only needed to decide if I wanted to pursue digging, even if it uncovered the images Kitty herself kept hidden.

Some of the images that would pop up in her quilts were so beautiful and amazing that she surely couldn't have conceived them without experience. And they were never half-finished like my memory portraits either. Kitty's quilts were tapestries rich and deep, even though the full meanings were known only to Kitty.

"Maybe she just made them up," I once heard an observer say.

Maybe so, I'd thought, *but probably not.* Kitty didn't make things up.

As those thoughts filtered through my mind, I gave my entire body to the piano keys, losing myself in the rhythms. After a little while, I abandoned the sheet music and started playing favorite tunes I knew by ear. I even played through the score from Harry Connick Jr.'s soundtrack from the movie *When Harry Met Sally*. I hoped Louise wouldn't mind, but I felt the need to play something different, something not so stuffy.

I closed my eyes and enjoyed the music as I went through each song. "Autumn in New York" and "It Had to Be You" were my favorites, but "Stompin' at the Savoy" earned me a round of applause. As I finished, I stood and nodded my head in thanks to the crowd. I was trying to hold back the embarrassed flush in my cheeks, when I saw Max standing only a few feet away. I nearly fell over the piano bench as I sat back down.

I felt my cheeks go warmer and had the sensation I was Sally in New York, seeing Harry in the bookstore. I wondered how long he'd been standing there.

"Beautiful." His voice was so deep I could barely make it out.

His smile broadened and he winked, then turned and walked toward the door. I had a panicky urge to run after him, but Kitty and Louise were suddenly at my arm, proudly telling the governor's wife that my name was Maria Lucero DiCamillo, Kitty's granddaughter, but she could call me Lucy. I was obliged to turn all attention to the first lady of California. I heard the click of the door as it shut behind Max and suddenly felt like I'd been injected with a four-day dose of caffeine.

Kitty and Louise didn't seem to notice that I'd discovered the first man I'd ever imagined could be my boyfriend.

I thought about Max all through the next morning, replaying the moment I caught him watching me at the gallery, and realized after class that I hadn't even taken notes. How does one keep from thinking about a crush every moment of the day?

I was scanning the cafeteria around me, watching for Susannah among the clang of trays and the chatter of students. Numerous backpacks were tossed over the backs of chairs and strewn across tables. Some students were bent over books trying to study, and I wondered how they could concentrate with all the noise.

Strangely enough, I felt nervous about talking to Susannah outside of class. For a moment I even thought about leaving. I was just reaching for my backpack when I spotted Susannah's curly blond ponytail bobbing through the crowd. She waved at me and headed across the cafeteria to my table. I'd never really thought about how I looked, but now I couldn't help noticing the contrast between us.

My own hair was long, brown, and wavy compared to her locks, which were hanging from a scrunchie, literally resembling those of Goldilocks. She was at least four inches shorter than me. And while I'd never had a reason to think much about my figure or how I looked in my clothes, I couldn't help but notice that she was no bigger than a large child, and she was downright cute. Beside her I felt like an Amazon woman.

Kitty had always claimed that I inherited Freda's curves and looks. Freda was the "beauty of the land" in her time, Kitty said. I was lucky to inherit her genes.

"What land?" I probed, partly joking but mostly serious.

Kitty frowned and changed the subject.

Susannah's chatter brought me back to the present, and I smiled appreciatively when a few minutes later we were standing in the lunch line and she selected two slices of lasagna and buttery garlic bread. I selected the same.

"I haven't got very far today." She sighed once we were seated and digging into our lunch. "Maria has afternoon kindergarten class and is home all morning. She wanted me to play with her, and I eventually gave in."

"You have a daughter? Maria?" I was shocked. Susannah didn't seem like a mom.

"Yes, Maria is five."

"My name is Maria too!"

"Really?" Susannah stopped, fork midair. "How did you end up being Lucy?"

"Maria Lucero actually. Lucy is short for Lucero."

"Like the legendary goddess of light? Hispanic? Latino?"

"Something like that," I said. "At least, I know *Lucero* means light. I don't know that Ruby cared much about goddesses or all that much about her roots, besides the obvious."

"Ruby?"

I felt warmth flood my face as I explained my mother and how she died.

Susannah reached across the table and grasped my hand for an instant.

"I'm sorry to have pried."

"Oh, you didn't. I was just thinking I was close to your Maria's age when it happened. Do you have pictures of Maria?"

"Of course!" Susannah reached into her bag and pulled out a lavender wallet-sized photo album decorated with colorful hand-print stickers.

I thumbed through pages of Susannah with her quite handsome husband, Troy, and mostly Maria.

"She is gorgeous!" I was surprised to see that she had darker coloring, actually more similar to my own and nothing like Troy and Susannah. "Does your mom have brown hair?"

"Maria's adopted."

I nodded. "You adopted her as an infant?" I was happy our conversation was coming so easily. The proud look on Susannah's face was one I wondered if Ruby ever had for me.

"Oh yes. I'll tell you all about it if you have all day." She laughed at herself, and motherly pride seemed to shine brighter in her blue eyes.

"Not all day, but a few hours."

"Well…" Susannah raised her eyebrows and smiled. "Maria's mother was a pregnant teenager who didn't feel old enough to raise her, but neither did she want to, well…you know."

"Get an abortion?" I said for her. The word rolled right off my tongue before I could even think of good manners. I smiled wryly as a few heads turned toward us. "Sorry," I whispered.

"It's okay, but, yes. It was a huge decision for Anna—she was only thirteen years old. She learned that carrying a baby takes a huge toll on one's body, and hers wasn't ready. I'm frankly surprised her mom allowed her to carry it to term."

I thought of Ruby and her unplanned pregnancy. "How was it for her, as far as the pregnancy?"

"We came into it at month five, and we only met with her a few times," said Susannah. "But her doctor said she had a terrible time of it from the start. It must have been scary. When I was her age, I was probably still playing with Barbie dolls."

Inside I tried to imagine having a baby that young or even now. Had Ruby's pregnancy been easy or difficult?

I felt heaviness in my chest as Susannah, eyes longing, wished aloud that it had been her giving birth to Maria.

Her eyes brightened suddenly. "Something that meant a lot to me was the prayer that little mother said for our baby."

I thought of Ruby and the prayer we used to say together, the one I wouldn't say with Kitty after Ruby died.

"Anna said the prayer in Spanish first." Susannah brought my attention back to the table. "And then in English. It was such a short prayer, asking Jesus to watch over Maria."

I thought about the young Anna giving up her baby for adoption. Ruby had been older when she got pregnant with me but was still young to be having a baby alone. Some things about motherhood, like each woman looking out for her baby in her own way, were starting to knit themselves together in my mind. Would Ruby have been praying for me were she alive?

I locked eyes with Susannah. "That's beautiful." When I said it, I really did mean it.

She smiled weakly, as if I hadn't responded the way she wanted me to, as if she'd hoped for more—to find some kind of kindred belief between us. I felt a little sad that I couldn't give her that.

I felt Susannah studying me for a while. "You haven't had an easy time yourself, have you? It must be hard without your mother."

I laughed, nervous about such a personal question. "Well, I have a grandmother for a mother. It's a mixed blessing, I guess."

"What about your father? Are you in contact with him?"

I shook my head no. "I know he exists because there's a picture." I paused. "It's funny. Kitty and I were just talking about him last night. Ruby was pregnant with me in the picture, but I don't remember him. It doesn't seem to be something Kitty thinks I need to know too much about. She told me he was a jerk."

"Were they married?"

"He sounds like a fling, and I know even less about him than I know about Ruby."

She remained silent, as if willing me to go on, but I was tired of talking about all the things I didn't know. That small bit of conversation was the most I'd talked about Ruby with anyone besides Kitty that I ever could recall.

Susannah grimaced. "Maybe he's dead."

It felt like a slap. The thought wasn't new—it was just that I'd never heard it spoken aloud. In fact, I'd never had anyone ask me directly about my father. It was as if he never existed, except through the photograph in Ruby's album. I'd memorized the photo: a tall, broad-shouldered, lanky, brown-headed leftover hippie with a bushy mustache standing next to Ruby. My Ruby, a tired smile on her face, her brown hair in two braids, and a pink tank top stretched over her tight, round belly, which was exposed above the elastic waistline of a flowing lime green skirt splattered with bright yellow flowers.

Susannah touched my hand and the introvert in me wanted to cringe, but I couldn't pull away. "Can't Kitty just answer all of your questions?"

I felt eight again as the blood roared in my ears. If only it were that easy.

"It would be best if I could get my memories to come back on my own. I don't think Kitty wants to share everything. There must be secrets that are too painful or something." I stared out the window at students walking back and forth to class, backpacks slung over their shoulders.

"You really think your grandmother would do that?"

I shrugged.

"Sometimes I get the feeling she's keeping things from me— maybe to protect herself. Maybe to protect me."

"Maybe she has her reasons."

"I'm sure she does. That's why I just wish I could remember on my own." For a moment I considered telling Susannah about the half-completed paintings hanging on my wall but decided not to for fear she'd think me odd.

"Do you feel her? Ruby?"

I sat back, trying to mask the surprise on my face. That's exactly how it was. "Yes. Every day."

Suddenly Susannah apologized. She had to go get her daughter. After a quick hug, we parted ways, promising to have lunch again soon. She said something to me about calling that I just barely caught as she walked away, but my mind was already distracted by thoughts of Ruby. Susannah, unknowingly, had stirred feelings I'd been trying to keep at bay.

Even if I couldn't find every memory of her in my mind, Ruby was everywhere.

I knew that Kitty, like me, thought about her every day. Ruby was part of our lives, always hovering in an uninvited comment from Kitty or beneath the quietness of the evening. During the stillness we always knew the other was thinking about her, but we rarely broke the silence with her name during those times.

They were the saddest times.

They crept up like the stealthy orange kitten I had that got run over when I was little. A beloved companion but constantly in the middle of everything, making everyone smile, making everyone cry.

That evening I sat in Ruby's blue velvet wingback chair and imagined she was with me. I imagined her sitting here pregnant, wondering what to do with her baby, feeling like little Maria's birth mother had felt. How many options had she thought of? Abortion? Adoption? How long had it taken her to decide to keep me? I glanced over at Kitty.

"What's so special about this chair?" I hoped she would tell me this time.

Kitty sat across from me on the couch, and the smile on her face brightened despite the dim light from the lamp near the now dark window. She paused for a long time before answering and looked up toward the ceiling as if she could see back in time. Leaning forward, I sensed some anticipation of a story, but I suppressed my hope that she'd truly share. I wouldn't press her.

Kitty's life seemed to revolve around me, but I knew it couldn't have always been that way. Before, she would say, her life revolved around Ruby. And maybe that's really how it was, but I needed to know how that came to be. How had it ended up just her and Ruby? In some ways I think her life still revolved around Ruby, and I was simply an extension of that.

I remembered what happened to Ruby in the hospital and that it had nearly destroyed Kitty, but what happened before that day? Where was everyone else after Ruby died? While we had not spoken about it over the years, the absence of other family members and friends was obvious. In the past, when I'd asked about Ruby's father or my father, I was met with a warning gaze.

"Not important," she'd say.

I watched Kitty as she turned her gaze to the azalea plant illuminated by the deck light, its flowers spilling over the edge of its pot, which was hanging just outside the windowpane.

Eventually she looked back down and past me. She spoke so softly I had to lean in even closer as she continued to stare back to a time in her past.

"I think I already mentioned that I was born in a tiny town near Sonoma Valley called La Rosaleda."

"No," I said, masking my awe and surprise. "You've never mentioned La Rosaleda. You're from the Sonoma Valley?"

"Yes. And so was your mother. A long time ago, Ruby was born there. There was an earthquake that night."

I felt the bottom of my reclusive, safe world dissolve beneath me. I stared at Kitty, trying to find my breath, but she still didn't look at me.

A long sigh escaped as her shoulders deflated, and the mask on her face fell away, revealing something more than sad, almost remorseful.

"La Rosaleda was a beautiful place. I should have never left there."

I stood then and moved next to her on the couch, my heart beating so hard I worried she could hear it. *This is the moment,* I whispered to my heart.

You are from La Rosaleda.

Your mother was born on the heels of an earthquake.

An earthquake was rising in me even as the room around me stayed dead still.

WHEN LA ROSALEDA
STILL BLOOMED

6

Kitty's smile was tender. "I thought for so many years that I could hide things," she said. "I know you think I hold a key that can unlock your past, dear, but you have no idea why things are locked up. Your mother's birth, like that earthquake, would shake the foundations of La Rosaleda and of my life.

"Back then I didn't think I could ever have secrets with the power to ruin lives, but that's because I was so young. When I lived in La Rosaleda, I still had hope…"

Katherine "Kitty" DiCamillo-Birkirt was sixteen, almost seventeen, when she was pregnant with Ruby in La Rosaleda.

She paced the creaking oak floor of the alley loft she and her new husband rented. The Irish restaurant below, popular with tourists, was already loud and lively with music and the rhythm of feet clogging to traditional Irish dances. It wasn't even dark outside yet, but the merriment had started, and from the sound of things one would think they were in Ireland instead of La Rosaleda, where the Mexican-American roots gave way to a blend of Hispanic, Latino, and European-American culture.

The Irish presence, Kitty would explain to me later, wasn't completely unusual considering the bohemian atmosphere the town took on during tourist season when anything goes, but it wasn't the dominant culture. Either way, she'd never minded the music because it made Blake, whose parents were from Ireland, feel at home.

The music from the restaurant below reminded her of Blake and those happy years when they were just children at Frances-DiCamillo, her parents' vineyard just outside of La Rosaleda.

La Rosaleda, or "The Rose Garden," was a small, sparsely populated northern California town set in the rolling hills and vineyards of the Sonoma Valley. It was also a tourist town, and with it being the season's peak, tourists were kicking up the nightlife, which is saying quite a bit for the laid-back town.

Kitty swayed clumsily from side to side toward the window and climbed as carefully out to the fire escape balcony as her pregnant belly allowed. One small chair fit in the space where she loved to sit and listen to the nightlife below. It wasn't the music itself keeping her up that night, and it wasn't the baby seemingly dancing its feet inside her. It was the fact that her husband would be coming home late that kept her from going to bed. It seemed she could never fall asleep until he was lying beside her, his breath warm on her neck, his hand draped across her waist, or what used to be a waist.

Breathing in the warm night, she gazed down at the alleyway below. She enjoyed how the fuchsia-colored azalea plant draped over the railing, partially shielding her from passersby who bothered to look up at the lone window above the restaurant.

She watched as a young man and woman shared a kiss before hurrying inside. Smiling to herself, she remembered when she and Blake first realized that their feelings extended beyond childhood friendship. They had been so enlivened by each other. How many times had they eaten at that little restaurant, sometimes even doing the Irish dances together?

She rubbed her tight, round belly and whispered to the fluttering baby. "Hear that music, little one? Are you dancing in there?"

She felt a quiver from within that gave her the sense of being tickled from the inside.

"You're already like your daddy."

She knew that soon he would come pounding up the stairs
from an entrance next door to the pub, and she would hurry inside
before he made it upstairs. He would see her first from the alley, of
course, and be worried, but she would be inside before he made it
up the stairway and then he would see she was fine. Until then she
enjoyed the fiddles dancing up from the pub. Judging from the
shifting in her belly, the baby was as well.

Just below the balcony was where they'd shared their first kiss.
As his lips had grazed hers that afternoon, she'd opened her eyes to
catch sight of the fire escape balcony and noticed a pot of flowers
peeking out through the railing.

Still breathless from the moment, she said, "What a charming
little place to live! I bet it's adorable!"

His pale cheeks held splotches of pink at the timing of her
response, but he smiled and promised to buy the loft. Before they
were even married, it became vacant and he grabbed the opportunity to rent it, hoping to eventually buy it before some tourist got
the idea to make it their summer home.

Blake had bravely asked Kitty's father for his blessing on their marriage. But her father had surprised them all and swiftly refused
Blake's request on the grounds that she was too young to get married. Too young! She didn't feel too young. His refusal had seemed
more than a denial of Blake's request; it was a rejection of her
dreams. He fired Blake from the vineyard the same day, and she
wasn't supposed to see him at all anymore, but as young men and
women often do, they found little ways to see each other without
her parents knowing.

There was no end to the excuses Kitty came up with to bump into Blake, such as running errands for her mother or going to the small library in town, knowing she would find him waiting for her near the cookbooks. When Blake showed her the loft and said he had rented it for them, she knew she was home.

On that afternoon, they spread one of Kitty's handmade quilts across the bare hardwood floor. Together they unpacked grapes, cookies, and cheese, so happy to be together and alone. But being away from prying eyes when they were forbidden to see each other, she suddenly understood how Juliet and her Romeo had felt.

A nice lunch was all they had planned, but being so completely alone with Blake made Kitty feel sentimental and sad. She'd missed him so much, and knowing that her father wouldn't allow them to get married filled her with a sense of being abandoned by her parents. She leaned into Blake as they sat on the quilt together, looking for reassurance, a promise that he would never leave her.

She would always recall how the colorful starry designs of the patterned quilt brightened up the empty loft, lifting them into a fantasy where no forbidding father's eyes could bore.

Sitting now on the balcony of their loft, she whispered down to her belly, "And that's how we got you, little one." Heat traveled down her neck at the thought of that day. How could she banish the memory any more than she could banish her baby? *All has been made right,* she told herself.

The second time Blake asked for Kitty's hand, he walked the two miles to Frances-DiCamillo from La Rosaleda, cutting through the vines. That time of year, the vine tendrils were already heavy with gleaming young grapes in the slanting sunrise across the hills. But Blake had no time to enjoy the hills layering the horizon throughout the valley, acre after acre of vineyards, or the venerable oaks surrounding the large estate house. He strode past the work buildings, and saying good morning to those picking grapes along the way, he tried to ignore the wild thumping in his chest. All this he told Kitty later, of course, when all was well, but for a while her normally strong Blake was extremely nervous about how her father might react when he found out that not only had they been seeing each other in secret, but they still wanted to get married.

He broke out of the vines just as the bell echoed from the tower across the hills announcing the beginning of the day, and he kept striding toward the imposing Mexican-style estate home. The walk across the yard seemed to be miles long, and he climbed the stairs to the large oak door feeling as if his feet were sinking into the porch.

The rap of the ornate door knocker echoed across the vineyard. She heard it from upstairs and looked out her window. *He's here!* she thought, her heart leaping through her body. He stood at the door waiting.

A few curious pickers had followed him out of the field. He recognized them and gave a slight wave. They nodded.

When Isaac DiCamillo finally opened the door, he wasted no time on formalities.

"Blake Birkirt. You dare step foot on this estate after I said stay away from my daughter?"

"But I want to marry her." He sounded resolute, and only the splotches of pink in his cheeks gave away his apprehension.

Isaac flung his arms upward.

"No!" he roared. "She's not getting married!"

Both men looked up as the screen door slammed.

Kitty's mother, Freda, stormed out onto the porch wrapped in a soft blue shawl, still wearing her nightgown.

"Blake," she pleaded. "Go back to town while we think about this."

Freda was beautiful, in her late forties with long brown hair, heavy across her shoulders and brown eyes that flashed as much when she was angry as when she laughed.

"I'm not leaving until I see Kitty."

"Yes, you are." Her voice was gentle.

Blake hesitated. Anger stung his eyes, and he bit his tongue to keep from saying something that might offend.

He walked away, back straight, stiffly nodding to the workers as he started back toward town.

Reflecting on those beginning moments of their few years together, Kitty said she sensed then that every fiber in Blake's body wanted to stay and fight the day Isaac and Freda sent him away. Watching him leave, the breath rushed out of Kitty's body. When he turned back and looked toward her bedroom window, she didn't even bother to hide behind the curtains. She tried to cheer him by blowing kisses.

He smiled at her that morning, not seeming to care who saw. The workers snickered as they parted for him to walk through them. There were good-natured slaps on the back and teasing words spoken in Spanish that she couldn't understand from where she was.

Then, before Blake reached the end of the driveway, Isaac amazed everyone by calling out to him. "Blake!"

They met halfway. Freda stood on the porch looking after the men, her arms crossed formidably over her chest, no doubt to make sure Isaac followed her instructions.

"Mija," Freda said later, sitting on the blue velvet wingback chair in Kitty's bedroom. "You are going to be so happy with Blake."

"I'm going to marry him!" Kitty sighed and hugged herself.

The wedding preparations had to be made quickly. Kitty glanced at her mother.

Freda placed her hand on Kitty's belly.

"I'm sorry, Mother."

Freda looked out the window at the sun setting across the valley and didn't say anything for a long while.

Finally she turned to Kitty. "Katherine, I know." She sighed. "I guess this child is meant to be born, and your father and I will be here for you. And so will your husband."

That evening Freda tucked Kitty into bed as if she were still a little girl. Kitty thought she was too old for bedtime prayers, but Freda's words in her ear were a blessing for the baby. She clasped her mother's hand tightly, glad she hadn't been rejected, and she dreamed about her childhood.

Blake and Kitty had spent their childhood years roaming Frances-DiCamillo, Kitty still in cotton dresses and curly ponytails. Their favorite game was hide-and-seek, which was how her nickname evolved.

"Here, Kitty Cat!" Blake would call.

Their favorite place to hide was in the bell tower, which was attached to the estate house. They got into trouble repeatedly for hiding in the tower and several times for ringing the bell when it wasn't time to call anyone home for lunch.

"The bell is for mealtimes, for emergencies, and for church!" Freda would exclaim. "It's for announcing news, not for playing! What news are you announcing when you play? That the bell is meaningless?"

Years later, on their wedding day, Blake and Kitty ran up the tower, her lace and satin wedding dress trailing behind her. Freda and Isaac laughingly called after them to stay out of that tower. But Kitty and Blake ignored those calls and rang the bell together, long enough to let the whole town know there had been a wedding at Frances-DiCamillo.

The night had turned chilly when Kitty woke to sirens.

Oh no, she thought. *Where is Blake?* She immediately imagined that he was possibly hurt and began to call his name. She saw red and blue lights shining on the walls of the alley and knew something had happened. She was lying on the ground looking up to where the balcony was now hanging by what must have been one bolt, and her beautiful plants lay broken around her, smashed in terra cotta. She thought, *I need to get those and put them in water or they'll die.* She tried to remember what had happened and vaguely recalled waking up as someone from the alley below yelled, "Earthquake!" That was when the fire escape gave way, and she fell straight down.

She lay on the ground a moment, stunned, and then looked around up at the buildings.

When reality sank in, she was in tears. Had the awning, now ripped and torn, softened her fall? That would have been like some sort of movie, she thought.

Then it dawned on her just how far she'd actually fallen. She pressed her hands on her belly. *What about my baby?*

A nurse knelt down and began to push gently along her expansive waistline. The nurse felt and listened with a stethoscope for a long time, ignoring Kitty's soft cries of worry. Suddenly there was a strong movement, and the nurse's face brightened.

She called out to the other emergency personnel, "It's kicking up a storm!"

"More like an earthquake," someone said and laughed.

Turning back to Kitty, the nurse said, "I guess your crying woke up the baby!" She beamed as Kitty's sobs turned to surprised laughter. Before Kitty knew it, Blake was beside her in the ambulance.

"Mike Larimer," one of the medical people said to Blake.

Blake tried to focus on the outstretched hand as he found a place beside Kitty's stretcher.

"Blake Birkirt," he said impatiently.

Mike motioned toward Kitty.

"Your beautiful wife will be fine. You are one lucky man."

"They're *both* okay?" Kitty heard the desperate hope in Blake's voice.

Mike nodded. "The hospital will want to keep her a few days, but right now the little one seems fine too." He reached across and gave Blake a stern pat on the back and talked on and on, perhaps just to fill the space.

"I have a little one myself."

"Is that so?"

"Three months old," Mike said. "A son."

"What's he called?" The driver had turned on the sirens, and their voices could barely be heard.

"Matthew!" He yelled his baby's name.

Blake smiled. "Ruby!"

"A name like Ruby will indeed fit a girl who could survive an earthquake. If she's a girl, she's a spitfire!"

Blake smiled. "Are you a doctor?"

"Just a glorified nurse really, but maybe my son will outdo me someday!"

"Maybe so!" agreed Blake.

Later, when Blake finally saw Kitty holding their baby, Ruby, safe in her arms, he became lightheaded. Freda led him to the chair beside Kitty's bed and gently handed him his Ruby. She hiccupped and he smiled, quickly overcome with a mass of emotion he tried to stifle, but with very little control.

SEARCHING

Lucy

7

Kitty was different to me after talking about La Rosaleda. Her dyed blond hair tied back with a sheer emerald scarf. Her lush figure still attractive in a curvaceous way under that loose muumuu. These features were still the same. It was what I knew I couldn't have dreamed about her only an hour before that suddenly made her different.

I wondered how in such a short amount of time she could have become a new person in my eyes. Was my strong, opinionated Kitty really the same Kitty as in the story? It seemed impossible. The girl in the story was so in love with a man that she had been willing to anger her father to be with him.

"Why did you leave?" I whispered, guarding my words because this Kitty seemed more fragile to me. She might decide at any moment to stop telling me her story, but what I was most afraid of was losing her. She gripped the handle of her cane, but it seemed not to be the arthritis that hurt her as she stood.

"It's hard to believe that was me, isn't it?"

She walked toward her room, and I wished I could take away her pain.

"Kitty?"

She paused and turned back, the lines in her face all slanted downward, her obvious exhaustion making her look older than she was. Her brown eyes were vivid in her dark face, and now I knew why her blond hair had never matched the darkness of her eyebrows.

"So we are Mexican-American then?"

She paused. "Does it matter, Maria Lucero DiCamillo? We are American."

My face grew warm. "I'm sorry, Kitty. I didn't mean…"

"My mother was Mexican-American, as your generation would call it, and my father was Spanish-American. The vineyard was in my mother's family, and my father met her in the same way I met Blake, who as you heard, was Irish-American. Isn't that a mouthful? We are first and foremost Americans, mija. Haven't I taught you that always?"

I stood and walked over to her, a deeper respect mounting in my heart.

"Will you finish the story?"

She reached out and put her hand on my face. "Another day, Lucy. When I am not so tired."

I nodded, holding out my arm to walk her to her room. I felt bad I'd kept her up late since it was the time she always hurt the most.

"Kitty?"

She paused, her hand on her doorknob. Her nails were red, a typical Kitty color that also reminded me of Ruby.

"What about my father? What was he?"

I'd meant his race or heritage. Was he Spanish, German, Irish? He'd looked more European to me.

"He was… He was not your father. Ruby said he was, but he never wanted you, so it doesn't matter, mija."

Calling me *mija* softened the blow. It had also been Ruby's pet name for me.

"You are part of me. You are part of Ruby, a part of all the people I have told you about. Why must you still ask me about him? Just because Ruby left us with the claim that he was your father doesn't mean he was any kind of father at all."

She turned her doorknob, then paused. "He doesn't deserve you."

I nodded in acceptance of her words, but in my heart I didn't accept it. I had to know, even if the truth was as bad as Kitty claimed. I just wanted to know.

"Not everyone wants to know who their biological parents are, Lucy."

Susannah and I had decided to grab lunch and sit in the park after class. As we were walking away from the classroom, I'd noticed Max's gaze. I met his eyes and smiled but didn't trust myself to speak. I was again nearly frozen to the spot as we both paused outside the door, a question in our eyes that I wasn't going to be the first to ask.

Fortunately Susannah jumped in to save the day. "Max, why don't you join us?"

His face broadened into a grin. "There's nothing I would like more than to escort you two lovely ladies to lunch in the park."

At the park we sat next to a giant oak tree on the manicured lawn that looked like a golf course. Max was busy feeding a squirrel, and Susannah had her day planner out, arranging her week. They'd both been listening to my story. I'd felt only a little bit uncomfortable that Max was there, but as I told the story, he pumped me with questions as if he were actually interested. The story was so new to me that I couldn't have contained it even if they both thought it was the driest thing they'd ever heard.

"Why would anyone not want to know who their parents are? Your daughter even knows. You even went to her mother's high school graduation."

"Troy and I are Maria's parents," she corrected gently. "And, yes, we know Anna well. I guess we aren't giving Maria the choice but are making it for her. However, out of the adoptive parents I'm friends with, some of their older children don't want to know.

According to their parents, some of them even live in fear that their biological parents will find them."

"That seems so strange. I so want to know who my parents are. Not only do I want to remember more of Ruby, but I want to know about my father and grandfather. I want to know them."

Susannah shrugged her narrow shoulders. "Some kids are just comfortable with the parents who raised them and feel no connection to their pasts at all, at least not a positive one. I think that's okay. And it's okay to want to see them. It's their choice at that point. Just like it is yours."

"I'm not adopted, so maybe it's not the same."

Susannah reached over and placed her small hand over mine. It was milky white, mine almost tan.

"You *are* adopted, Lucy. You were an orphan, and Kitty took you in."

"Of course she did. She's my grandmother. My only living relative." I laughed halfheartedly. "At least *known* relative."

"Believe me. If you were familiar with adoption, you'd know that not all relatives are interested in or even capable of caring for the orphaned children in their own families."

I didn't say anything. How could I argue with her reply? I had never really acknowledged that I was an orphan, and I had never even bothered to ask Kitty what legal steps she'd taken to get me. Knowing her, I doubted she'd taken any.

I glanced over at Susannah, who was still planning her week.

"Midterm exams! I have three in one day!" She clucked her tongue. "Troy is traveling, and my mom has doctor appointments. I'm going to have to find a sitter."

"How do you even manage to go to college?" I asked her, somewhat envious.

She shrugged. "Oh, it's not a big deal. I try to grab chunks of time at night or when Troy takes Maria on a date. The rest of the time I let my mom watch her."

"That is so cute about the father-daughter date." I smiled, sneaking a look at Max. He was stretched lazily on his side, still tossing fries at the squirrels. *Kitty would be aghast that we are eating fries,* I thought.

"Well," said Susannah, "motherhood and being a wife come first."

I wanted to protest, but how could I? I wasn't a mother and I didn't really have one.

She saw my chin rise and smiled. "What's the matter?"

"Well," I said, choosing careful words, "I think women should not forsake their dreams for anything or anyone."

Out of the corner of my eye I saw Max stop throwing fries as he turned to listen to our conversation. I found myself wondering if he would be the type who would expect a wife to stay home with the kids and not enjoy her intellectual pursuits or a career, or if he would encourage her interests. When I realized I was thinking in the context of being his wife, I felt my face warm and I looked away.

Susannah didn't get angry. "I never said I was forsaking my dreams."

I felt my face darken with embarrassment.

"For me," she continued, "what I did say—or mean—was that being a wife and mother comes first and everything else second."

"But that's not fair," I said.

"Why not? Kids are helpless. They need someone to take care of them."

My heart cracked a little, but I knew Susannah couldn't have meant for me to think of Ruby and how much I had missed having her in my life to take care of me. Kitty had been wonderful. I couldn't have a better mother, except for Ruby. My real mother. She, I imagined, would have been even better.

I let my mind roam. Ruby had worked part time at the library. If she'd been married to my father, would she still have worked? I realized with a sense of peace that it didn't matter to me whether she would've worked outside the home or stayed with me. Just having her there would have been all I needed.

Max seemed to squirm in his place on the grass.

"I like being a mom and a wife," Susannah quietly added.

I had to admit that Susannah had a good life. Who wouldn't enjoy being her?

"Kitty got the shaft when it came to choices," I said, some negativity creeping into my voice. I looked over at Max, who was still listening but remaining quiet. He probably didn't want to get in the middle of a conversation between two women about this subject.

"Kitty," she said softly, "is a grandmother who has been standing in as your mother. Motherhood came before her personal pursuits when she was young, and it does now." She sighed. "I don't see how that's much different than what I'm doing by staying home with Maria and juggling school, I might add."

I looked up and realized I'd offended her. "I'm sorry. That's not what I meant," I apologized. "I think it's great if you want to stay home with Maria. I guess that's what people who go to church prefer to do."

Susannah giggled. "I don't know about that. Some mothers at my church work, and some don't."

"I've noticed that at church too," Max said.

"You two go to the same church?" I asked incredulously. I was beginning to wonder if they were trying to convert me. "Is this some kind of intervention?"

They laughed.

"No! Max could be Jewish for all I know."

I looked at him. "Are you Jewish?"

He shook his head.

I raised my eyebrows. "Christian?"

Max raised his hands like he was under arrest. "Guilty as charged."

I learned that Max was a youth minister in his spare time and part of a rock band. What a shocker that news was, but it explained the days he showed up in disheveled dress pants as opposed to his regular student outfit of jeans and a T-shirt.

My heart sank. I could never date a minister, could I? Not that I was dating him, of course. But maybe if he asked me, I might consider it.

I suddenly felt prejudiced, which is the exact opposite of what I'd always envisioned myself to be.

"It's okay with me that you're religious," I said to Max and Susannah.

They both looked at me with bemused expressions, but they wore smiles.

"Well!" Max said. "Glad we got that out of the way!"

Susannah dismissed Max's comment with a wave. "I'm glad you aren't offended, Lucy," she gushed. "Because I like you."

I dropped my gaze to the ground. Susannah certainly wasn't afraid to dole out a compliment when warranted, even if it was a little on the syrupy sweet side.

"I like you too, Lucy!" Max said, grinning broadly. He cocked his head in mock drama as if he were an employee of Disneyland. Susannah chuckled at his silly imitation of her.

It was all ridiculous and sappy, but it did make me smile. I felt my face turn an even deeper shade of pink at Max's compliment even though he'd only been teasing. There was nothing I could do but concentrate on plucking blades of grass.

Max spoke seriously, "You know, they have groundskeepers to do that, and they have these things these days called lawn mowers."

Susannah and I both laughed as she stood up and tossed her backpack over her shoulder.

Max and I moaned. "You're leaving?" we asked in unison.

"Yes, I need to pick Maria up from kindergarten."

I nodded. "Call if you need anything," I said standing. "I hope your mother is feeling better."

"Me too," she said. She studied her painted toenails. "It could be breast cancer."

I gasped, not knowing what to say. Max offered to pray for her. I wished I could say I would pray, but then I would be a liar. Instead I stood up and reached for her. We hugged, which was coming naturally between us more and more these days, and she walked away, her usual bounce gone.

Max and I sat in silence. I took a deep breath and willed him to speak.

His tall, lanky body was stretched out closer to me now, with his back leaning against the tree.

"So, Miss Maria Lucero DiCamillo, what's new?"

I laughed. "Basically nothing. I lead a mundane life," I joked.

"I can hardly believe your life is mundane, Miss DiCamillo. What do you do every day?"

"Well," I said, liking the way he said my name, "every day, I go to school, go home, study, and my grandmother and I usually visit the Market Square, the bookstore, the park, or the library. And sometimes we just hang out in our kitchen or garden and have tea."

"Sounds like you two are close," he said.

"We are," I responded seriously. "Kitty is not only my grandmother, but she has been my mother and my best friend since I was eight."

"And she's given you a topnotch education," he added.

"You think so?"

"Let's see," he said glancing up into the tree's branches. "You are a senior in a private university, which I might add isn't easy to get into, and you're only nineteen."

"Yeah, so?"

"Okay, Miss Modest, it's normal to be nineteen and almost entering grad school?"

Not comfortable with talking about myself so much, I tried to change the subject.

"How old are you?" I asked.

"Twenty-four."

"Twenty-four?"

"Well," he said in mock defense, "I'm on my second degree. The first was music. The second is business. I'm taking your humanities class as a filler by special permission of the instructor."

He winked. "I'm still in my twenties. It's not like I'm an old man."

Looking down at the grass, I busily plucked away again. "I'm sorry. I didn't mean you were."

"I'm just teasing anyway. But seriously, do you think your grandmother would approve if you went on an outing with an 'older' man?"

I laughed, feeling silly. I thought of the minister thing and wondered if I dared.

"Technically I'm old enough to go somewhere if I want, you know, with or without Kitty's approval."

"But somehow I get the feeling you wouldn't," he teased.

I shrugged. "It depends on what an 'outing' is." I was unfamiliar with the dating world, and I had no idea what he meant by outing, so I remained cynical. "I'm not twenty-one, so I can't go with you to a club or anything like that."

"I don't drink," he said, as if that solved everything.

"And Kitty is afraid of cars; she thinks I'm going to die in a car accident."

"We'll walk."

"And I think it might freak her out to know I would be alone with a man."

He grinned sheepishly. "I am perfectly safe. And you're alone with me right now."

I laughed at his observation. "Yes, I am," I responded. My heart roared in my ears.

"But," he said, "I am old-fashioned. I don't mind having to work for your attention. It'll be like courtship in those old novels you say you like to read." He waggled his eyebrows at me as his perfect mouth turned up into a captivating smile.

I raised my eyebrows back at him. "You mean like in *Pride and Prejudice?*"

"Something like that," he said, laughing at my example. "Which means I wouldn't even mind inviting Kitty to come along. We would need a chaperone. Then she wouldn't have to worry about us being alone together."

I smiled back at him, suddenly at ease, and very formally said, "That would be wonderful, Mr. Sheffield."

"Then I'll pick you and your grandmother up Saturday at eleven, and we'll walk to the nearest park. Where do you live?"

I told him my phone number and address, ignoring Kitty's warnings to me about men.

"Then since you're close," he said, "we'll picnic here in the park."

We soon collected our things and, as awkward as usual, I started to stand when I noticed his outstretched hand. I reached out and took it, letting him pull me up, all the while reveling in the warmth of his hand encasing mine. We stood facing each other, and he let go of my hand as quickly as he'd grabbed it, shoving his hands in his pockets. I was disappointed, but I guessed I had no business holding hands with a man I barely even knew.

And did people even hold hands anymore?

I felt like I needed to go read a stack of romance novels to learn what was expected of me.

"I'll see you tomorrow." He saluted and walked away.

As I walked through the rest of the park and turned down my street, I dug around for my inhaler. I wondered if I was feeling lightheaded and breathless because of Max or my asthma. I figured it was both.

8

I didn't build the confidence to ask Kitty to go on the picnic with Max until the next day. I'd been sitting in our garden having my usual morning routine for about an hour, watching the humming-birds, dreaming about what the rest of Kitty's story would yield. Would she divulge some seed that would prompt me to remember Ruby? Part of me wanted to run off to La Rosaleda and find Kitty's family—my family. But part of me also feared they wouldn't want to see me. Maybe like the children Susannah told me about who didn't want their biological parents to ever find them.

There was something else I wanted to ask Kitty about her story. It was now obvious to me that Kitty's story wasn't hers alone, but also mine and Ruby's. The stories were one, interconnected...like the vines Kitty sewed into her quilts.

The quilts. Of course. Kitty's quilts were about La Rosaleda.

I watched the sunrise over the neighborhood behind our house, and just when I thought I might go in and make my own cup of tea, Kitty wandered out in an orange-and-yellow Hawaiian-print kimono. I smiled at my grandmother's style, which was sim-ply anything she found beautiful, and that usually leaned toward loud, large prints. Again I was reminded that she seemed so differ-ent than the newlywed Kitty who had lived in La Rosaleda.

"I love that robe."

"Oh, silly Lucy, you've seen this a thousand times."

"Yes, but I wasn't sure if I'd ever told you how I love the rich fabric. Where did you get it?"

"Well, you may not believe it, but from Dr. Larimer many years ago."

"No! My doctor? Our family doctor, here in Sacramento? The one who writes me prescriptions for inhalers? Are you kidding me?"

Kitty nodded. "No, I'm not."

"Wait a minute… Dr. Larimer's name is Matthew, isn't it? Then, is he…?" I was afraid to ask, but it made sense. It was just too weird, but I'd always wondered why Dr. Larimer was so nice to us.

"Matthew is the son of Mike Larimer from La Rosaleda. The one who rode in the ambulance with Blake and me on the day Ruby was born."

"You've kept in contact with the Larimers?"

Kitty scoffed. "I can keep in touch with whomever I want."

"I'm sorry," I said quickly. "I just meant if you hadn't told me—"

"It's okay."

"Have you kept in contact with others at La Rosaleda?"

"No, definitely no. And I don't keep in touch with the Larimers either, only Matt."

I reached out and touched her hand. "Was Blake somehow unkind to you? Is that why you won't go back?"

She cocked her head sideways and stared at the bees buzzing along the marigolds, seeming to consider whether he was or not.

"No, at least not exactly. Really I was the one unkind to him."

I didn't try to hide my confusion. "Why all the secrets?"

"What did you say?"

"Why have you kept so many secrets from me?"

"I'm sorry, Lucy, but these are not things I like to dig up. It was hard to leave it all behind. I did mean to tell you where I really came from. Someday."

"The quilts with the grapes and vines and the Mexican-style houses—those are about La Rosaleda?" I muttered in embarrassment that I had never put it together before this day—me, a lover of the arts, a humanities major! I knew her quilts were dubbed "signature" by many people, but I'd never fully appreciated that they were also an artistic expression of herself. How blind I'd been to my own grandmother's art. I began to feel like I didn't really know as much about Kitty as I imagined.

"Yes, the stories in those quilts are about me—about us actually."

Us? If these are my stories too, why didn't I know them? What could have gone so wrong that Kitty would keep so much from me? In the silence I could hear the bat of hummingbird wings in time to the beating of my heart. Would Kitty ever know how much I needed to understand the past?

"Lucy," Kitty said finally. "Nothing is a secret."

I watched anxiety shadow her usually sharp, bright eyes and wondered if that was the truth.

"At first, you were grieving Ruby and just a little girl, not really of an age to understand. If you didn't ask about Ruby's past out loud, what makes you think you would have listened to me talk about my own?"

"But that's what grandmothers do, isn't it? Pass on stories about the past?"

Kitty was quiet several minutes more. "Yes, but not when the granddaughter is already filled with pain. I didn't feel like my stories would help you out of your own anguish. I thought only remembering your mother in your own way could do that." She shook her head, resigned to something. "I haven't done everything right in my life, but with you I tried to do it better. I've sheltered you too much, too long. I hoped I could make your pain go away by filling your life with beautiful things like music and art. I didn't have time or energy to go back and revisit my own sorrow. My troubles began before your mother was ever born. These things have little to do with you and Ruby."

"Sorrow?" I couldn't believe what I heard. "How could your past *not* have anything to do with me and Ruby?"

Kitty looked away, and I knew she was finished with the conversation. "I'm not going to talk about it anymore, not today. I realize now that maybe I need to tell you some more about my life in order for you to really understand Ruby's, but you have to be willing to take a little at a time."

I wanted to protest in frustration, but Kitty was already making her way back into the house. If I were younger, I would pout. Now...

My date with Max forgotten, I sighed in exasperation over the top of my teacup. Kitty had always given me only what she felt I needed and only at the rate she could give. The hummingbirds drew my attention again. They were working so hard to find the sweetness, flitting from flower to flower. How like Kitty, I realized, and her words echoed in my mind. *I didn't have time or energy to go back and revisit my own sorrow.*

I wouldn't know until later, but Kitty knew I struggled to understand.

"I have to give my story to you a few squares at a time," she said. "Like I do on the quilts I sew. It's so much easier to tell my stories in those quilts. You don't look closely enough at my quilts, Lucy. You think you need to get all of the information direct from my lips. And maybe you do, but I wish you would think of my quilts and notice that it takes a long, long time to finish one of them."

BUILDING A HOUSE
IN THE VINES

9

Our little apartment became much busier after the earthquake, Lucy," Kitty said. "But it was definitely a house of love. Your mommy—Ruby—grew and was the delight of the La Rosaleda locals every time her blondish-brown curls bounced through a doorway."

Ruby was two when Blake mentioned to Kitty he might like to build a house on her parents' land, the land that would be theirs and Ruby's someday.

"It won't be as big as the main house," he explained hopefully. "But I would still make it beautiful, and you'd be close to your mother."

"But what about the loft?"

"We'll find a way to keep it. Maybe your parents will help, just for a while."

Kitty thought of her mother. Even with weekly visits, she did miss her and could also use a hand with Ruby, who was getting rambunctious at her age.

As he spoke, Kitty sat in front of him on the kitchen counter, where he'd lifted her for a welcome home kiss.

Maybe it would be nice to be home again. She hugged him with all four limbs to show how much she loved the idea. "Okay!"

"Really? But I know how much you like town."

She looked at him, stocky, tall, muscular from working. His ash blond hair was combed over to the side, and she loved the way he cocked his head when waiting for an answer.

"Yes, silly. I'm sure!"

"Hot dog!" In one swoop he grabbed and spun her. Then he set her down gently and kissed her mouth. "I love you, Kitty Cat." His voice was a warm whisper against her cheek.

"Oh, really? How much?"

He kissed her forehead.

"Only that much?" Her eyes dared him.

He kissed her chin.

"Is that all?"

He leaned closer, kissing her neck, his hands sliding up her arms.

"Is that how much you love your wife?" she beckoned. He smiled, and she let out a soft sigh and wondered if they would ever get tired of their game. She hoped not, but then she didn't know yet how wicked life could be.

HE MUST BE A FINE BOY

Lucy

10

The morning of my date, I found Kitty in her usual chair on the back porch. I decided if I wanted her to meet Max and go with us to the park, I'd better warn her now.

"Kitty—" I stammered. "I, uh—"

"What is it, dear?"

"Well, um, would you like to meet my friend Max?"

"Who is Max?"

I could feel my face turning red. "A guy in my class, a really nice guy who's invited you and me to lunch."

"He's trying to go the old-fashioned route, is he?"

Kitty always put me on the defense when it came to men. "I don't think he's trying any route."

Kitty looked at me. "If you believe that, Lucy, then I guess my overprotective ways have made you naive."

My cell phone rang, and Susannah, on the other end of the line, told me quickly, breathless, that her mother, Mary, had breast cancer.

Kitty watched my frown as I clipped the phone shut. "Bad news?"

"Yes." I told her the news. "And she already has a mastectomy scheduled for next week."

"Oh." Kitty was sympathetic. "How horrible."

"It seems really fast, doesn't it?"

Kitty frowned. "Yes, they do move quickly when they know it's breast cancer."

I felt terrible for Susannah, knowing how close she was to her mother—and how it felt not to have one.

Kitty shook her head. "It's so hard being a woman. I'd like to meet Susannah and Mary sometime." Her frown deepened. "When it's appropriate," she added.

Kitty stood and walked into the house.

Pushing aside concern for Susannah and nervousness about the date with Max, I followed Kitty to the kitchen and reached for her elbow to help her into a chair.

"Really, Lucy," she chided. "I'm not that old. You don't have to help."

"I know you aren't, and I know I don't. I just like an excuse to hold your elbow."

Kitty smiled at that. "So are we going somewhere special for lunch?"

"Actually we're having a picnic. Really, it's a date sort of."

"Sort of a date? For both of us? I thought we were just going to meet him at the park."

"Yes. No! Well, yes," I answered. "It's complicated."

"Men always are."

Kitty's sudden humor about men surprised me, and I laughed. Sobering, I took a deep breath. "This nice guy I told you about— Max, well I mean Maxwell Sheffield—invited you and me to have lunch in the park."

Kitty tapped her cane steadily on the floor. I couldn't tell what she was thinking. When I couldn't take the silence any longer, I blurted, "He looks like Harry Connick Jr."

"Now, you know that if he looks like Harry, he must be a fine boy!" Kitty laughed and I joined her, relieved.

But she was serious when she added, "Lucy, I do want to meet your Max, but you need to be careful about men. I'm glad you were smart enough to let me meet him."

"It wasn't my idea," I said quickly. "It was Max's—he's sort of old-fashioned."

Kitty raised her eyebrows. "I guess we'll see. Speaking of manners, how about I bring *Mantecadas*?"

"Mmm!" My mouth watered at the thought of the crumbly almond cookies Kitty said her own mother had taught her to make. "Are you sure you don't mind?"

"Of course, I don't mind. You know I love to bake."

"No, I mean the dating…or possibly dating Max."

Kitty was quiet.

"That's just possibly, not for sure," I said.

Kitty took a deep breath. "Of course, I care. I'm scared to death to let you date any man."

I felt my heart sink.

"But if you're going to date someone, I want to know the fellow."

My heart swelled with the anticipation of seeing Max again. Kitty's permission meant everything to me; I couldn't contain a huge smile as I helped get the cookie ingredients and worked myself into a frenzy thinking about what to wear and how much time I had to get ready. Would Kitty have enough time to make the cookies? I glanced at my watch. We still had two and a half hours.

In my bedroom I stared at myself in the mirror, an act that Kitty always said was vain. My long, curly brown hair was a constant mess of tangles; my brown eyes seemed dull; my skin lackluster. I couldn't imagine what Max would see in me, so I looked for just the right outfit. I settled on a light yellow sundress and gave second thought to many of the hats, shoes, and outfits on the rack that had belonged to Ruby or Kitty. *This closet is like having my own vintage clothing store.* I took advantage of it. I grabbed a small-brimmed straw hat adorned with a sunflower, grabbed some strappy sandals, and hurried to the kitchen only to be met with the aroma of Kitty's Mantecadas. I reached for one and was surprised when she didn't slap my hand away.

She did stare at me though, eyes wide.

"What?" I said, putting down the cookie.

"Oh, honey." She put her hands on each side of my face. "You are so beautiful. You look so much like your mother in that hat." Big tears came to her eyes as I hugged her neck. "Lucy. My Lucy. You are as beautiful as your name."

I pulled away, shaking my head, and rolled my eyes.

"Now don't do that. You're too old for getting your eyes stuck up in their sockets."

She let me go and handed back my half-eaten cookie. "I have kept you too close, dear. I didn't realize you'd turned into such a remarkable woman."

"I'm hardly…remarkable…Kitty," I said between bites of the Mantecada.

"You are."

"Well," I said, "I guess I am daughter of Ruby and grand-daughter of Kitty. I can't be too bad, can I?"

"Exactly right!" proclaimed Kitty as she began to clean up the kitchen.

"Kitty?" I couldn't resist taking advantage of the mood. "Who was Ruby's first boyfriend?"

"Well, you wouldn't believe it if I told you."

"Who?"

"Dr. Larimer. When they were just little kids, Ruby called Matt her boyfriend. That was before…"

"My father came along?" I interrupted.

"Before a lot of things."

I sat down at the table and looked at Kitty. "Tell me," I whispered. "Tell me about it, please, Kitty."

She glanced at the clock. "Your date will be here in an hour."

"I don't care."

She sighed. "Well, as they say, there's no time like the present, right?"

My chest tightened with excitement. I wanted to know everything I could about Ruby.

I was surprised that Kitty seemed a little nervous, or maybe just sad. I wasn't sure. I could tell that as much as she'd always wanted me to know about my mother, visiting her memories was painful.

"She believed in God."

"What?"

"God. You know I'm not big on God stuff, but Ruby was. Shortly before her death, she'd gone God crazy."

"God crazy?"

"That's what I called it. I still feel so bad; it's one of the things we argued about in the end."

This was something from my past, a thread I wanted to follow, a thread that always seemed hanging there at the edge of everyday things. Part of me wanted to know about God, but Kitty had left faith behind, along with her family. I hoped he was real. If not, then Kitty's anger was displaced. Mine too. Who could we blame? A part of me needed someone to blame, but another part needed someone bigger to hold on to—someone even stronger than Kitty had always been to me.

I didn't want to drag Kitty through pain, but I needed to know the truths about my life.

"What is it, Kitty? Was Ruby part of a religious cult or something? What do you mean 'God crazy'?"

Kitty sighed, tracing the wood grain across the table. "She found God even though he had never been there for us. She defied me."

"Was she some sort of zealot?" I felt the bile rise in my throat knowing that Ruby relying on anyone but Kitty would have offended.

Kitty shook her head. "No, not Ruby. Now that I reflect on it, she was simply peaceful. She wanted me to be also."

"You are peaceful, Kitty." But as I saw the creases at her eyes deepen, I knew she wasn't, not really.

Kitty shook her head, as if confronting a big mistake. "Maybe, my Lucy, I was jealous of your mother."

"But she was your daughter. You said you were best friends."

"Yes, I did say that, but Ruby, with her joy, was the better friend to a mother who wronged her."

LOST IN SAN FRANCISCO

Kitty

The day was beautiful, and the wind off of the San Francisco Bay was slight. "You are my best friend, Mommy," Ruby told Kitty, holding her hand as they waited to get an ice-cream cone at Fisherman's Wharf. Kitty had taken the day off from her waitress job to take Ruby sightseeing at the wharf.

"What flavor, kid?"

Ruby giggled when they got their ice creams, both pistachio, and bounced off to see the seals.

Ruby squealed and pointed at a big seal as it rolled itself off and splashed into the bay. When a baby poked its head up from the shiny pile of seals, Ruby screeched such a loud scream of delight that a few observers put a hand up to rub their ears.

"Oh!" she said, suddenly whispering. "A baby."

Ruby knelt down low to peer at the baby and began talking to it as if it could understand her. When it nodded her way, Kitty laughed out loud. It appeared that the baby seal was talking to her daughter!

She suddenly jumped up. "Mommy! Take its picture!"

Kitty obliged.

"What about us, Mommy? Let's take a picture of us!"

"How, sweetie? Who will hold the camera?"

"I'd be happy to do that." A tall, slender blond man dressed in business attire offered his hand for the camera, which Kitty handed over. He was very attractive, very friendly. The usual fleeting moment of guilt passed through her as she thought of Blake, but it had been so long…

"Why, thank you."

"My pleasure." He aimed the camera and paused a long time, as if he were trying to get the right angle, before he clicked. He handed the camera back and remarked, "Two princesses to be sure."

Kitty noticed Ruby giving him a suspicious look. Ruby would never allow anyone to take her father's place.

"No," Ruby said, "Kitty is the queen. I am the princess. And Matt is the prince, and Daddy is Mommy's king. You may leave us alone now."

Kitty smiled as the man's expression changed from being taken aback to amused.

"Thank you, Mr.…"

"Mr. Thompson," he responded and extended his hand in greeting. "Mrs.…?"

"DiCamillo," Kitty said quickly. "*Miss* DiCamillo."

"Well, *Miss* DiCamillo, it has certainly been a pleasure to meet you and your…niece?"

Kitty watched Ruby's face, embarrassed that Ruby might have noticed his eyes roam Kitty's curves. She knew that Ruby had instantly decided not to like him. "This is my daughter, Ruby."

"I'm sorry. She called you Kitty, so I thought—"

"She is my Kitty," said Ruby, eying him suspiciously.

He looked confused.

"I am her Kitty. I'm her mother, and she calls me Kitty."

Ruby tried to cover her face. Debris from the wharf had been swept into her eyes, and as the wind died back down, Kitty leaned down to help.

"What is it, baby?" Kitty tried to make her voice sweet so Ruby would feel less worried about talking to Mr. Thompson.

"Mommy," Ruby wheezed.

Kitty produced the inhaler, which Ruby sucked in instinctively. "She just has a little problem with asthma."

"Ah." Mr. Thompson nodded. "I understand."

But really Kitty knew he didn't. Nobody ever did because Ruby was so young to have developed this problem, or so the doctors at the free clinic said.

The next morning Mr. Thompson sat at the breakfast table with Kitty and Ruby. Kitty didn't know how she had so easily let down her guard again. Maybe she was lonely, she reasoned with herself.

Ruby ate her eggs in silence, and Kitty could tell from her glares that she despised him.

After a few weeks he was still coming over to the house. Kitty had never told him to stop.

One night Ruby cried for Kitty to stay home, and she did. She convinced Mr. Thompson that a dinner at home would be nice for a change.

Ruby sulked, and right in the middle of the meal she picked up her plate and calmly dropped it to the floor. The porcelain shattered, taco shells and lettuce spreading like confetti across the kitchen floor. Ruby looked at the mess, stood up from her chair, and walked calmly to her room, and then slammed her door.

Kitty was shocked. She apologized as she headed to Ruby's room. "I don't know what got into her."

In Ruby's room, Kitty demanded an explanation.

"Is he gone?" Ruby asked, hugging her favorite floppy bunny.

"No! He's not, and dinner is not over."

Ruby began to cry as she tried to burrow into her tattered princess pillow with her bunny.

A feeling of guilt swept over Kitty, and she was quickly by Ruby's side. But she spoke firmly, "Sweetie, you're acting like a spoiled brat. This isn't the Ruby I know."

"Mommy! I want my daddy."

Kitty's heart dropped. "I'm sorry, baby. I really am."

"Then take me back! I want Grandma and Papa. I want to play with Matt. Can Matt come over, Mommy?"

She had decided that handling Ruby's fits with authority would teach her how to accept the reality that they were never going back to La Rosaleda.

"Young lady, go back in there and apologize to Mr. Thompson."

She walked into the kitchen and stood beside his chair.

"I'm sorry," she said sweetly.

"It's okay, sweetie." He picked up his fork and began to eat again.

"Now go back to your room, Ruby," Kitty said firmly.

Ruby just stood there staring at Mr. Thompson, who, obviously uncomfortable under the child's scrutiny, put down his fork and turned toward Ruby.

"You aren't my *daddy*," she said emphatically.

"Ruby! Go to your room!"

Ruby ignored her mother and began to shower Mr. Thompson with six-year-old-themed obscenities.

"I hate you—you stink!" Her childish voice rose louder. "I wish you would leave. I hate you. She is my mommy! Not yours." Ruby pressed her arms against her sides and balled her hands into fists until she began wheezing and her insults came out as squeaks, but she wasn't stopping.

Kitty had to carry her, kicking, into her room, forcing her to take her inhaler.

"I want my daddy."

"I know. I know, sweetie. Mommy does too, but we can't have him, okay?"

Ruby cried for herself and for Kitty until she finally drifted off to sleep, sniffling for her daddy and calling out quietly in her sleep for her friend Matt.

Kitty knew she should have made the man leave. She still didn't know what possessed her to let him stay again when her daughter so obviously hated him—never mind that she was married.

In the middle of the night, Ruby crawled out of her bed like she was prone to do when she was scared and came into Kitty's room.

Kitty woke to her soft voice. "Mommy?" she whispered. "Can I sleep with you?"

Remembering her visitor, Kitty sat up abruptly. "Oh, baby, not tonight, but I'll come tuck you in."

"But why?" Ruby rubbed her sleepy eyes.

"Because—"

At that moment her guest chose to turn over heavily. He sat up too. He stared at the little girl standing beside the bed.

Ruby began to cry as her mother whisked her to her room, sat her on the bed, and walked back out, slamming the door behind her.

Kitty worried the whole time that Ruby could hear them fighting and wondered how she had come to this horrible place, cheating on her husband, her daughter in the next room. Because she was lonely? She should have realized that nothing could fill the cavern she'd dug in her own heart with her separation from Blake.

"Then get out of here if you don't like it!" she shouted.

Mr. Thompson stood, pulling off a blanket to hold at his waist. "I'm not saying I want to go. I just have trouble dealing with your kid."

"She's part of the package! If you can't deal with her, then you can't deal with me. Get out!" Her voice rose in a shriek, and she barely recognized it as her own. This was detestable, a sound she'd never had reason to make when she lived with Blake, when their whispers and quiet laughs escaped so easily but never would have woken their daughter or alarmed her if they had.

Kitty cracked open Ruby's door. "You awake, baby?"

"Yes," Ruby whispered.

Kitty crawled into Ruby's bed and lay cradling her.

"Don't cry, Mommy. I'm sorry I hurt your feelings."

Kitty responded with a kiss, hoping to reassure her precious Ruby. At least, she would always try to keep Ruby away from men if she even dared date one again. She shouldn't, she knew, but…

"I forgive you, sweetie." She hugged Ruby closer. "What you did to Mr. Thompson at suppertime was not nice. I don't ever want to see you do that to anyone again."

"Okay," Ruby whispered.

"But you didn't hurt me, honey. It's not your fault he's gone."

Kitty stared at Ruby's profile in the light of the streetlamps flickering into the room and wiped away the tears on her plump cheeks.

"Then whose fault is it?"

"It's his fault, honey. I don't want him around here anymore."

"Me neither," whispered Ruby. "I only want it to be you and me, Mommy."

Kitty was silent until Ruby voiced what was on her own heart.

"Unless…" She hesitated for just a moment. "Unless Daddy finds us someday. Then maybe he could stay. Could he, Mommy?"

The guilt wrapped around Kitty like a heavy cloud. "If he finds us, sweetie."

"Are we lost, Mommy?"

She shushed Ruby and snuggled in beside her but couldn't voice her answer.

The Grieved Are Many

Lucy

Kitty pushed herself away from the table and began to place the Mantecadas in a plastic container.

"How did you and Ruby get to San Francisco? What happened to Blake?"

"It's not something we can talk about right now."

Kitty was resolute. So we packed some other things in silence, napkins and forks in case Max forgot them. Our mood had changed, and inside I couldn't reconcile the story of Kitty in busy, crowded San Francisco with the quiet life she'd had in La Rosaleda. Why had she told me this? This wasn't what I wanted to hear. I wanted to hear about how beautiful Ruby's life had been and how mine would have been if she had lived to raise me.

I tried to break the spell. "My mom could be ornery."

Kitty chuckled. "Oh, not so much really. I deserved it for bringing men into my house. I realized years later that it was something I never should have done."

She paused as if remembering something. "I should have listened to Ruby and let it be just me and her. Dating men all those years was one of my biggest mistakes. And as you're learning, I've made more than my share."

"Nobody's perfect," I offered.

She laughed cynically. "Certainly not me."

"So is that why you didn't date when I was a kid?"

Kitty nodded. "I don't regret it." She smiled.

She patted her full hips. Kitty wasn't really large but had put on a few pounds since she was young. "It's also not like my youthful figure would really attract a man now."

"Hey!" I said protectively. "You are still beautiful. You look pretty good for your age!" And she did. I wasn't just saying it to make her feel better.

I reached out and touched the ends of her hair, now cut in a shoulder-length bob and bleached blond. "Is it gray underneath?" I asked.

"A little but not so much. It's still brown."

"Auburn," I corrected.

She chuckled.

"Why blond?"

"Oh," she mused. "I guess I've had it this way all these years because I was hiding."

"Are you still hiding?"

She hesitated to answer. "I'm not sure. Most days I am, but some days I wish I could throw it all aside and go back."

My heart leapt. "Why don't we?"

"Oh no, Lucy." She shook her head sadly. "I can never go back. It will never be the same. Blake might have remarried by now, or perhaps he's moved on. Besides I'm old now. I'm not the same girl he married. I left him. I've done things no married woman should ever do." She paused. "I broke our promise." The lines in her face were suddenly deeper.

"Are you still married?"

She massaged the place where her wedding band should have been and frowned. "I really don't know. I wish we were."

I cautiously challenged her. "But I thought you didn't need men?"

"I don't. I don't need men. But Blake was not...'men.' Blake was my husband."

We were both silent for a long time. The strong woman who

didn't need anyone except me didn't really exist. She needed my grandfather. The prospect of going back hovered between us.

Could I dare go without her?

She ran her hand through her hair. "Maybe I should let it go back to grayish-brown."

"That's a great idea! You'd look beautiful natural."

"Oh, Lucy." Kitty reached out and touched my arm. "You have turned into such a lovely young woman. Ruby would have been proud."

"Do you think so?"

"I have no doubt." Kitty patted my arm again. "Even though it's hard, it's so nice to share these things with you now. You aren't a child anymore, are you?"

I felt a small burden lift.

"It's true," she said. "I wanted you to remember her, but as far as my secrets…? I knew they would affect you someday. A little girl shouldn't hear such things about her grandmother."

"I'm glad you told me about Blake…my grandfather."

She looked away for a moment and then met me with a grin I knew was forced. "Speaking of dashing men, where is your admirer?"

I looked up at the clock. Max would be here in five minutes. My hands flew to my face, and I felt silly and embarrassed about my giddiness.

Kitty grasped my hands. "Don't worry. Don't think of it as a date. It's just an outing to the park with your old grandma tagging along."

"With my Kitty," I corrected.

We laughed as the doorbell rang, and Kitty headed toward her room to freshen up.

I hung my hat on the coat tree with the thought, *God, please let him be as good as he seems*—then laughed at my little halfhearted silent prayer. I definitely was not myself.

I swung open the door to Max, who was leaning against the doorjamb, his hands shoved in his pockets and his thick hair swept over to one side. I couldn't stop the flush that crept over my skin.

"You look incredible." He held out his hand. "Lunch delivery."

I took the soft-sided cooler and set it beside the coat tree. I could hardly believe how nervous I felt. Would I ever get used to this feeling? My eyes fell on his sandal-clad feet, and I thought they looked like Jesus sandals. I giggled nervously at my twisted humor.

"What?"

"I was just thinking that your sandals are appropriate for a youth minister. They look like something Jesus would wear."

He sighed in mock exasperation. "You don't like my sandals?"

"No, I do!"

"But you're making fun of them."

"No! It was just—" I gave up. "I didn't mean to offend you."

Max laughed. "Believe me, I'm not offended. It's funny. I'm far from resembling Jesus, but being a youth pastor does keep me humble. I'll have you know these sandals were a great buy from the Bargain Shoe Outlet."

I laughed and then realized that we were still standing in the doorway. "Let's wait in the garden—Kitty isn't quite ready yet." I ushered him through the living room and out the sliding glass doors with pride. Kitty had outdone herself with the flowers this year. Petunias in all shades of pink, all sorts of daisies, and an assortment of healthy herbs spilled over their containers—like part of a Home and Garden TV set.

"Wow, this is beautiful. You and your grandmother did all this?"

"Mostly Kitty, but I help her. She's an organic gardener, so no pesticides or anything. It's cheaper to garden that way too."

"A smart way to go. Maybe I can get some tips."

"Do you get paid for being a youth minister?"

"Barely. That's why I'm going back to school. I'm hoping

that if I get my education degree, I'll be able to supplement my income. Right now I substitute-teach on the days I don't have classes."

I was impressed. "When do you have time to do homework?"

"In between classes and on weekends."

"Except when you're taking girls on outings to the park," I observed.

"Actually," he said, his eyes twinkling, "this is an exception. I've never taken a girl on a date to the park."

"Really?"

"Really. So be patient if I mess it up."

I was flattered.

He started. "Oh, that reminds me. Do you have a blanket? I forgot one."

I excused myself to look for one and found Kitty placing the container of cookies next to the cooler. She'd added a red scarf to her hair, pulling it back from her face smoothly and curling it into a small bun.

"He's handsome," she said, looking over my shoulder. Her eyes wandered farther back into the yard, like she was lost for a moment.

"Kitty? Is everything okay?"

She waved away my concern. "I was just thinking that besides visiting with Dr. Larimer at the hospital, it's been a while since I've spent time with a nice young man. I think I'm looking forward to today." She frowned. "I let you grow up too fast, Lucy. You deserved to enjoy your youth."

"Oh, Kitty," I protested. "I've enjoyed my youth. Between violin and piano lessons, reading, and art museums, I couldn't have had a better life. How many girls get to do their schoolwork at the art museum where their grandmother works? And it's not as if I've never seen men before."

"Having a friend, boy or girl, wouldn't have hurt you."

"You," I said, "are my friend, my best friend."

Her eyes lit then. "Just like Ruby," she said and put her arm through mine.

Being around this new, more laid-back Kitty was a different experience. I was used to seeing her cold or indifferent to people in public—not exactly rude but just not warm and personable like she was at home. I guess I really shouldn't have been surprised since, according to the things she'd told me about herself recently, she'd once been a more social person. It seemed as though she hadn't lost her enjoyment of people after all, but had just hidden it away for a time.

We rounded up a Blue Star quilt Kitty had sewn a few years earlier and headed out the door for introductions.

"Did you make this?" Max asked, pointing to the quilt.

I could tell that Kitty was pleased by his attention to her handiwork.

"She did," I said. "Each one really is a piece of art. Kitty makes them all by hand. We probably shouldn't even be using this one."

Kitty waved away my concern. "Don't be silly, Lucy. Quilts are made to be used."

"Uh-huh," I said. "Sure. That's why some of yours are hanging in the university art museum."

Max turned to Kitty. "I saw your latest exhibit at the university museum—beautiful!"

I ignored my leaping heart at the memory of Max watching me play piano.

"She even sells them. People can buy them in six different highbrow shops around the country."

"It's just part of our bread and butter." Kitty always downplayed her skill. She laughed. "When Lucy gets out of school and gets a job, maybe her old grandmother can stop stitching her fingers to the bone."

"You better not," I said to her and then turned to Max. "Some of her quilts are traditional patterns like the Wedding Ring or this

Blue Star, but many are signature tapestries." I looked at Kitty. "They tell our stories."

After the slightest pause, Kitty smiled. "And some of them are for having a picnic on! Now enough about my quilts. I'm hungry. Help me across the road, please."

Max seemed impressed by Kitty's way of ordering people around, so I followed behind, grateful to observe, as he obediently offered his arm and escorted my grandmother across the street. I'd never seen her so enamored with anyone. I loved this new Kitty and wondered if this was how the young Kitty had been with Blake: funny, happy, talkative.

At the park we sat beneath a towering oak, its branches sprawling far enough to shelter three different picnics. But I was glad ours was the only one in this corner of the park this day. Max helped me spread the quilt for the three of us to sit on.

As Kitty and I enjoyed the shade, Max unpacked bottled waters, a cluster of grapes, several containers, and a loaf of bread wrapped in paper unmistakably from our favorite bakery.

"Martha's!"

Max smiled. "You like Martha's baking?"

"And her coffee and tea. Hers is our favorite shop." Kitty beamed. "And Martha is a friend of mine. Did she pack everything up for you too?"

"No, Max's deli did that," he said with a chuckle.

"A man who knows his way around even half the kitchen is a blessing in my opinion!" Kitty exclaimed. "There was a time when my Blake—" she stumbled over her words as I looked up. This was a new Kitty indeed. "My Blake..." she said quietly.

We all sat in uncomfortable silence, and my heart dropped.

I wasn't sure what I should say or do. Kitty looked confused and embarrassed. I reached over and touched her hand. She softly brushed it away.

Max and I exchanged understanding glances. He looked decisive as he took a deep breath. "Blake Birkirt?" he asked.

My jaw couldn't have dropped any further. I was horrified. Why would he just come out and ask about Blake?

Quickly I reached over again and put my palm on top of her shaking hand; this time she let me squeeze it.

I thought it might help to change the subject. "Kitty, are you hungry?"

She turned her hand over, still shaking, and clasped mine. She finally looked straight at me, her eyes glistening. Then she raised her chin and adjusted her hat as if recovering from a fall.

"Why yes, Maxwell. Mr. Birkirt was my husband."

I wanted to correct her. *Blake* is *your husband, Kitty.* But I was surprised she had acknowledged my grandfather at all.

"I guess you've heard about him before since you're Lucy's friend." I hoped silently that Kitty wouldn't be angry I'd shared her business with someone who might as well be a stranger to her.

"Yes ma'am."

"Well, you are correct. He was my husband, and he knew his way around the kitchen like you seem to. When I was pregnant with Ruby, he used to help me cook. A very romantic thing to do, you know, cooking together. A good time to talk, a time you can make one another feel cared for."

My jaw dropped again.

"I'm sure it is." Max leaned back on his haunches. He talked so easily about all of this. "I've never been married, so I don't really know. What did you and your husband like to make?"

Kitty began to talk about different occasions in the kitchen with Blake as I busied myself unpacking the rest of the picnic basket. I found the conversation flow intriguing but disconcerting too.

How could a stranger bring out so many details of Kitty's past seemingly easier than I could? I listened to every word about my grandfather.

I didn't know if I'd ever figure out where my father was, but I now knew that I had a grandfather who was practically a neighbor in the Sonoma Valley. Hearing Kitty talk about him tugged at my heart, and I wondered if a part of her wanted to run to him as much as I did. Of course he could be dead, but I had a feeling that somehow Kitty would have known if he was.

I pulled out containers filled with what looked like red potato salad, sliced vegetables, some kind of dip that must have been for the vegetables, and baked chicken that smelled like lemons and rosemary. I was surprised. It certainly appeared that Max was something of a gourmet cook.

With Max's spread and Kitty's cookies, we would be eating like royalty. When I pulled out three blue floral porcelain plates tied together with red ribbon along with three sets of forks and cloth napkins also tied in ribbon, I decided that if Max was trying to impress Kitty, he'd outdone himself. It was exactly the kind of thing Kitty would have done if she were packing a picnic. Then the warmth in my stomach reminded me that Kitty might not be the one he was trying to impress.

"So this blanket is a replica of the one you and Blake used to use for picnics?"

I glanced down at the tiny stitches perfectly holding together blue stars in an array of hues and patterns that reminded me of the night sky. I remembered when Kitty had made the quilt a few years ago. She'd worked on it day and night, and even though it wasn't nearly as intricate as many of her other quilts, she'd seemed very driven about not finishing until every stitch was perfect. Why hadn't I seen before what Max so easily put together? This was just like the quilt Kitty had described in her memories of time with Blake— maybe even the quilt from when Ruby was conceived. I flushed with the reminder that Kitty had not been perfect and with the knowledge that she'd once been part of a grand love affair, one that had resulted in a very special marriage—interrupted by what I didn't yet know.

I ran my hand over the stars. How gifted Kitty was to recall the design so clearly. I longed to see the original and compare the two, but it must have been left at the Frances-DiCamillo estate. If only I could get Kitty to go back someday…

"Oh!" I suddenly exclaimed with a mouthful of potato salad. My hand flew to my mouth. "This is divine! Kitty, you have to taste this!"

I reached over and offered her a bite. Her face lit up. Kitty was an amazing cook herself, and I could tell she was surprised. The texture of the salad was wonderful. Just firm enough and the red skins soft enough that they didn't interfere with the chewing.

My stomach was doing some odd flip-flops. I wondered if Max would cook if he got married or if it was just a bachelor thing to impress us.

"Delicious!" Kitty agreed. "Not only do you cook, but you cook so well! Where did you learn?"

"Oh, I take a gourmet cooking class here and there, but living on my own I've had lots of time to practice."

"Rehearsal for the future," Kitty said knowingly. "But don't forget, if you win a girl over with this cooking, you'll have to continue after you marry."

She winked. I knew she wasn't referring to me, but my face reddened. I thought I might toss up the potato salad when he caught my eyes. I tried to look away, but it was impossible.

Kitty came to my rescue. "Well, I'm hungry. What else do we have here?"

She passed us each a plate, and then Max seemed to remember that he was the host as he started to dish up our food and hand out the waters. It was so nice to be waited on. What a treat. We rarely, if ever, had been doted on so much, especially Kitty.

I reached for my fork, glancing at Max. I could tell he wanted to say something. Then it hit me. He was a minister. He probably wanted to say a blessing. I looked over at Kitty, who was busy spreading her napkin across her lap. What would she think? Would she be upset? Max seemed to sense my unease. He closed his eyes for a fleeting moment, then picked up his fork. "Shall we eat?" He smiled warmly in my direction.

A hazy memory surfaced in my mind, like the light filtering through our patio doors at sunrise: Ruby praying over a breakfast of eggs and toast. Ruby, barefoot, in a jade green robe, head bowed and clasping my hand. Ruby's beautiful hair, each auburn wave falling forward as she turned and leaned toward me.

"Whose turn?" she had asked.

"Yours."

"Okay. Close your eyes. And don't peek! Father, thank you for this lovely day, for my beautiful Lucy, and for your Son."

"Amen," we both said.

We raised our heads at the same time to look out the window.

"The sun is up now."

Ruby chuckled. "Yes, that sun is up and ready for you to come out and play."

Kitty's laugh shook me from the memory. I tried to figure out what she and Max were laughing about, but remembering Ruby's prayer had transported me somewhere.

"What is it, Lucy?" Kitty noticed my lostness.

"Oh, nothing." I glanced up and was horrified when Max reached over and brushed his fingers across my cheek.

A few stray tears had rolled down my face.

Kitty was digging out one of her embroidered handkerchiefs. I pressed it to my cheeks and then stared at the cloth in dismay. I always hated soiling Kitty's handkerchiefs. I never understood why she preferred them over tissue. They were much too pretty to mess up, but burying my face in one was better than looking at Kitty and Max.

"I'm so sorry. I…"

"What?" Kitty implored.

I felt my cheeks flush. How embarrassing.

Max's eyes locked with mine when I looked up, and I knew he understood.

"Really, Kitty. It's nothing. I just remembered something, is all."

"Wonderful, dear!" Kitty again came to my rescue, actually holding her hands in the air. "You remembered something!" She laughed. If anyone understood the power of a diversion, it was Kitty.

The growing sensation, which began the day I first heard about La Rosaleda, was drifting through me and slowly filling some of the empty place Ruby had left. And there was another new warmth in my chest created by Max's presence this afternoon.

I looked over at Kitty, now laughing with Max about something he'd said. I was happy that she seemed to be having so much fun long after finishing lunch.

"So tell me," Kitty asked Max. "What else do you do? You're too old to be a full-time college student."

He dropped his jaw in mock insult. "What are you saying?" he asked innocently.

I laughed, recalling my similar conversation with him the week before. Kitty and I could be so alike sometimes.

"I work with teens."

"Wonderful! What kind of work do you do with them?"

Oh no, I thought. Here it comes. Kitty will be ready to toss him out, gourmet picnic and all.

"I'm a youth minister. So I mostly take teens on cool trips—hiking, rock concerts, that kind of thing."

Kitty was quiet a moment to give the idea a chance to roll around in her head. I gave Max a reassuring look when he glanced nervously my way. After she made us squirm for several minutes, she said quietly, "I can picture you working with kids. I bet they love you."

I watched as he exhaled in relief, and my heart began to slow its thundering beat.

"They only like me because I can play the guitar, and that makes me cool."

"Really?" Kitty exclaimed.

"Well, the first time I went to college, I earned a degree in music."

I watched as Kitty's eyes glowed. I braced for her announcement.

"Lucy plays the violin and the piano—beautifully, I might add."

Max's face lit up. I have to admit I was embarrassed.

"I've heard her play piano at the museum. She's amazing. I didn't know about her gifts with the violin."

I smiled at his wink.

"I have a band. Nothing too serious, but we do play several instruments. I can also play the piano and the saxophone, but we have other people in the band who handle those instruments, as well as bass and drums."

Interested, I asked, "Who sings?"

He spread his hands out before him. "Me."

Kitty clapped her hands, and I thought I might be hallucinating. Who was this jolly person who had taken over my grandmother's body?

"So," I challenged him. "Sing something."

"Is that a dare?"

"Of course not," Kitty said protectively. "It's an invitation!" She grinned at me.

"Well…" Max grew modest. "I usually don't sing in the middle of the park—"

"Nobody will notice," I joked even as another family spread their blanket under a tree near ours and a couple of kids threw a ball back and forth close by. "Please?" I asked.

Kitty kept smiling, but she was too dignified to beg.

He took a big nervous breath, exhaled loudly, then sent a low, sultry hum into the tree branches. His singing was even lower than his speaking tone, but it was a soloist's voice.

I nearly fainted when Kitty joined in, harmonizing with him perfectly to the tune of "Amazing Grace."

14

Kitty…?" We sat out on the porch a few mornings later, and I was hesitant. "Did you once have faith?" Since hearing Kitty sing the song in the park, I'd become convinced that Kitty had once had some kind of faith. I realized it wasn't simply the words of the song after all but the ease with which she sang them. And skill.

Surprised, Kitty looked away and sighed with a kind of resignation. We sat in silence for a while.

"Once."

I absorbed her confession. "What happened?"

"Oh, I don't know." I could tell she really didn't. Her secrets seemed to be collapsing around her. "I either left it behind or it left me behind. I can't tell."

"Do you resent people who have faith?" I was afraid of her answer, but I had to know how she felt about Max.

"I guess I have in the past," she admitted. "There have been several times in my life when I've wanted to seek refuge in faith only to end up being judged by people of faith. I seemed to keep running into the overzealous types, so I just started staying away."

"I don't think Max and Susannah seem zealous," I suggested.

"No." Kitty shook her head sadly as the chimes hanging around our back garden clinked in the slight breeze. She seemed carried away on that breeze for a moment. "I remember once when I walked into a church in the center of San Francisco. I'm not sure what denomination it was, but when I confessed my troubles and asked for help, the preacher offered to comfort me in a way very unbefitting a spiritual leader."

I gasped. "You're kidding!"

"No." She looked deep into me, trying to convince even me, and I could see the fear she'd kept hidden with this revelation. "I'm not. So the next time I tried looking for help, I went straight to the women in the church. I guess I should have gone to them first, but one would expect a preacher to have higher standards."

"Did the women help you?"

"No. They were too busy taking care of their husbands and children. In all fairness, I guess they tried a little bit, but they didn't know what it was like to raise a child on one's own. I told them I was a widow, but one Sunday morning Ruby announced to a group of ladies in the church kitchen that I took her away from her daddy. I was mortified at the looks of pity they gave to Ruby and the disgust on some of their faces when they looked at me." She laughed halfheartedly. "I suppose lying to them didn't give me a good start."

"That had to be embarrassing."

"It was. I was ashamed. There was this one lady who actually lectured me. 'It's shameful, utterly shameful,' she said and stormed out of the kitchen, dragging her little girl, Ruby's new friend, behind her."

My heart ached for Ruby. I guessed she must not have had many friends when she was little, just like me.

"But there was also another lady. I guess she was just about my age. She'd been very nice and accepting. This woman, Carrie Bingham, really was a widow, and she would save a seat for me at church on Sunday mornings. I've always felt bad for not going back. I wonder how many Sundays she continued to save a seat for me?"

I smiled. "I think Susannah is kind of like Carrie Bingham."

"I thought she was married. Is she a widow?"

"No, oh no. But she reaches out like that—it's like she glows with her faith. She's just as normal as everyone else except she has this attitude of hopefulness and peace I can never understand."

Kitty considered this, brows knitted.

I told Kitty the adoption story of Susannah's daughter, Maria.

"She's had hard times." Kitty seemed to have new respect for my friend, whom she'd not yet met.

I cocked my head. "I guess I hadn't thought of it like that. She seems, well, almost perfect to me."

"Dear, nobody is perfect. Peel back the layers of any person, and you'll find pain and suffering well-hidden in their soul. It might be low self-confidence for one and cancer for another. It's all relative."

I nodded. "So my mom was a Christian? Is that what you meant when you said she was God crazy?"

The guilty look on Kitty's face surprised me. I could tell she was measuring her words carefully. "She was. And I hated it. I almost despised the way she was always praying for everyone. She would tell me, 'I'm praying for you, Mom.'" Kitty paused. "It just rubbed me wrong."

"Did Ruby pray for me?"

"Every day, from the sound of it."

I couldn't hide the small smile that played at my lips. I felt a wave of relief washing over me. I hadn't expected it to matter so much, but it did.

"And what about Freda? Didn't she pray for you when you were pregnant with Ruby?

"Yes." Kitty nodded, lost in her thoughts. "She prayed for me, Ruby, my family…"

"So if she prayed for you and your family through the generations, would that include me too?"

Kitty sighed again. I wasn't sure if she was only trying to humor me when she said it or if she meant it. "I don't see why not, dear. I've heard the prayers of a mother are the loudest to God."

"What about you?"

"I left my faith in La Rosaleda, Lucy. When I did pray for Ruby, it didn't work, as you know."

The wind caught the chimes and lifted them in a crescendo that gave Kitty a welcome pause. "So faith? I've never been able to get it back. I'm not sure God would even want me back."

I wondered if that could be true.

"But, Kitty, aren't prayer and faith the same thing?"

She sighed. "Child, shouldn't you ask Max these things? He's a minister—surely he would know more than I do."

My insides grew warm at the mention of Max.

"What do you think of Max?"

She smiled then, her defenses coming down. "I think it's wise not to blindly trust men, Lucy, but he's a fellow I think you should definitely give a chance."

I let a sigh escape my throat, relieved to know that Kitty approved of Max.

"Just remember," Kitty said, setting her cup on the garden table between us. "People can put on a good front. Sometimes they can trick you. Make sure you get to know Max, and don't trust him only because he is nice or because he says he has values." She looked at me seriously. "Make him earn it. Make him show you his heart. Then wait and see."

She sounded like a mother then. "Trust me, I know."

I was learning that real life was seldom like the novels I read or the love songs I'd heard. Art was just a snapshot of everything that was good, sad, or bad about love; it rarely encased everything romance was all at once.

I suddenly had the urge to bring a canvas into the garden. I wanted to fill in the memory I'd had of Ruby during the picnic. "I think I'll paint today," I said, changing the subject.

Kitty's face brightened. "That's a girl. Be true to yourself."

"Kitty." I waved her wizened words away. "I'm still me."

"Of course you are," she said, but I wasn't really sure what she meant. "But you are in love."

My eyes widened, and I looked at where the roses bent low toward the ground. "I do really like him," I admitted.

From the corner of my eye I could see Kitty smiling. "So do I."

"What do I do?" I asked.

"Nothing, dear." She reached over and grabbed my hand. "Just be yourself, and don't ever feel the need to do anything different than what your heart tells you to do."

"But how do I know it's my heart speaking?"

"You'll just know."

"Kitty, did my grandfather have—?"

"Yes. A true faith. The real thing. If all Christians were like him…" Her thought trailed off, and we sat quietly then.

I thought of a lady in one of my courses who had told how her family became Jewish. Her grandmother, a Catholic, had fallen in love with a Jewish man, she said. But his family had refused to give their blessing to the relationship unless she converted to Judaism. Her grandmother began a long journey to learn about the Jewish faith, eventually breaking away from her past religion and embracing the faith of her fiancé. Theirs had a happy ending.

Could I—would I even be willing to—embark on such a journey? If not, could two people who loved each other give up their beliefs for each other?

As soon as the thought entered my mind I wanted to dismiss it. Asking Max to choose between me or a God I wasn't sure of, a faith I wasn't ready to leap into, would be wrong.

A breeze caught the chimes again, and I realized I was already exhausted and I hadn't even had lunch. I needed to eat and get my paints.

"Grilled tuna and cheese?" I offered.

Kitty looked amused. "Of course! I look forward to your gourmet skills in the kitchen, dear. Let's have your best meal."

I laughed at her reference to the meal I knew how to cook best. We didn't have full meals except on Friday and Saturday nights and Sunday afternoons, and those were only cooked by Kitty, with me, her lovely assistant, helping out.

"Well," I joked, walking into the house, "it looks like there are some men out in the big world who like to cook, so maybe I'll be okay after all."

We both laughed, but I wasn't completely joking. If I ever did get married, it would have to be to someone who liked to cook or who didn't mind grilled tuna and cheese several times a week.

Kitty took her usual spot in the kitchen, and I soon had the sandwiches toasted and had heated two servings of leftover tomato soup Kitty had made from her garden tomatoes the day before. Just as we sat down, the telephone rang. We both stared at it. We were together, so who could be calling?

I got up to answer the phone, my heart quickening at the thought that it might be Max. My voice was disappointed when it was Susannah, even if I was glad to hear from her. And then I panicked as I remembered I'd never called her on Saturday.

When I hung up, I asked Kitty if she'd like to meet Susannah at the hospital to visit with Mary this afternoon.

"Absolutely. But why at the hospital?"

"Her surgery, remember? It was yesterday."

"But she was only just diagnosed. I almost forgot," Kitty protested.

"I know."

We ate in silence, both of us lost in thought. There was so much to think about lately. I wondered where our simple, reclusive life had gone. Having friends kept people busier than I'd ever imagined.

At the hospital, Susannah, Kitty, and I all sat around Mary's bed talking. Mary had responded warmly to Kitty, and the two had hit it off immediately. Susannah seemed happy I'd brought Kitty with me.

I hadn't gone through anyone's death since Ruby's. I didn't

know Mary that well personally, but I felt I did through Susannah, and I hoped Mary wouldn't die.

After a while I patted Susannah's hand and got up. She started to follow, but I shook my head and whispered, "You need to be with your mom."

She nodded and sat back down as I headed out the door. I didn't know where to go; I just knew it had to be away from seeing Mary's sad face. It reminded me too much of Ruby and the day she died. And I still remembered Kitty's pain more than my own, how it had surrounded us both like a thick mire of blackness.

15

I found my way into the cafeteria, ordered a latte from the café cart, and sought out a table in a quiet corner where I could be alone. I let the hot liquid seep into my bones even as it scalded my throat. I didn't care. The pain kept me in the moment, where I wanted to be, instead of back in Mary's room or back even further in Ruby's room. I bowed my head and allowed my eyes to close, willing myself to relax. I needed to relax; I could feel the familiar tightening in my throat and chest, but I'd forgotten my inhaler at home again.

So much like your mother, Kitty had accused before.

I needed to concentrate on taking deep breaths.

"Excuse me."

I looked up. The familiar voice belonged to Dr. Larimer.

"Are you okay? I haven't seen you in a while."

I realized it had been nearly six months since I'd had a checkup. "I'm sorry, Dr. Larimer, Kitty has been trying to get me to go, but I've been so busy with school…"

He sat down beside me and patted my back.

"How are you, Lucy?"

"Oh, fine." I smiled weakly.

I recalled Kitty's comments about Ruby's connection with Dr. Larimer. I hadn't had time to follow up on it with all the excitement about Max and the other new revelations.

I shook my head. "It's so hard to sit in a hospital room. Do you know Mary in room 215?"

"I do. She's in good hands."

"I'm glad for that."

"She's your friend, right?"

I nodded. "She's my friend, but it's so much more, Dr. Larimer."

"So much more of what?" he pressed.

I felt awkward. "You're my doctor—you don't have time to hear my personal problems."

"Not true," he said. "You're a special patient, Lucy. I've been treating your family for years. In fact, did you know it was my father who helped Kitty during your mom's birth?"

I raised my chin. The unspoken was finally being said.

"Yes." I felt relieved. "I mean, I didn't know before, but I've been asking Kitty questions. It's all just too…crazy, you know? That Kitty never told me who you really were. I'm not sure what to believe." I coughed and he patted my back.

"Where's your inhaler?"

I looked guilty and didn't answer.

He smiled knowingly. "Come with me. I'm on a break and have a half hour."

We made our way to the pharmacy, and I waited outside. He came out with my prescription filled, and I wasted no time inhaling the passage-opening medicine. We walked out to the hospital garden and sat down by some rosebushes that were showing off deep pink and red blossoms.

"When I was a resident, sometimes your mom would come meet me here. We'd talk."

"About…?"

"About you," he said.

I tried to imagine Ruby, sitting here by what might have been those very same rosebushes. I caught a trail of their sweetness in the air.

"She liked roses." A sudden memory flashed through my mind,

how we would pick roses in our garden and put them on the kitchen and coffee tables. I thought of the vase on the table the day Ruby died, where she normally would have left her inhaler. Roses were one flower variety that didn't bother her too much, not that she ever would have gone without flowers anyway. She loved them too much.

"You still have the garden?" he asked.

"Yes, it's beautiful. Kitty takes such good care of it."

"Your mom did too."

I glanced at him. "How do you know?"

"Do you really want to know?" he asked.

I nodded, relieved that this unspoken tie between us was finally being acknowledged. I had a feeling that even Kitty might not know everything that had gone on between Dr. Larimer and Ruby.

"Do you remember when I came to visit you at your house, Lucy?"

Surprised, I shook my head. "I still barely remember anything before…"

"That day," he finished.

I nodded.

"Did you know I was friends with your mom when we were children?"

I smiled at the thought of him and Ruby being childhood playmates. "I know that you were friends until she and Kitty left La Rosaleda, when Ruby was really young. You were her best childhood friend."

"Yes." He nodded. "It was strange. Years after she left La Rosaleda, we ran into each other at Pier 39. That's where she and her friends liked to hang out on Saturdays. I recognized her right away. Even though she'd turned into a woman, a very beautiful woman."

"Did she recognize you?"

"No. She was busy watching and talking to the seals."

I smiled, the story Kitty had told me about Ruby talking to the seals when she was little still fresh in my mind.

"I watched for a while. It had been more than ten years, maybe fifteen. Then I couldn't stop myself. I strode up, meaning to say hi, but I was so nervous I couldn't say anything."

I smiled at the thought of Dr. Larimer being at a loss for words. He'd always been so professional and well-spoken. Of course, I'd only known "Doctor Larimer," not Matt.

"What did she say?"

"Nothing, she and her friends just laughed at me." He chuckled. "It was pretty embarrassing. But finally she asked who I was, and as soon as I said Matt, she threw herself into my arms."

I tried to picture Ruby wearing one of her worn pairs of jeans and a few colorful tank tops layered on top of each other, the way she would be in our memories forever, throwing herself into young Dr. Larimer's arms. I couldn't say anything. Hearing about her, like she was a real person and not just Kitty's ghost daughter, was…glorious.

"After that we spent every day together, at least every day we could until I had to go back to school. It was the best summer of my life."

"But you were just friends, right?"

"Did Kitty tell you that?"

"Ruby told Kitty that." I wondered at his expression.

"That explains a lot." I waited for him to say more, but he seemed finished.

"Please," I said. "I need to know."

"Okay, but Kitty probably won't appreciate my telling you."

"It's okay."

"We were in love," he said somewhat shyly. Since he was now married with children of his own, I wondered if it was embarrassing for him to talk about a past relationship.

"I was away at medical school, but every free weekend, I flew back to see her."

"Really?" This new bit of information amazed me. It wasn't at all what I'd expected.

"I stayed with some friends of mine, but they hardly saw me because Ruby and I spent every minute we could walking along the shore, going to the wharf, and of course eating, especially at Mexican restaurants."

I smiled, not surprised. "She had my grandmother's taste for good food?"

He glanced at his watch. "Look, Lucy. I don't want to leave you hanging, but I'm running out of time. Promise me we'll talk more later if I don't get to finish?"

I nodded.

"There were several weeks when I couldn't go see your mom. I had finals, and well, some other things I'll have to explain later, but Ruby had a really hard time. We got into a fight, and while she was mad at me she started hanging out with this older man she'd met."

I nodded. "Kitty told me about George Fields. He's my father, right?"

He looked hurt. "Is that who she said he was?"

I nodded.

"I'm sorry to say he wasn't a very nice man to Ruby. I'm sure he would have made a terrible father."

His words stung.

"It's a really complicated story, but…" The sound of the beeper made us jump, and he looked regretful. "I'm sorry. Do you want to talk more about this later?"

"I do."

"You're a good kid," he said, ruffling my hair like he had when I was twelve. "Listen, I have most weekends off, and maybe after church on a Sunday I could get my family settled and we could meet at that coffee shop—Martha's, is it?—down the road from your mom's." He paused. "I mean down the road from your and Miss Kitty's house."

He winked and ran off while I sat feeling dejected and insignificant. Everyone knew so much more about Ruby than I did. How could I have seen him for years and not known? It made perfect sense as I thought of many comments he'd made about knowing Ruby, how he'd been so affectionate with Kitty.

I wondered if he knew the whole story of how Ruby died— and if he too blamed me for her death?

16

I was painting near the patio doors when the doorbell rang the first time. I leaned in closer to the canvas, trying to finish the last few strokes needed to fill in an area of a backyard garden. The second time I took a breath and hoped it was just a salesman who would go away.

But when the bell rang a third time, I gave up, put the lid on my paints, and flung open the door.

My hand flew to my chest as a spray of deep red roses materialized—the fragrant kind, tied together with a silk ribbon.

"Oh my goodness!" I called to tell Kitty to come see but remembered she was at the museum. When I turned back I caught sight of the deliverer's footwear. Jesus sandals. "Max!"

The roses now hung by his side. "Guilty."

He opened his arms. "A hug?"

I only hesitated a moment. I raised myself on tiptoe till his arms were snug and warm around me and his breath on my neck sent little shivers crawling down my spine.

"Are you going to invite me in?"

"Oh! Yes!"

I rushed to the kitchen to get some scissors and a vase, and we took turns clipping the ends of the roses and arranging them in the vase.

"Breathtaking!" I exclaimed, setting them on the coffee table in the living room.

"Like you."

I was amazed at how he could make my insides bubble and pop like I'd swallowed a Mexican jumping bean. I sat on the couch, where Max sat beside me and took my hand.

"Susannah and her husband asked me to go to a food festival with them in Old Town this evening."

"Oh really?" I asked, surprised at how stiff my voice sounded.

He nodded, seeming more nervous than the Max I was used to. I hesitated. "Are you asking…?"

He seemed to come to his senses then, and I couldn't stop myself from grinning.

Turning toward me he said, "I'm asking if you want to go too. It sounds fun. And…we could invite Kitty too."

"Or maybe Kitty doesn't need to come along this time."

"That would be great. I mean, not great that she isn't going, but…"

I needed a moment to collect my own nerves, so I excused myself to go change; when I returned, Max was looking through the photo album Kitty kept on the coffee table. "You were a cute kid," he said.

"Thanks. Not hard to do when you're a little girl."

"You still make it look easy." He kept turning pages.

I took a breath, promising myself I wouldn't hyperventilate in front of him. I sat down beside him to view the album even though I'd thumbed through it nearly every day and already knew the details of every photo without even looking. Then, as Max turned the final page, I noticed one of the pictures coming loose from its holders. I reached over to push it back into place, and it popped up from the page and flipped onto the floor.

"Uh-oh," Max said. "Now I've done it! I'm sorry."

"You didn't do it," I assured him. "The album's old. This was bound to happen eventually."

As I reached down to pick up the picture, I gasped. The eight-by-ten photo of Ruby and me had landed upside down, and taped on the back were two smaller pictures. The people who stared at me were strangers but at once completely familiar.

The first photograph was black and white and pictured Kitty and Blake—it had to be him—on the porch of what might have been the vineyard estate Kitty had described. Kitty was dressed in the most gorgeous wedding gown I'd ever seen, with yards and yards of lace. I stared at the man I was sure had been my grandfather. He was handsome and had the easygoing look of a casual man, which his fancy suit couldn't hide.

The other portrait was in color and was of Ruby with a man and a little girl. I was absolutely shocked to see a picture of Blake and me sharing the same lens. He had more lines around his eyes and looked to be about as old as Dr. Larimer. Ruby looked to be in her early- or midtwenties.

"Is that little girl with the curly pigtails you?"

I took a deep breath. "I think so."

"But I thought you didn't know your grandfather."

"I don't… I didn't… At least I don't remember him. I have barely any memories before Ruby's death."

"Do you think Ruby might have known him?"

"Maybe. I think Ruby could have had a connection to La Rosaleda. I had an interesting conversation with Dr. Larimer when we went to visit Mary yesterday. Do you remember my telling you about him?"

"You said your mother and Dr. Larimer were friends as children."

"Right, but Dr. Larimer and I got interrupted by his beeper, so he couldn't finish telling me about his time with Ruby. He made me promise I'd talk to him later. I was hoping he'd tell me if she'd ever gone back."

"Apparently she did."

"And I guess she took me with her."

Max turned my chin toward him. "You guess? Lucy, you're so used to not remembering that you can't even see the proof you hold in your hands. Of course you've been to La Rosaleda with Ruby. And you met your grandfather. Just look at how happy you must have made him!"

I looked back at the picture. Blake was in the center holding me in one arm with his other around Ruby. She had one arm wrapped around him while her other arm rested on my leg, like she'd been patting my thigh. I was laughing! We were all laughing at something.

"Look," Max said, pointing to the banister in the picture. "It's the same as the picture of Kitty and Blake."

I couldn't believe my eyes. It was. The potted plants and outdoor furniture were different, but it was the same porch. Even the big door and ornate knocker in the background were the same in both pictures.

"Ruby did go back," I said quietly.

After I'd studied the pictures for a while, I retrieved some tape from the drawer, and gathered the pictures to reposition them in the album.

"You're putting them back?" Max seemed incredulous.

"Kitty isn't ready to tell me about all of this yet or she would have shown me these."

Max said nothing as he helped me stick new tape on the back of the photo where the old tape had been. It looked like it had been removed before over the years and had slightly torn away the paper. At least I didn't have to worry about damaging it. We replaced the album on the coffee table, and I tried to mentally rearrange my thoughts to think about our date with Susannah and her husband.

I hurriedly wrote Kitty a note to tell her where I was.

"Ready?" Max asked, holding the door. We stepped down the walk, and he guided me to the curb and a yellow minivan.

An appropriate vehicle for a youth minister, I thought.

"I wonder why Kitty didn't tell me I had been to La Rosaleda," I said, buckling my seat belt.

Max shrugged. "I don't know Kitty very well, but from an outsider's point of view, there must be something in La Rosaleda she doesn't want to go back to."

I knew. "She can't face Blake—my grandfather doesn't know she has been—" I hesitated, not wanting to smear my Kitty's reputation.

Max cleared his throat "That she's dated other men since…La Rosaleda?"

"Yes," I replied simply. I didn't want to voice the question troubling me: *How could Kitty have been unfaithful to Blake?*

"Maybe that's enough for her to deal with. She's probably too ashamed to face Blake."

"Perhaps, but why didn't my grandfather come for her? If he'd reunited with Ruby and had a relationship with us, then he would have known how to find Kitty."

"Maybe Kitty has a reason to doubt that he would welcome her. Maybe he didn't want to find her."

Perhaps Max was right. Kitty's sins might be too big to be forgiven. Perhaps my grandfather hadn't wondered about her at all, like I'd imagined.

We drove in silence for a few moments. I attempted to change the subject. "So how did you get so wise?"

He laughed. "You want my life story? Let's see…my grandmother was the child of German immigrants who made a living on the coast and still do. My mother is a lawyer, and my dad is still a fisherman. I grew up in San Francisco and graduated with a music degree from Berkeley before moving to Sacramento three years ago to get my bachelor's in business. Meanwhile I've joined the symphony, done some student teaching, found God, and become a lowly youth pastor, much to the chagrin of my mother."

His hands swiftly turned the wheel at an intersection. "I discovered it was hard to make a living as a youth pastor and figured

I might never be able to find a wife if I didn't learn how to make some money on the side."

We laughed, and he flipped on the radio, tuning from a rock station to one playing classical music.

"But your parents both have good jobs. Why would you worry about making ends meet? Don't they want to help you in your ministry?"

"My parents are loaded," he said, as if only half joking. "But I don't want to just live off of them."

I was thoughtful for a moment. Kitty and I had always lived a very simple life. She seemed to have a very strict budget; I'd always had the feeling there couldn't be much extra. The idea that Max had access to money that could make his life easier but instead refused it was interesting to me.

"Are your parents still married?"

"Amazingly, yes."

"How on earth do they make that work? I mean the life of a lawyer doesn't really fit with being a fisherman."

He shrugged. "It doesn't. Notwithstanding her disappointment in me, my mom's a pretty amazing lady really. She puts up with a lot from my dad and his job, but he does the same for her. They haven't spent a lot of time together over the years, but they share a strong work ethic, and one of these days I think they'll both throw their careers out the window and spend their time on what they both love." He leaned in toward me. "Sailing."

"How romantic."

"Well, they deserve romantic. Law and stinky fish don't exactly allow for a lot of romance."

I wanted to ask what he meant about his mom's disappointment in him, but we'd just pulled up to Susannah and Troy's house. *Always questions,* I thought. *Never enough time for answers.*

"I'm so glad you came," Susannah said, climbing into the backseat.

Troy extended his hand in a warm greeting, and we were on our way to downtown Sacramento.

The aroma of barbecue wafted through the Western-looking Old Sacramento, which teemed with people, but it was a booth of Chinese food that made Max stop.

"Are you a fan of Chinese?"

"Yes," I said. "And Vietnamese and all kinds of sushi."

"You're just full of surprises."

"Lucy! Come with me!" Susannah grabbed my hand.

It was the dreaded girls-heading-to-the-bathroom-together moment. I hated the way Max and Troy looked at each other knowingly as we walked away. Why did girls do this? Couldn't we just go for a walk? But I had to laugh when Susannah said before the bathroom door even shut, "He so digs you!"

"Digs?"

"Max is so into you. Are you interested in him too?"

"Just between us?"

"Just between us girls," Susannah promised.

"I'm really into him too."

We stepped outside as my stomach growled.

"I'm in serious need of some sushi," I said, hoping to deflect the attention from me to what I knew Susannah loved—lots of food.

Max and Troy shot an amused look at one another, and Troy poked teasingly at Max.

"Do they know we were talking about Max?" I felt my face go red.

"Of course!" Susannah laughed. "But we'll keep them wondering." She turned serious for a moment. "Listen, Lucy. I just wanted to talk to you about one thing real quick."

"What is it?"

"I know your grandmother—"

"Kitty."

"Yes, Kitty is very cautious of men, and that's good. But I just want to vouch for Max. He's a great guy. We've had him over for dinner and…"

"Hey!" I said accusingly. "You haven't even had me over for dinner yet!"

"I will! Soon! But I want you to know that Max seems so great—nice, the real thing."

I wanted so much for that to be true.

"What is it?" I could tell she sensed my hesitation.

"I'm just a little worried about our difference of beliefs."

"Our difference of beliefs?"

"No, I mean Max being a minister." I shrugged. "Maybe we could be one of those two-belief couples?" I tried to laugh.

Susannah smiled, but I had the feeling she disagreed. "Lucy, don't worry over this. It will work itself out. Worse things could happen than you converting to Christianity."

I raised my eyebrows. "I didn't say I would ever convert to anything."

"I know," Susannah said. "I wasn't saying you would. And if you don't, I still love you—you're my friend." She gave me one of her spontaneous hugs. Her total acceptance of me always surprised and moved me.

"Come on, you two!" Troy called. "We're starving."

Eventually the quiet sound of the river drew us away from the food booths and storefronts. We walked along the riverfront for a while. I watched Susannah and Troy curiously as they teased and cuddled. *How lucky their Maria is,* I thought. *How good it must be to see your parents in love.*

I tried to imagine Blake and Kitty at Susannah and Troy's age, and my heart went out to Ruby. How much she missed, never seeing her parents in love. Before I could feel too sad for myself, Max pointed out a particular floating restaurant.

I was reminded that his father was a fisherman. "Did you go out on your dad's fishing boats much?"

"All the time."

"And you liked it?"

"Loved it."

"Do you know how to fish?"

"Does Kitty know how to quilt?"

I laughed. "Then where in the world did you learn music?"

"My dad started teaching me how to play the guitar when we had time. When I showed some talent, my mom decided I needed to learn as many instruments as possible, so she signed me up for everything."

"I know the feeling," I said. "Kitty did the same thing. It was exhausting sometimes."

"Yeah," Max agreed. "But you must have loved it to excel at it. I know I did."

"I did. I still love music, especially the violin."

"Have you thought about auditioning for the symphony?"

"No, I only play piano in public at the gallery. Kitty didn't have the money to invest in the performance part. Last year I dropped all the lessons in fact. Now I just play on my own."

Ahead of us Susannah gasped. "The baby-sitter is expecting us in twenty minutes! Do you mind if we go?"

We headed for the car, and I looked at my watch. I hadn't realized it was so late.

"Past your curfew?" Max teased after dropping off Susannah and Troy.

"I don't know if I even have a curfew."

"Well, you'd better go in before she comes out chasing me away with the broom." He pulled up to our walkway.

I laughed. "Oh, she wouldn't even need a broom."

Max hopped out of the van to escort me to the door.

I smiled up at him. "Well, good night." It seemed so inadequate to end the night with those words, but I knew if he tried to kiss me, I would duck. I'd never kissed a man before and wasn't sure what to expect. Besides, was kissing on the first date even appropriate? What were his religious convictions about that? There were so many things I wished Ruby were there to help me understand.

"Hug?" he asked sheepishly, but his brown eyes twinkled.

I stepped into his arms and liked the mixed scent of soap and cologne on his T-shirt. His arms around me felt safe and secure but dangerous in a way I had no experience at dealing with.

After a long minute, I gently extracted myself from his arms.

"Good night, Lucy girl."

"I'm nineteen," I protested with a smile.

His gaze lifted me closer.

"No," he whispered. "You are not a girl."

His lips brushed mine before I could think of what was happening. Then he reached behind me and turned the doorknob. "Bye," he said as he gently pushed me through the door, like he was tucking me in, back safe at home.

I peeked out the door to watch him climb into his car; he waved before driving away.

Watching his van disappear, I found myself wishing the kiss, if it was that, had lasted longer. *When one waits her whole life for such a moment, she wants to savor it.* So I touched my lips trying to feel what was left.

I shut the door and found Kitty sitting asleep in the blue velvet chair. I hadn't realized she would wait up for me. I walked over to her, hesitating to wake her up. The album was on my desk beside her chair, and I wondered if she'd been looking at the photos. Had she noticed I'd retaped them? Would she say something to me if she had? I reached out and rubbed the velvet of the chair she sat in.

According to Kitty's story, my great-grandmother Freda had

given the chair to her before she gave it to Ruby. Now the chair was mine, but in Kitty's story there had been two chairs. What had happened to the other one, and how had this one ended up here? Even though Kitty claimed she'd given it to Ruby, how could that be possible if Kitty had never gone back home to get the chair? Could Blake have given it to Ruby after they reunited?

Kitty looked tired when she opened her eyes.

"Hi," I whispered. "I'm sorry you stayed up—you should have gone to bed."

"On your first date?" she asked incredulously. "Of course not!"

I smiled. "I'm glad I wasn't thinking of it as a real date, or I would have been even more nervous!"

"Tell me all about it."

I perched on the arm of the blue velvet chair and told her about the food, meeting Susannah's husband, Troy, our walk along the riverfront. I kept the good-night hug and what may or may not have been my first kiss to myself, and she didn't ask.

Kitty smiled. "Susannah and Max are such nice kids. I'd like to meet this Troy too. It seems as if you girls make better decisions about men than I used to."

"But you chose Blake," I said. "He was a good decision."

"Yes," she agreed. "Besides Ruby he was the best decision I ever made. His decision didn't turn out so well though, did it?" Her eyes glistened.

"I don't believe that." I leaned over to hug her.

"Believe it, Lucy. I'm glad you love me, dear. But I can't erase some things I've done. I've made too many mistakes. Blake would have been better off if he had never met me."

"How can you know that?"

"I just know, that's all."

"Maybe you should let him decide."

She pushed me up from the chair and stood up as she shook her head no. "If you're suggesting I go back to La Rosaleda, Lucy, it won't do you any good. Your mom tried the same thing, and it didn't work."

"I know," I said. "I found…"

"The pictures," she finished. She looked disapprovingly at me.

"Max and I were looking at the pictures together, and they fell out. I'm sorry. I wasn't snooping. "

"I believe you," she said. "I suppose you need an explanation."

I nodded and sat down on the couch. She limped over, her muscles stiff from sleeping in the chair.

Putting her arm around me, she said, "Are you tired?"

"No." And I wasn't. There had been too much excitement in my life lately, especially today, to go to bed. "But you are."

"Fiddlesticks. Go put on a pot of tea."

My heart raced. Was I going to hear about how I'd met my grandfather? I nearly scalded myself as I poured the tea and carried two cups back to the living room. I found Kitty staring at the photographs I'd found earlier that evening.

"They were taken on the same front porch," I said.

"Yes."

"I don't understand. I thought La Rosaleda had been left far behind." I thought of Dr. Larimer's revelations but didn't want to overburden Kitty's feelings any more than they already were.

"La Rosaleda was left far behind for me but not for Ruby." Kitty shook her head. "Never for Ruby. She missed her father so much that she never let go. I think now that I should have left her with him."

"Kitty! You never could have left her!"

"No," she agreed. "But I should have tried. I shouldn't have subjected her to my mistakes. They weren't her fault, and she never understood. She never knew the full truth, and she blamed me for depriving her of her father."

"Why did you?" I regretted the way it sounded.

Kitty stared across the room at a picture of Ruby smiling from a place in a rose garden where she seemed to be pulling weeds. She was wearing cutoff jeans, her brown legs tucked underneath her and her bare toes digging into the ground.

"That's not an easy answer."

The clock ticked a sad beat that matched my pulse, and I waited.

"I so loved it when Blake moved us back to Frances-DiCamillo. I was so young and wanted to be with my mother. I knew I would miss the loft, but my need to be near my family at such a young age overwhelmed me, and Blake knew it. It's really hard to be parents when you're practically still teenagers. I had grown up so fast. I just wanted to go back and hold on to my mom for a little bit longer."

17

I know what it's like, Kitty, to try to hang on to your mom. At least you remember yours." I looked at her, and she was staring at her hands. "Don't you, Kitty?"

"I do. I think of her every day, but going back, well, it just wasn't an option, dear. But Ruby did go back. She tried to get me to go too, once she made the connection, but I never would."

"I don't understand," I said. "But then I don't know why you ever left."

"Well, something happened that I wish I could forget, dear. I did things…"

"Bad things happen to everyone, don't they, Kitty?"

"They do, but…"

When Kitty finally told me the things she had done, I wished she hadn't. I tried to remain neutral as she spoke, but I admit it was difficult to hear what at first sounded to me like huge indiscretions.

Of course, in the day and age we live in, Kitty need not be so ashamed, but it was still shocking to me, if only because it had happened to my own grandmother.

It had happened gradually, but the first encounter had set the tone for what would happen later. She said it had been a warm day, almost sultry, in the vineyard when she decided to walk into La

Rosaleda. Ruby was with Freda, and Kitty wanted to visit some of her favorite shopkeepers.

Blake had suggested that she call their friend Mike Larimer to drive her into town when there was nobody else, but she preferred to walk. Maybe she was just shy, but something about Mike had always bothered her. She didn't like the way he looked at her. He stared longer than he should or would hold her arm too long as he helped her out of his car. I can just imagine how this infuriated Kitty, especially since she was even more reserved back then.

Kitty said she wondered why Blake had never noticed how cocky Mike was. Perhaps it was because of his help the night of the earthquake. Whatever it was, she told me, Blake never seemed to notice that Mike was a shameless flirt—no matter that he had a wife, Charlotte, and his little boy, Matt, at home.

"After my shopping," Kitty told me, "I still somehow found myself walking back toward home accompanied by Mike Larimer."

"I thought you didn't call him," I said.

"I didn't, but he *just happened* to be walking that day."

"Was he interested in you?"

"Yes, he was. I guess I knew it, but I just tried to ignore that fact when I saw him."

She said Mike made small talk for a while, and she kept noticing how he would place his hand at her elbow even when he didn't need to. She tried to distract him by asking about Charlotte. In turn he asked about her family and about the home Blake was building for her at Frances-DiCamillo.

"Oh yes," said Kitty. "It's gorgeous. It's what I've always wanted. He and my father did a wonderful job."

Mike was thoughtful. "That is downright sweet," he said.

Kitty said she thought she caught sarcasm. *What an odd response from him,* she thought.

"Whatever do you mean?" she asked.

He dashed a lock of blond wavy bangs off his forehead. She

said he really was exceptionally handsome compared to most men, even her Blake, and it would have been easy to be caught unaware of his bad manners. "It's just I figured your dream home would be the one your parents will give you someday."

"My new home, well, my husband built custom, just for me."

"I'm sure he did, right along with your daddy. He is Blake's benefactor after all, right?"

Kitty, incensed, quickened her pace. "My husband certainly works very hard for everything he has received. He is my father's most valued and trusted employee. And he is a co-owner of the estate, as am I."

Mike raised his eyebrows before changing the subject. "That Ruby of yours is growing," he said.

"She sure is." Kitty was suddenly relieved at the turn in conversation, glad to be talking about something more innocent. "How is Matthew? We haven't seen him or Charlotte in a few weeks."

"Well, he is fine. Matt's mom and I don't live together at present, but I do see him once a week."

Kitty was appalled. "That must be hard for Matt. And Charlotte…"

Mike just shrugged his shoulders, as if resigned to the way things were. When they reached the gate, Mike tipped his hat to her and continued walking.

"Sad, isn't it," she told Blake later that day.

"Yes. Very," he said. "Especially for Charlotte and Matt. I didn't even know there were problems."

"Well," Kitty hesitated, not wanting to sound like a gossip. "I hear he can be a bit of a flirt sometimes. Maybe…"

Blake scoffed. "Oh, Kitty, it's probably just rumors. Has he ever flirted with you?" He placed his arm around her shoulders and guilt swept through her. For some reason she told him no.

"Then I bet he'll be back with his wife in no time. It's probably just a lover's spat, like we have from time to time."

"Hardly ever," she said.

"Often enough to keep me on the straight and narrow," he joked.

Kitty said she felt silly for misunderstanding Mike's intentions and that Blake was probably right.

"I don't think you misunderstood the situation, Kitty," I assured her. "Mike Larimer sounds very rude and disrespectful, nothing like our Dr. Larimer. I don't understand why Blake would have trusted him though."

"Well," Kitty said, "Blake only saw the good in everyone. That is until he couldn't see it in me."

"What happened? Did he think you had an affair with Mike Larimer?"

I saw her chin drop. She reached a hand to one temple and slowly massaged. I took her silence as guilt. Was this a confession?

"*Did* you have an affair?"

BITTER GRAPES

Kitty

18

It was a Saturday evening when Blake took over story time for Ruby, giving Kitty the rare opportunity to sit out on the porch and relax. As she took in the rolling countryside around her, the leaves lush on the vines and the grapes themselves emerging, she listened to the sound of Blake's songs coming through the open window of Ruby's room.

All she needed was her shawl that evening as she sat on the porch swing and watched the sun setting over the vineyard. She loved being near the grapes, and the longer she sat breathing in the sweetness of the air, the more convinced she became that she needed to take a stroll, even if only through the yard.

She walked slowly toward the gate, enjoying the warmth of the evening, before turning back to the house and walking along the vineyard's edge, enjoying the hush that fell over the vineyard this time of night. She took a few turns through the vineyard and was humming her favorite song, the one Freda sang to her as a child, "Amazing Grace," when she heard a rustle among the vines.

"Oh!"

She jumped back, not having expected anyone else to be near. Turning around, she saw Mike Larimer step into her path.

"Mike! You nearly scared me to death!"

Kitty attempted a laugh that stuck in the back of her throat. He smiled at her, his charming grin full and friendly.

"I'm sorry, Mrs. Birkirt."

"What are you doing?" she asked sternly.

She was baffled at why he was out strolling at this time of evening. "What are you doing here?"

Mike had inched closer to her, and before she realized what was happening, he'd reached out and laid his hand on her shoulder.

"Well," he said, as he squeezed her shoulder through her shawl, "nobody has to know I'm here."

She cocked her head, wondering what he meant as she felt the warmth of his hand through the fabric of her clothing. Then she noticed something else in his eyes that caused her heartbeat to quicken. This is the moment when she should have turned and walked away, but confused, she instead found herself rooted to the spot.

"Why, Mike Larimer…" she said in surprise.

He stepped close enough for her to feel the heat through his shirt and then yanked her quickly into the shield of the vines.

"I had to see you alone."

Seven weeks later, young Kitty sat at the doctor's office in town.

"Absolutely not," argued the doctor. "It's wrong and illegal. Not only that, but your father would destroy me if he found out."

Kitty had no doubt that if he found out, he would. But what choice did she have? "Please," she implored. "I have to. This would disgrace my family. And my husband." She whispered his name.

"Kitty, you don't believe in this."

She fought to keep control of the tears. The doctor held her arm.

"What is it, Kitty? I'm your doctor. Please tell me. How did you come to be pregnant with another man's baby?"

Her sobs deepened. "I…I can't say!"

"And how do you know it's not your husband's?"

"I just do. It happened during a time I wasn't feeling well, so we...uh...we were sort of taking a..."

He frowned. "Of course, you were taking a break until you were over the flu you had a few months ago."

She looked up at him, her eyes a well of grief. His eyes looked sad, and she knew in that moment that she could trust him.

"I could lose my practice. You could get hurt."

She nodded. "If you help, I will never tell."

He was quiet a long time. Then he grabbed a pen and a sheet of paper. "It wouldn't be me."

Her eyes widened.

He patted her leg. "Don't worry. I would go with you," he assured, "and I would attend the procedure if I approve it."

"I see," she said. Her stomach felt queasy.

"I want to do it." And she knew she did. She was so desperate that she pushed her beliefs away and let her fear of losing Blake and disgracing her family outweigh her fear of the procedure.

"Are you sure?"

"Yes."

"There are many risks," he said. "Girls have actually died."

She looked frightened but answered "yes" again.

"Kitty," he said. "If I do this, you must first tell me who the father is."

"Why?" she cried.

"Because I have to know the truth of this before I can feel right about it. Before I can approve it."

She sniffled and slumped over as she sat across from him. Raising her eyes, she looked desperately in his direction.

"Will either one of us ever really feel right about it?" she choked.

"No." He put his hand on Kitty's cheek. "We'll never feel right about it, but let's face our consciences now."

She nodded and took a full breath. Kitty couldn't stop the tears pouring down her face, and then, to her surprise, tears trickled down the doctor's cheeks too as, filled with shame, she told him about Mike and the vineyard that evening Blake was putting Ruby to sleep.

"I shouldn't have gone for that walk."

The doctor seemed overcome with emotion.

"Dear girl," he said grasping both of her hands tightly. "I will keep your secret."

A Secret Told

19

Kitty leaned heavily on her cane to push herself up from the blue velvet chair. I watched inconsolable tears roll down her cheeks as she walked to her room and shut the door softly, leaving me shocked and feeling helpless. I was still trying to fathom the fact that my grandmother had had an abortion.

What should I do? I wanted to rush in and hold her, but since the day Ruby died, I'd rarely been the one comforting Kitty. While I had always been free to cry and feel afraid, Kitty had been the rock who was sure and staid and made everything right. I couldn't cry but was overcome with her loss.

How could I have missed seeing such terrible pain in Kitty? And how had she held it in for so many years? Had I been too wrapped up in myself to notice how Kitty felt?

I knew I needed to be the comforter, but I didn't know how. I went to Kitty's room and lowered myself onto the bed behind her, curling around her body. She reached back and took my hand, pulling it around her waist. I could feel her heart beating while my own was breaking for her.

We lay together in the silent room for a long time. I stared at the outlines of Kitty's hats propped around the room on stands, her jewelry lined up neatly on a mirror lying flat on her dresser, and her scarves draped on pegs and the bedposts. Kitty had always been one to dress up with accessories, and now these things seemed to be part of her disguise instead of her fashion statement.

"Kitty," I whispered.

She squeezed my hand in reply.

I took a breath, not sure what would help. "Kitty, I know it's a horrible thing what you went through, but you aren't a bad person."

She didn't say anything, so I continued, reaching for an answer that might make her forgive herself.

"These days, Kitty, you don't have to suffer through stuff like this alone. Girls go to counseling; they work through it. Even families love them through it. When girls do this…"

She interrupted. "I'm no longer a girl, Lucy dear."

I pressed my lips together and snuggled close to her, not sure how to respond to that.

"It was a long time ago, Kitty. Things are different now."

"True," she said. "But it seems like yesterday. It's the real reason I kept you and Ruby from La Rosaleda. It's the reason I can't go back."

"But," I tried to reason, "it's past. You can put it behind you. People's mistakes aren't as stigmatized these days as they once were, Kitty."

"Some things will always hold a stigma, Lucy."

"Yes, but you might be surprised how easily many people can accept your past."

"Do you, Lucy? Accept my past?"

"It wasn't your fault…was it?"

No, I reminded myself as I went over and over Kitty's confession. *She'd had no choice.*

In order to forget about what had transpired, Kitty said she began to take long walks around the estate, feeling sure Mike wouldn't dare approach the estate again. Even when he'd appeared with Charlotte around town, he seemed to go to great lengths to avoid her, Blake, and her father.

Most of the time Blake would go with her on her walks, but sometimes she'd walk alone, only the slightest bit nervous. On one particular August night, Blake had prompted her to have a few moments alone while he tucked Ruby in. She'd gratefully hugged her husband, kissed Ruby, and headed out of the house.

Shedding her shawl on the front porch, she'd set off across the yard with long strides. Beads of sweat had formed across her forehead by the time she stopped at the edge of the vines. She ran her fingers over a cluster of grapes nestled in the tendrils, still green and tight, before stepping around the end of the row and walking up the center.

She walked up and down the rows for quite some time, taking in the fullness of the fruits around her and watching the sunset over the edge of the fields. It felt good to get fresh air and enjoy the smell of the rich earth between her feet.

She heard the bell of the main building ring over the fields. Her mother still used it to let the vineyard workers know they could go home if they hadn't already. Those who didn't have homes often joined her and Isaac for meals—picnic tables beside the main house covered with white cloths and bowls of food.

The bell echoed and died away, and Kitty reached down to remove her sandals. She dug her toes into the cool earth and breathed in the familiar smell of the grapevines—the scent filled her with warm thoughts of Blake and her parents—and then she wrinkled her nose at a different odor. What was that? Someone smoking a pipe?

She turned slowly, hoping to see her father.

Mike Larimer tipped his hat and smiled warmly, but ice flickered in his eyes. "You never speak to me anymore, Kitty."

Her hand went to her chest, and she felt the slick spot where perspiration had gathered along her neckline. Panic crawled its way to the back of her neck, but she remained calm.

"You shouldn't be here."

"And why is that?"

Kitty backed quickly to the edge of the vineyard where she might be in view of others.

"That's what you said last time." He grabbed her arm.

"You've already caused enough trouble in my life."

"What do you mean?" His voice was harsh now. "I told you not to tell anyone."

"I didn't. What I mean…" Kitty trembled, wanting to run to her husband but wanting to let Mike Larimer know what he had caused.

"What I mean," she said, her voice cracking in her throat, "is there was a baby."

"A baby?" he asked, his face confused.

Silence grew heavier than the peace that usually settled across Frances-DiCamillo in the evening. She heard a rustle nearby.

Then a different but familiar voice, confused and angry, carried across the rows to her.

"A baby?" She turned to see Blake rounding the corner and walking toward them up through the rows of vines. She was relieved he'd decided to join her. Maybe he could… She paused and her heart fell. She knew what it looked like.

"*Was* a baby?" Blake asked. He was incredulous.

He and Mike both stood staring at her, obviously confused.

"Blake, dear, it's not… I know it sounds bad, but it's not that." She reached out to him.

He brushed her away and stepped toward Mike. A moment later Blake took a swing that landed squarely on Mike's nose. Kitty's cries disturbed her parents, who were sitting out on their porch swing.

Within minutes Freda was quickly walking Kitty back to the house.

"Mother, I know it looks terrible, but it's not what it seems."

Freda looked intently at her daughter. "I believe you, Katherine. So tell me what it is then."

Kitty erupted into tears. "I can't!"

"Of course you can, child. You can tell me anything!"

"Blake will never understand."

Freda reached for her daughter and wrapped Kitty in her arms.

Soon the men were in the house speaking in hushed tones; Isaac raised his voice to Blake. "Impossible!"

Isaac stormed into the living room, where the two distraught women sat on the couch holding hands. "Impossible!" he repeated. "Kitty was not pregnant with that man's baby."

Kitty's mouth dropped. Her father's disgust was apparent, and her mother was aghast.

"You aren't pregnant, are you?" Freda laid her hand on Kitty's shoulder.

"No." Kitty looked away in shame.

"Because," Blake tried to explain, "because she…" He looked at the floor but not before glancing at Kitty. The disgust in his eyes said enough.

Freda stood; her voice was calm but stern.

"I don't know what's going on here, and Kitty won't tell me, but my daughter would never be unfaithful to her husband or"— she threw her hands up in confusion—"get rid of her husband's child! Shame on you both!"

"Then explain what I heard!" Blake demanded, his hands shaking beside him and his face mottled pink with humiliation and rage.

Kitty had to look away from Blake's pain and her parents' stares. She couldn't stop crying, and regret fell over her like a river flooding the bank after heavy rains.

She couldn't explain.

"It was those walks," Blake said, his voice catching and sputtering. "Those rides you took with him, wasn't it?"

Kitty looked up, a pleading look in her eyes. "You wanted me to ride with him. To walk with him. You told me to, even though…"

"I trusted you," he whispered, his eyes wide with grief.

The house was quiet and dark now, and when she entered the bedroom she and Blake shared, she felt new relief and despair that he was gone. A note on the pillow fluttered slightly in the breeze coming through the open window.

I need to think, she read. *Be back in the morning.* It was so like Blake, she thought, to be mad at her but want her to know he would return.

He would return! Kitty panicked. There wasn't much time. She knew Blake had probably left on his motorcycle or was walking and not far away. Maybe he was sleeping in one of the buildings on the estate. But he would be back and quickly.

She couldn't let him know the worst of what she'd done. She paused for a moment before turning the note over and scribbling a short letter back. She was careful not to make any promises. She'd already broken enough.

Blake,

I'm sorry. Please tell Mother and Daddy I'm sorry. I do not care for Mike Larimer. You will always be my only beloved. There is so much I wish I could explain, but I cannot. I have Ruby. I love you dearly.

Kitty

CROSSING OVER

20

Kitty had never planned to be gone for so long, but years passed without writing home to Blake. Her secret was too awful, and as much as she missed her family, she couldn't let them find out. She would lay awake at night dreaming of Blake and wishing he would come for her. Then she would wake in a sweaty panic, afraid he had.

Ruby cried almost every day from missing her daddy. She could never forget him even though Kitty tried to distract her.

"She seems very tired," one of Ruby's homeroom teachers said.

"That's because sometimes she stays late at the baby-sitter while I work, but she handles it fine."

"She falls asleep in class," the teacher persisted.

"She misses you," the baby-sitter, Janet, said one night. Her wrinkled eyes were kind but serious. "You work too hard."

"But, Janet, I don't have a choice."

"Then give Ruby something that is just hers, Kitty. She needs to be a girl. Right now her life revolves around waiting for you."

Kitty knew it was true, but there was no way Kitty could do what Janet was suggesting. Taking her to mother-daughter brunches or putting her in ballet lessons was out of the question. Kitty would probably never even get to attend the recitals.

"What about piano?" Janet had asked cheerily.

"We can't afford it, and we don't even have a piano."

"I used to be a teacher," Janet continued with a grin. "And I have a piano in my living room, see? I just need to dust it off!"

"Oh, Janet. I couldn't let you."

"Yes, you could. And you will."

Sometimes Kitty would daydream about going home as she wiped down the tables around her. But who would want her now?

She observed the daily comings and goings of people in the coffee shop, running off to work, meeting their girlfriends, their husbands, and listened to their conversations. She read and heard about events in the *San Francisco Chronicle* and on the television sets at the diner. She continued to change with the times; from presidential elections to plane crashes, feeling swept up with the passing years.

The world was reshaped, and she felt she was being pushed farther away from her family.

One evening a young man had wandered into the diner where she worked. He looked around for a moment, baffled at the aging clientele, and with a shrug seated himself in the corner and stayed until closing. He was handsome but looked sad, and Kitty recognized that look in his eyes as grief, the same as hers.

He was waiting for her at the back entrance as she left, and at first she had the good sense to be afraid.

"Coffee?"

Kitty hadn't answered, but she also didn't turn around and go back inside.

He held up his hands and grinned at her sideways. He was handsome, dressed casual, like a father might dress if he were taking his kid to a ball game.

"I'll walk ten feet away."

"Okay, but I pick the coffee shop."

And so she led him to the all-night coffee shop where she worked on weekends. They'd talked for hours, and since Kitty was off the next day, she didn't worry about sleeping.

"Oh my," she'd said, looking at her watch. "I have to get out of here or the regulars are going to start asking me to get their coffee."

And somehow his offer to walk her home had turned into walking to his house instead. He'd opened the door for her as she left later.

"I'm sorry," he said, grabbing her hand. "I can't see you again. I have a wife and a daughter. At least I did. She took her from me...but I—"

Kitty shushed him.

"I understand. I'm so sorry."

And she'd left knowing that he would do the right thing by his wife, but she wondered if her husband would have done the right thing had she gone back. The strange man's pain haunted her always, and having seen it, she knew more of Blake's pain than she had ever allowed herself to imagine. She only hoped that he wouldn't make the same mistake as this man had made with her, and for a precarious moment she'd cried at the thought of it.

Bad relationships with men continued for her after that, and they, like Mr. Thompson, were never as nice as that first man had been. In fact, he was the type she avoided. Instead she'd been inexplicably drawn to date men who ended up controlling her every move, which convinced her she was insignificant, and took advantage of her insecurities, always leaving her desperate and nearly destitute.

She felt in her heart that Blake wouldn't be able to love her the way she'd become. To him it would be biblical to divorce her—she was sure of it—if he hadn't already found a way.

When she allowed herself, she sometimes dreamed of the old days. Not for long but for a while, and that's what Blake became— a mirage in her dreams that would never be real. Kitty had grown convinced that Blake and her parents were better off not knowing the transgressions she'd found herself participating in. She hoped they could remember the Kitty she once was to them, pure and innocent—except for the one thing that had driven her away. She hoped they would never have to know about the new Kitty, used and worthless.

To make matters worse, this was when Ruby was first diagnosed with asthma, and Kitty found herself wishing more and more that she had her mother to help. She had to carry medicine with her at every moment, never knowing when Ruby would start gasping and run out of breath. So Kitty added the fear of losing Ruby to the pile of worries she carried, and with each desperate asthma attack she witnessed in her daughter, she clung to Ruby even more tightly.

When Ruby was old enough, she decided to move out on her own with some girlfriends. Kitty received the news from Ruby like a brick hitting pavement.

"Most definitely not!" she'd exclaimed.

"Mother! I am a woman now. You cannot stop me!"

"Please, Ruby," Kitty had implored. "You don't understand what is out there. It's not safe."

"Mother, it will be different for me. I won't make the same mistakes you have."

The words had hurt Kitty, but what could she say in response? She had made more mistakes than she could count, and she hoped her daughter had at least learned from her poor example if nothing else. And there was nothing else really. Nothing else she could do to go back and give Ruby what she really needed, a father. Not just any father, but Blake.

Kitty had somehow entertained a fantasy over the years that Ruby would never leave home, but as she packed Ruby's bags and put them into the trunk of the small beat-up red car she'd bought for Ruby, she realized how silly she'd been to think she could keep Ruby back.

She was too eager, too full of life. She was looking for answers that Kitty had no doubt she would find, whether they should be found or not. Getting away from Kitty was the only way Ruby could search, and Kitty knew this without either of them acknowledging it out loud.

Kitty had run back into the house for Ruby's box of paints and a few clean canvases and a new easel.

Ruby's smile was warm, and Kitty knew her gift had been the right one.

"Never stop painting, Ruby. You are so gifted."

Ruby took everything and set it in the backseat on top of some suitcases.

"Mother, you act as if we'll never see each other again."

"Well, we'd better." Tears welled in Kitty's eyes.

"It's okay, Mother." Ruby stood with a bag over her shoulder. "We'll see each other on weekends, at least a few weekends a month."

Ruby looked so pretty, Kitty thought, with her curly brown hair bound in a ponytail; her sun-browned arms bare in a sleeveless red shirt. Her figure was like Kitty's had once been. Curvy in all the right places in her faded jeans, complete with her favorite beaded sandals. How had she grown so beautiful?

"I should have moved out a long time ago. I'm too old to live with my mommy."

Kitty had laughed with Ruby, not agreeing with her at all, and held her tears in check until Ruby turned the corner at the end of the street. Then she'd turned and run back into the house. She'd thrown herself into the recliner she'd saved so much money for and cried into the night. She'd woken up the next morning a mess and called in sick to work.

Kitty wanted her own mother and had almost called home, but when she spied a man's hat tossed on the coatrack where it had been left, she remembered her secret. There were so many now—so many men who had come and gone in the night. The real secret, the most horrific one, was buried beneath all the hats and socks left behind.

It was old grief Kitty felt but lived with every day. It made her dull inside but never failed to bring new tears each time she was reminded of how far that secret had taken her from her family. She could never go back, she knew. She was too messed up, too enmeshed in her mistakes, to ever expect her family to understand.

As days passed without Ruby, Kitty would sit at the piano and peck at the keys wishing for a song from Ruby, and this made her think more about her mother, who had taught her to play the piano as well, although she had never been as good as Ruby was. But her mother had been patient. She would have been proud of Ruby now had she been able to hear her play. Kitty wondered if her own mother felt the same emptiness—this same worry about her absence over the years. Only how much worse had it been for Freda, since Kitty at least knew where Ruby was?

Fortunately, hard work and worries about Ruby often managed to crowd Blake and everything else in La Rosaleda to the back burner, but her heart always filled with more pain during the nights. It weighed on her each morning as she got out of bed. Even as she tossed it away with yesterday's laundry, it would show up again in the folds of her clothing.

Ruby had always been wrong about Kitty. When she was angry, she would accuse Kitty of not missing Blake at all. In reality Kitty missed him constantly.

His hold on her heart didn't diminish with distance or time, and the sweetness of her memories was bitter in her mouth every time she thought of La Rosaleda. Her demanding job, where she now lived just outside San Francisco, seemed to be the best way to deal with it since she no longer had Ruby to devote her time to every day. She started working long hours, and her days fused into one empty journey.

The day Kitty was finally jolted out of her carefully constructed wall of lies, she'd gone to San Francisco for the afternoon with a new boyfriend named Stan. The day had gone okay, and they'd just enjoyed (if one could call spending time with Stan enjoyable) a Chinese dinner and were leaving to visit Ruby and her friends at their apartment.

Kitty pushed open the door, and the breeze lifted her highlighted brown hair, now cut in a shorter bob, to float around her face. She tried to brush it away from her eyes as she vaguely heard the chime of the bell above the entryway of the restaurant. She scoffed silently at her date's rudeness at not holding the door open for her as she struggled to smooth her hair back in place. Struggling with the weight of the door as she tried to step out onto the sidewalk, she bumped softly into another person.

Glancing up, she drew in her breath and held it.

Staring back at her was the man who had become a dream.

She would have known him in a sea of people, but there was no doubt who he was now. Her heart rose up, filling her chest and throat, as she stared straight into Blake Birkirt's blue eyes.

For a moment she doubted his presence. This was only a man who looked like her beloved, but it couldn't be him, she thought. Not this way. Not this accident of what...? Fate?

But it was Blake, dressed in slacks and a tailored brown jacket, an ensemble he would only wear if he had important business to do. She knew he normally would be wearing blue jeans and a denim shirt for working, and that's also what he would have been wearing had he been coming for her. So he was not in San Francisco to look for her. He was on business.

This was an accident.

She became frozen together with him but not touching as people bustled around them and disappeared from focus.

They didn't need to touch to feel each other. This was her husband. She couldn't believe he was close enough to reach out to, but she didn't dare. He was still as handsome as in the years before and in her mind, his ash blond hair combed neatly to the side with only a speck of gray at the roots. She knew by the definition of his arms and chest, which rose and lowered rapidly beneath his white button-down shirt that he'd stayed working at Frances-DiCamillo. He'd been working the vineyards, and if he'd stayed on with her father, she knew he must still be part of her family.

She wanted dearly to ask about the vineyard and her parents, but she was afraid to open her mouth. She'd dreamed of this moment, of going back to him and begging his forgiveness, of telling him everything she'd kept silent for so long. In her fantasies she'd imagined that he would take her into his arms and say he understood everything. He'd been waiting for her to come.

She could tell now by the look of shock, amazement, and disappointment in his eyes that her fantasy wouldn't come true. He would never accept her now. She felt this deep within her, and in one way it wasn't a surprise at all, but the crushing awareness shocked her. Of course he wouldn't want her, she realized. She was standing in front of him now, still legally married as far as she knew, with another man's slimy hand resting on her waist, as if this new man owned her. All this right in front of her husband.

Kitty was sure that each detail told Blake everything he needed to know. She risked glancing down and noticed that he wasn't wearing a wedding band, so even if he hadn't found a way to legally divorce her, he had probably divorced her in his mind.

How could he not have divorced her? It's what she deserved, and even if her heart still loved him, had she not already divorced him by her actions?

For an agonizing instant Blake looked long into her eyes, as if searching for an answer. His jaw was clenched, and the place between his eyebrows creased as if in the same pain as the day he'd discovered her talking to Mike Larimer in the vines.

What was he waiting for? What answer could she give him now?

She couldn't open her mouth to say what she'd dreamed of saying for years. Her heart cried these things silently, but he did not hear them.

I'm so sorry, she cried inwardly.

I love you.

I love you more than you can ever know.

She looked down then for a long moment as Blake held the door of the restaurant open for her. When she finally met his eyes a second time, the pain that filled his was too big for her to acknowledge.

It was beyond an awkward moment when Stan reached out to shake Blake's hand and introduce himself as her "boyfriend."

Kitty was mortified at the look in Blake's eyes. His face hardened, and he silently refused to extend his own hand but instead stepped through the door to go around Kitty. He paused as he passed close to her side, just long enough to brush her elbow softly with his fingertips.

Years of repressed passion for her husband rose and fell in a wave that nearly collapsed her. She felt his hand on her waist then, holding her up. Stan reached out before she could stop him and took her by the shoulders, turning her back into the restaurant. Blake turned and walked brusquely down the sidewalk, leaving Kitty to drown in the bottomless well of her own regret.

Blake's touch had left her trembling.

She wanted to go after him and beg his forgiveness, so she tried to step away on shaky legs but was rooted to the spot by Stan's hand on her arm.

"Well," Stan snarled. "What's his problem?"

"His problem is you," Kitty snapped. The spell was broken.

She stared at his ugly sneer and knew her life had become repulsive. She felt a moment of panic now as she thought of Blake, who had run away from her so fast that it was as if she were rubbish. What if Ruby did the same? What if she went back to La Rosaleda and decided she had no mother worth having? A cloud of memories and thoughts circled Kitty's mind. What must Blake think of her? Had he noticed how sickly thin she was? How she'd cut the hair he'd loved so much?

She was concerned and for a moment thought maybe she could finally explain it to everyone and be forgiven. Only a few minutes had passed—maybe he wasn't gone yet. She reached for the doorknob.

Stan grabbed her hand to pull her in.

"No," Kitty said. "Leave me alone!"

She ran out the doors and stared in the direction Blake had gone. She could see his distant figure walking away quickly and wanted to cry out, but he was walking too fast. It was obvious he wanted a quick exit. This time he was the one running.

Tears poured from her eyes, betraying the tough, no-nonsense approach to life she'd worked so hard to portray. *I am dead to him,* she thought, feeling sixteen again, sitting in the blue velvet chair beside her mother, Freda, who had told her it was all okay, that she and her father loved her, and that she was special because she was God's child.

Kitty didn't feel like God's child right now. She shuddered at the thought of her mother knowing how her life had become— desperate and faithless. God's child would not have done what she did. No good child would have. She stared down the sidewalk where Blake was disappearing in the distance, knowing that Stan too had already taken off.

"Get out of the way, lady!" a man shouted as he bumped her arm.

Kitty didn't care. She stood on the sidewalk, immobile, crying until she couldn't cry anymore.

Later, when Kitty stood at Ruby's apartment door, Ruby pulled her mother into her arms without a word.

It was then that Kitty really understood how lucky she was to have her Ruby.

21

The chance meeting with Blake seemed to have opened the floodgates to La Rosaleda even as Kitty continued to fight to keep them closed.

It was only a few months later that Ruby told Kitty the story of meeting her childhood friend Matt Larimer.

"And, Mother, as soon as he said my name aloud, I knew it was him! Can you imagine that? Matt! My friend Matt!"

Tears had glistened at the corners of her eyes at her revelation, and while Kitty's breath was sucked out of her the same as it had been on the street when she'd seen her husband, she couldn't tell Ruby not to see her friend. Hadn't she been the one who'd ripped the two apart in the first place? Would they not have been the best of friends for years to come? Maybe the two would have grown up and married had she not taken Ruby away. Who knows, thought Kitty, what wonderful things she had kept from Ruby since the day she'd taken her away.

"Oh, Ruby."

Kitty had pulled her to her chest then and wept. She cried for all she'd taken away from Ruby, and she knew she could not step in to take this away from her now. Her daughter had always longed for family, never believing what Kitty had said about her being all the family she needed. Matt was, in Ruby's mind, family.

"I know about La Rosaleda now. I had forgotten the name, but as soon as I started talking to Matt I remembered. I just said, 'How are things in La Rosaleda?' And it was back, just like that."

"I know," Kitty said.

"No, not only the name of it, Mother. I remember all of it, and I want to go back."

Kitty's slight smile faded. "No," she whispered, a quiet appeal.

Ruby had turned her head at an angle to stare at her mother, baffled. "What is in La Rosaleda, Mother? What is it you left behind besides Daddy?"

"I never wanted to leave your daddy, Ruby."

"Then why?"

"Let's leave it unsaid. You don't want to know."

Ruby had squeezed her hand.

"I do, Mother. I do."

"No, it's not something you need to hear."

Ruby looked at Kitty, waiting, but Kitty only shook her head.

Ruby remained silent until Kitty, shoulders drooping in resignation, said slowly, "Can you keep it a secret, even from your friend Matt?"

"I promise."

"From your father, if you are to ever see him?"

Ruby hesitated.

"He can't know, Ruby."

"Okay, I promise."

And so Kitty told her, and it was Ruby's turn to weep. And then after her tears had dried up, she still begged Kitty to go back with her and tell her secrets to Blake.

"He would understand! And besides, so much time has passed. You don't know what has changed in his life that might make him accept this."

"No, dear. I can't. Not ever."

"But what about Grandmother Freda? Don't you miss her?"

Kitty stifled a sob.

Ruby had sat there, staring at the vase of red and yellow ranunculus bending from the vase to kiss the table. She reached over to grasp Kitty's hand.

"I am sorry, Mother. I have been so selfish thinking you just wanted to leave Daddy, and I knew you were a good person, so I didn't understand. I haven't been very nice to you at times."

Kitty smiled slightly, unable to speak.

"Don't worry. I promised. I'll keep your secret, but I won't like it. I hope you'll change your mind, but I won't tell Daddy when I see him."

Kitty's shoulders dropped. "You're still going back?"

"Please," Ruby said. "I must. Please don't take this from me, Mother."

"Give me time." The panic on Kitty's face was unmistakable. "Give me time to think before you go. Don't go until I have some more time."

"Oh, Mother, please—"

"Please," Kitty interrupted.

"I'll wait, but it's not fair." She softened, seeing the tears again.

"I am so sorry for all of this, Mother. It's worse than I ever imagined, but I still love you. I love you even more."

Kitty began to worry every moment that Ruby would do something that would reveal all she had worked to hide for so many years. But Kitty knew she couldn't keep Ruby from going back— Ruby was on her own now.

Kitty tried to prepare for the day when she would tell Ruby to go to La Rosaleda, but for some reason she could never bring herself to give Ruby her blessing. Each time she considered it, she was filled with a new fear that Blake would come for her and demand the truth, and a more complicated fear filled her that he would do nothing at all now that he'd seen her with the other man's hand on her waist in the city.

She worried so much because she knew Ruby's love for her

father would draw her back, even if it meant going against her promise to Kitty. And now Ruby had Matt in her life to escort her straight into her father's arms—she didn't even need Kitty's help.

"Sit down," Ruby said one Sunday. "I have a present for you." She handed Kitty a box tied with a pretty bow.

Kitty tried to smile as she untangled the ribbon. Ruby said she'd brought it back from her weekend outing. She was happy for her daughter's new friendship with Matt, even though he was a tie to La Rosaleda and all of Kitty's secrets.

"Where are your roommates?" Kitty asked, suddenly noticing the silence. "Didn't you all go away for the weekend together? They must be tired—"

"They're still away, Mother." Ruby's face flushed red. "I was away on a trip with Matt." Kitty stopped fussing with the ribbon.

"Relax, Mother. Nothing happened."

"I didn't even say anything," said Kitty. "But I am your mother."

"You didn't have to say anything." Ruby's tone changed as she tried to switch the subject. "I like your hair that way. You look dressed up. Do you have a date?"

Kitty smoothed her dress in exasperation. It was a plain gold-colored sheath with a matching jacket and black pumps. She hated the styles these days and had to look in the nicer boutiques for the classic-cut dresses she lately preferred. Even then it was hard to find a color that wasn't so trendy looking.

It was the same with haircuts, so she'd cut her hair into the same old bob style and had it highlighted so it was almost blond now. She reached up and flipped at the ends. Even then she didn't like how trendy it looked. She hated to look like a woman in her forties trying to look like she was in her thirties. Of course, she hated looking forty as well.

"No." She felt the frustration and anger rising again. "You know I stopped dating a long time ago."

"A long time ago?" Ruby had followed Kitty into the bedroom to help her unpack.

"Yes, a year ago," Kitty reminded Ruby.

"Yes. And your decision was long past due."

Kitty stopped and looked at Ruby—hard. "I'm still your mother, and I can date any time I want."

"You've certainly done that my whole life, haven't you, Mother?"

Kitty, who had tried so hard to throw her mistakes behind her, flushed with shame. Even if she deserved it, she always felt hurt when Ruby talked to her so boldly.

Ruby knew it. "Let's not talk about it," she said more softly. "Let's open your present."

"Ruby, please promise you've not done something you'll regret."

Ruby looked away. "Mother, please open your present."

It had been wrapped in red paper.

"An early Christmas present," Ruby declared proudly.

"Oh, really?" Kitty tried to remain neutral, but she'd longed for the day when Ruby would stop pushing her away, and moments like this one reminded Kitty that they were still mother and daughter. "What is it?"

"It's a surprise, but first I need to explain something." Ruby paused a moment. "The gift is from Matt too, Mother."

Kitty frowned. She was no longer touched. "A gift from Matt? What's that boy up to?"

"Nothing, Mother. It's a sort of peace offering."

Kitty sighed. She hated that Matt felt a need to buy her a peace offering. Nothing was really his fault. It was the fact he was the son of the man who ruined her life that bothered her, as if Ruby were rubbing elbows with the enemy. In reality she knew

Matt was a good young man just as he'd been a good boy, but Kitty worried constantly that he might have a touch of his father in him—or worse, that he would interfere with her efforts to keep La Rosaleda out of her life and Ruby's.

Reluctantly, she opened the box.

"Well." Kitty smiled in spite of herself, pulling at a fold of fabric that slid from the box. She stood up and held the orange and yellow kimono in front of her. "Beautiful," she said, staring at the light yellow silk fabric with tiny orange flowers. Her fingers followed the line of the white satin piping, which glowed against her caramel skin. She wrapped it around her and cinched the waist. Kitty still had her shape, and more than once Ruby had lamented that she wished she'd gotten curves as great as her mother's.

"Nonsense," Kitty would say. "You've got more than enough. Besides, they just get in the way, don't they?"

"The men don't think so," Ruby would respond.

Kitty would scoff. "I was dumb to…" She would fumble for words during those conversations.

Now Kitty was glad those days were over. Dating had been hard on her, a huge mistake. She'd had no right. Even if she wanted to pretend she had no past, she'd had no right to take it that far. She was glad to leave dating behind.

"It's really lovely," Kitty said as she stared at herself in the mirror that hung above the red velveteen couch. "I guess Matt is kind of sweet to have bought it for me. How did he know I would love this? Did you tell him?"

Ruby didn't answer right away.

"Well?" Kitty pried. "Did you?"

"Well," she said. "No. Actually Daddy helped him pick it out."

Kitty whirled around and stared at her daughter in shock. She tried to speak, but no words would come. The room began to spin.

Ruby rushed over to her. "Mother, sit down. Just sit down and hear me out."

"You…you went back…without telling me? I…I, uh…you shouldn't have."

"Mother, calm down." Ruby was back on her feet.

"How dare you!" Kitty finally sputtered. "I left La Rosaleda behind for a good reason! I needed more time."

"But you took too long, Mother."

Kitty pointed a finger at her daughter. "That boy is no good, just like his father. Was this his idea? Does he want to humiliate me?"

"That's not true!"

"Yes, it is. Boys always turn out like their fathers."

"That's not fair, Mother. Do girls turn out like their mothers then?" Ruby spat the words and Kitty stepped back.

Is this what Ruby was afraid of? "No," she said finally. "You are nothing like your mother."

"Oh, Mother." Ruby tried to take Kitty's arm, but Kitty shrugged her away.

"Please just sit down and listen for a minute!" Tears streamed down Ruby's cheeks.

Kitty looked down at her, a much younger and more beautiful version of herself wearing jeans and a T-shirt. She looked a lot like Kitty these days, but her smile was still her daddy's—the big beautiful smile, which Kitty rarely saw on her anymore. Right now Ruby's pretty mouth was turned down in hurt, and every time she said "Daddy" Kitty felt like running out of the apartment. She sat back down and dug her hand into the loose, cheap fabric of the couch.

"I knew when you and Matt ran into each other that something like this would happen."

"Why, Mother? Because he's part of your secret past?" She emphasized *secret* like it was something ugly. And it was ugly.

"That's exactly why. The two of you might have romantic notions about my going back to La Rosaleda, as if we can all go back and pick up where we left off. Well, Matthew Larimer doesn't know everything he thinks he knows. Nobody does."

"You told me! I understand, and I didn't tell anybody. Not Matt and not Daddy. I would love for you to go back, Mother, but you don't have to. That doesn't mean I shouldn't be allowed."

Kitty stood up again and paced the living room, her hands wild. "How dare you go and stir things up for your father! I left so I could protect him!"

Ruby looked hurt. "Protect him? You think leaving him protected him? Mother, Matt asked if I wanted to visit La Rosaleda, and I did. What do you expect? It's where my home is, and you never let me contact Daddy—ever! Don't forget, it is you who took me away!"

Kitty sat down, and Ruby offered her a tissue. She hadn't realized she was crying but accepted the tissue and began to dab at the mascara streaking its way down her face.

Mother and daughter sat silent for a long time before Kitty spoke.

"Did you really see him?" Despite her dismay and fear over Ruby's trip, so many questions were forming in her mind about Blake, her parents, and her home that she was afraid to ask.

Ruby sat down beside her. "So you do care, Mother."

"Of course I do! Did you really see him?"

"Yes."

"And...how is he?"

"He's wonderful, Mother, just like I remembered. It was so— so like yesterday. He saw me, and I was in his arms and cried, Mother. Cried because he was holding me again."

Kitty half smiled. "And where does he live?" She looked away, afraid to ask the obvious.

"At Frances-DiCamillo. Alone. He doesn't have a girlfriend or anything if that's what you're wondering."

Kitty looked up slowly. "Alone?"

Ruby reached out and touched her mother's small hand. "Alone, Mother." Ruby's eyes filled with tears now too. "And I'm afraid I have terrible news. Grandma and Grandpa…" Ruby stopped. "Mother, they died in a plane crash seven years ago. Remember the one that went down over Maui?"

The words dazed Kitty. "My mother and—" She choked, and grief rocked her body.

Ruby didn't know what to do except lean over and hold her mother.

"I'm so sorry," she said. "I'm so sorry."

Kitty struggled to breathe. How could she have left her parents without an explanation? How could she have let her mother and father die without saying good-bye? The guilt she'd carried for so many years fell down around her like the coffee cups that day she'd passed out from fatigue at the diner—they'd shattered and cracked in sharp jagged pieces, the handles lying unattached from their cups. That's how she felt now, shattered and separate and unattached. She'd been so wrong.

Kitty barely noticed her steps toward Ruby's bedroom as her daughter guided her into the bed, silently removing her jacket and shoes and pulling the blankets up and around her. Sun filtered through the thin red fabric curtains Kitty had helped hang. But she couldn't look at them now. She turned into the pillow to shield her eyes.

Kitty woke up hours later. It was dark inside the room. She turned over and found Ruby, in her old Snoopy pajamas, asleep beside her. The breeze lifted the curtains, and the street noises far below drifted up. A siren somewhere wailed, and she wished again that her daughter didn't live in the city.

For a moment Kitty wondered if having Ruby move back to La

Rosaleda would be a better idea now that she had reunited with her father. La Rosaleda was a nicer place. Ruby could have a different life, a much better life. But they would never get to see one another.

Kitty smoothed Ruby's dark curly hair back from her face. Maybe Ruby would only visit La Rosaleda. Maybe they could start over somewhere else, and Ruby could just visit her father on special occasions. Kitty wondered if she could get Ruby to move with her to Sacramento someday. She'd been thinking about relocating again, and then she could talk to Ruby about going to college. There were some good colleges in Sacramento. Even though Ruby would be a little late starting college, her grades had been high enough that if she wanted to go to the elite private college there, she could probably get in. Blake would certainly have the money to send her. It was a possibility Kitty couldn't ignore. She knew Blake, and as soon as he saw how hard Ruby had to struggle financially, he would want to help. And if Ruby didn't want to attend a private school, there were always the state colleges. Sacramento wasn't as big as San Francisco either, and it might be a nicer place to live.

Kitty's heart stirred at the thought of starting over in a place where there were no bad memories. She watched the curtains wave in the breeze and remembered her bedroom in the main house at Frances-DiCamillo. Had Ruby slept there? Had her mother kept the blue-flowered curtains in her room with the eyelet tiebacks?

She had an image of her mother sitting in one of the blue velvet chairs, staring out the window at the acres of vineyards and chatting as Kitty got ready for her day. The memory brought new tears to her eyes, and she choked them back, not wanting to wake Ruby. Kitty's mind swept back over the vineyards. Old memories of her parents and a new longing for Blake flooded her consciousness. She closed her eyes and tried to go back to sleep.

Sleep never did come that night or for many nights after.

Several days passed before Kitty and Ruby talked about La Rosaleda again. On the weekend Ruby talked Kitty into driving to Point Reyes. Kitty had agreed, hoping the fresh air and the salt smell of the ocean would clear her mind.

The city grew distant behind them, and Kitty tried to concentrate on enjoying the day with her daughter. She had a feeling that she might see her less and less. La Rosaleda had beckoned, and Ruby would go there. Kitty's heart lurched again as she thought about Blake.

When they reached Point Reyes, the views from the huge gray cliffs lifted Kitty's spirits, freeing her momentarily of her personal incarceration. For a while, she actually felt some of the anxiety being washed away with the rolling waves of the ocean. Only fragments washed back to lodge in her heart, the familiar fragments that had always been with her and would never leave but would instead work themselves into her heart in the areas that couldn't be flushed clean, even by an ocean.

Kitty and Ruby walked along a well-worn path high above a stretch of beach inaccessible by land due to jagged rocks below. Kitty enjoyed the view over the bluff as she carefully picked her way along the trail, enjoying the exercise until her muscles demanded that they take a break and Ruby's lungs screamed to rest as well.

They looked for a place to sit, and the wind whipped the scent of brine and beach wafting through their hair. Sea gulls and pelicans flew high above the beach but seemed close enough to touch. Kitty felt free this high up—far, far away from her past, from the present. She sat on a large sturdy outcropping of rock, and Ruby sat beside her. Kitty thought about how passersby might have thought they were more like sisters than mother and daughter. But if Kitty needed a sister, Ruby needed a mother more.

Kitty listened to Ruby's shallow gasps and waited for her to use the inhaler. She watched Ruby breathe in the life-giving medicine and rubbed her back affectionately, waiting for it to fill and open her lungs. Ruby's asthma was a sort of mystery to Kitty. She wasn't aware of a family history of the disease, but it had struck her daughter hard at an early age.

Kitty reached over and held her daughter's hand and stared into the rolling waters, forcing herself not to close her eyes, pushing back images of La Rosaleda. Instead she let her mind be swept away with the swoosh of the waves, but as much as she wanted to avoid talking about La Rosaleda again with Ruby, she knew this was why Ruby had asked her to come along.

In some ways Kitty ached to find out how Blake really was. What had he been doing over the years? Who was he now? Even though she could never face him, she needed to know. "How is he?" she finally asked.

"He's good, Mother." Ruby's voice was a little bit annoyed. "Just like I said. Doing really well."

The freedom Kitty had felt earlier between her and Ruby turned stilted; the tone of Ruby's voice hurt her.

"What's he doing now?"

"Running the vineyard." Ruby paused. "It's hard to believe, but it's really your vineyard. That's what he said. Your inheritance."

"It's not mine anymore. It's his or yours. Either is fine with me. I don't care. I don't deserve it anyway."

Ruby shook her head. "You should care. It's legally yours, and he calls it yours too. Daddy says he's taking care of it for you until you're ready to come home."

Kitty's heart swelled. "He said that?"

"Yes."

"Well, he can have it," Kitty whispered. "It's his too. He was my husband."

"He's still your husband."

"Never mind that. Tell me more. What did you do when you went to visit him?"

Ruby turned and looked doubtfully at Kitty. "Do you really want to know?"

"Yes." She reached over for Ruby's hand. "I do want to hear. I'm sorry I've made life so difficult for you. I admit I'm worried about this reunion between you and Blake, but over the years I've also worried that you would regret not seeing him. I didn't really want to take you from him. You needed him and he you, but there didn't seem to be a way that was right. So, yes, I want to hear."

Ruby shrugged. "Matt and I were just going to drive by the vineyard on Friday so I could see what it looked like, but when we did, I decided I wanted to get closer." Ruby closed her eyes. "It's so beautiful, Mother. The vines were even lovelier than I remembered."

"The big house?"

"The house still looks like the same big white Mexican-style home with large columns and roses all around it. Grandmother Freda's gardens are still magnificent. Daddy says he keeps them up so they'll look beautiful if you ever come home. He said Freda wanted that for you. She wanted everything to be just so for your homecoming."

Kitty's chest tightened. "And our house?"

"Oh, Mother, the cottage is breathtaking. Daddy's planted these beautiful red rosebushes next to the house, all around it. He planted them the year we left and says they're Ruby-red roses, for me and for you. They've taken over the entire front porch. There's barely a path to walk along, so we had to enter through the back door. Hardly anyone ever goes in there anymore. He keeps it locked up, except for when it's cleaned once a month."

Kitty was silent.

"He looks the same, Mother. Just some gray hair is all."

Kitty knew it, remembering her accidental meeting with him. "Did he really see me that day I bumped into him in San Francisco? Did he mention it?" Kitty's heart pounded over the crashing of the waves. Did she want to hear this?

"What he did say was that you are still beautiful. He wanted to speak to you that day, but since you were with a friend, he figured you'd moved on and wouldn't want to speak to him."

The guilt weighed on Kitty's heart. "What did you tell him?"

"I told him I didn't know about moving on but that you were not with that man. I told him you aren't dating. I told him that I knew you missed him every day but that you mostly avoided talking about him. I didn't say much about your life. I didn't know how to explain..." Her voice began to trail off. "He seemed uncomfortable talking about it..."

Kitty felt awful. How else could he feel? She longed to apologize, to tell him he was the only man she had ever loved, who had ever loved her. He was so good and wonderful, and all the other men had been meaningless, just men she'd used to try to hide from her past mistakes. "You didn't tell him about my coming to your door? How upset I was?"

"It wasn't mine to tell," Ruby said softly. "It's for you to tell him, Mother. You can apologize and tell him how you still need him." She paused, tears forming in the corners of her eyes. "He will forgive you. He misses you so much. Please go home. I'll take you. We can go together."

"Oh no, Ruby. I can't ever see him again."

"Why?"

"So much has changed, dear. Too much. I've done so many bad things."

Ruby stared deep into her mother's brown eyes. "But mostly a lot of people have done bad things to you."

"But I've made terrible choices that allowed those things to happen."

Ruby didn't protest.

How could she? Kitty thought. Poor Ruby had been the victim of many of Kitty's bad decisions.

"He wants to see you."

Kitty covered her mouth with one hand. She struggled for a long moment before saying, "I can't. I'm tarnished, completely soiled as a wife, Ruby. I could never go back to him this way."

"Mother, he knows."

Kitty shook her head. She knew he really didn't.

"Mother, I think Daddy thinks you had an affair with Matt's dad."

"Is that what he told you?"

"No, Matt thinks it's what Daddy had heard."

Ruby had to strain to hear Kitty's voice above the wind whipping up the rocks from the shore. "You know it's more complicated than that. Things happened so fast. I hardly had time to think. When I found out about the pregnancy, I knew your father would be brokenhearted. That's when I had the abortion."

Kitty couldn't stop the tears. She wondered what her daughter thought of her. Too many terrible things had already been exposed. "Blake misunderstood some things when he heard me talking to Mike in the vineyard. He reacted in anger, which was unusual for Blake. I guess I don't blame him. What else was he to think? I guess he acted how any husband would have."

"How do you know it wasn't Daddy's baby?"

"Because, dear, I'd been sick with the flu, and it had taken a long time before I felt up to...well, you know." Kitty was surprised that she was shy to talk about being intimate with Blake after the kind of life she had lived, but this was her husband, or had been. And this was her daughter she was talking to.

Ruby nodded. "I rang the doorbell, and when he first opened the door, he thought I was you."

Kitty looked astonished.

"Yes. But then he said my name very quietly. And he started to cry."

Kitty reached over. "It's okay," she told Ruby. "You don't have to explain. I forgive you for going back, but...I can't. He is better off without me."

"No, he isn't!" Ruby wiped at her eyes. "Why don't you tell me why you won't go?"

"I've told you enough!"

"But it's okay now. You can go back."

"You don't know what you're asking, Ruby."

"What if he asks to see you?"

"Tell him no. Tell him I'm not in love with him. Tell him I've moved on. Anything. I had sex with Mike Larimer, for God's sake, child! How can I love Blake?"

"But it's not true! I know you love him. You said so!"

Kitty sat up straight. "It's true," she said with all the conviction she could muster.

She stood up and turned back down the trail.

Ruby soon followed and stormed ahead of her to the car; they rode home in silence.

Kitty hated to lie to her daughter about how she really felt, but she had to stay away from Blake. She wasn't the same woman he had known. Her choices could only hurt him even more if she went back and told him everything.

RUBY KNEW
THIS BREATHLESSNESS

22

The clock on the wall struck twelve times, and I was reminded of the bell at Frances-DiCamillo, which Kitty described as echoing across the fields like a church bell. I looked over at her slumped and tired form. She looked exhausted.

I, on the other hand, was wide awake.

"So will you ever go back to La Rosaleda?" I asked, hoping she might answer differently.

Kitty frowned and glanced around the room, desolate eyes eventually resting on mine. "Things have changed too much."

"Yes, they have," I protested. "You're different now. You've been living a good life. He might still be waiting for you. He might be able to forgive you."

"It's not only about forgiveness. It's about acceptance."

"If he is as great as he sounds, I know he would accept you!"

"Maybe things have changed for your generation. But when I was your age, there were things that no one could be expected to forgive. Some things are that bad."

"Kitty, I know that what you have told me is not unforgivable."

Kitty smiled, a sad smile. "My Lucy, what would I do without you?"

"You'd make it, but I wouldn't without you." I hugged her gently. "You look beat. You'd better go to sleep."

"Aren't you going to bed?"

"I think I'll stay up and watch something."

Kitty frowned. She no longer followed the news, and she hated television. She thought it was a bad influence and preferred that I read a book any day rather than watch.

"Just the gardening channel," I promised her.

She nodded.

"Go to bed soon."

"Okay," I agreed. "Good night."

I left her room and settled on the couch. I clicked on the channel, but instead of concentrating on the television, I thumbed through the album. Studying the pictures of my grandfather caused the lost space in my chest to open up anew.

It had been the same when I thought of Ruby—a feeling I wished could be filled up with something else. In the photo I was looking at Blake, my grandfather, smiling that special smile that must be reserved just for grandparents. Ruby too looked happy in the picture. Her smile looked like a laugh, as if he'd just said something funny that made her happy.

I thought of her then, as Kitty had described her. She had been like me. Not as quiet of course, but she had longed for something that had been taken away from her. She'd longed for her father and for La Rosaleda. It had in some ways been the same for her even though she'd never truly forgotten like I had. She'd never forgotten the vines, the house, her family, or her friend. She'd known what had been lost to her, and she went back to get it.

I looked into the photo at the image of me, very small, with her, and even if I couldn't remember it, I imagined I could feel their skin on mine. I could imagine smelling the earth and vines around me, perhaps the aroma of cooking streaming from the house. I could smell the roses growing up over the cottage and hear the creak of the front porch as I walked across to get to my mother. And I heard the bell gong, and its echo resonated so far that they could hear it in town, the announcement that the Frances-DiCamillo family was almost whole.

I leaned forward then and placed the album opened on the coffee table. If at some point in time communication with La Rosaleda was reopened to us, then how had Kitty managed to stay away from Blake? Wouldn't he have insisted on seeing her? Wouldn't she have gone? I was amazed that her fear was so strong that she would let it intrude on her obvious love for Blake. I had read stories about people whose bad memories were so heavy around them they became hardened and sad, but in those stories the characters were usually given over to their hardness. I didn't think Kitty was there yet, although she was close.

The romantic in me wanted to believe there had to be something more, some other reason that had kept them apart, and that if I could figure it out, I could bring everyone back together. Except for Ruby—but even then her memory would be with us all, and we could talk openly about her, and I could be in the places where she and I had been. I wondered what had happened to communication after Ruby died. Kitty must have let Blake know about his own daughter's death, but what about me?

Was my grandfather at Ruby's funeral? I wanted to know what Kitty had done to keep him away. Instinctively I knew it had to have been her doing to keep him out of my life. The idea angered me, and I struggled with my love for Kitty and a new frustration at her. How had she kept everyone away from me?

Feeling a little bit out of breath, I reached over to the coffee table and picked up my inhaler. With deep breaths I imagined what it had been like to be Ruby. She knew this—this breathlessness I lived with. *Of course,* I thought. *Matt Larimer, Ruby's friend.* He hadn't been kept away from me, although he must have honored Kitty and her desire to keep secrets from me for some reason. I needed to talk to him, and he had already opened those doors.

Why now, I wondered, had he brought up the past and his connection to Ruby for me? He had sensed my curiosity. He knew it was time now. Had he been waiting to tell me all these years?

I remembered all our doctor's appointments, his gentle way and his kindness. It hadn't been just because he was a doctor. It had been more.

He knew about me. He and Kitty had remained friends, and he kept secrets for her, but maybe he wanted to tell me those secrets now. I felt a peace within that there was this one person I had who might help me with going back, with learning more. After all he had been the one to help Ruby go back.

And he knew about my mother and father. The realization sent flutters through my mind. He knew a lot about my mother and even some about my father.

I had a father, I realized. I knew he wasn't the best father one could wish for, but he was out there. Did I want to find him too? Kitty would be angry, but it was my choice now, wasn't it? It sounded as if Matt had a low opinion of George Fields, just as Kitty did, but I wondered if maybe he'd been jealous of George's relationship with Ruby.

I ached to know the truth about my father, good or bad. I wanted to find him or lay him to rest in my heart. Maybe he wasn't even alive, as Susannah had suggested. That would make sense because surely he might have searched for me if he was.

My thoughts rambled on until I turned the television off.

Of course, I thought, *Kitty could have made it impossible for George Fields to contact me.* If she could keep my grandfather away, then surely she could have kept someone who didn't even know me away. Maybe Dr. Larimer would tell me more of what I needed to know. Maybe he wouldn't keep holding on to secrets as Kitty did.

I wondered how much Dr. Larimer knew about Ruby's death. Did he know I'd been poking around the morning she died, not getting her inhaler fast enough? My thoughts unwittingly went back to the remorseful feelings I'd been battling since I was so young. Thinking about those things always sent me back to the pit of grief.

My heart picked up its heavier beat again, and I leaned back in my chair, taking deep breaths and trying to be calm. I needed to train myself not to use the inhaler so much.

"Always stopping to smell the roses," Kitty had often said to me.

Doing so had literally wasted precious time the day Ruby died. If only Kitty knew how true her teasing words had always been.

I coughed as I let my mind swim backward.

Every time Kitty mentioned something about Ruby that I couldn't recall, I felt like a stranger staring through the windows of my own life. It tore at my soul.

I suddenly jumped up and reached again for the inhaler. Letting the medicine fill my passageways, I tried to relax.

I picked up one of the photographs and mused at how small I had been when the picture was taken. I was stronger now, I reminded myself. It was time I took control of my own memories, my own life.

Kitty found me sleeping on the couch the next morning, the photographs in my hands. She gently shook me.

"You're going to tear them," she said, softly prying the photographs away from me. She leaned over to place them back in the album.

"Do we have to keep hiding them?

She looked up, surprised.

"Well, I don't know. I certainly don't want to display them."

"Why not?"

"Because I'm not married to him anymore. This picture is just a sad reminder of that fact."

"I think Ruby was right. You are still married to him."

"Lucy, that is a fantasy. You need to stop thinking that way."

"No, it isn't," I said. "I think it's the truth. If Blake knew where

Ruby was, he must have known where you were. If he had divorced
you, you would've received papers. He knows our address now of
course, doesn't he?"

She was quiet.

"You didn't receive divorce papers, did you?" The thought had
not really occurred to me before, and I was suddenly worried that
this was another secret Kitty hadn't told me about. She shook her
head, and relief rushed through me.

"Then what? Did he tell Ruby something bad about you? Did
he say he didn't want to be married to you?"

"No," she whispered. I noticed how tired her eyes were and
knew her muscles must be screaming for rest. It was hard to imagine her as the woman she'd spent hours the evening before telling
me about. She was still beautiful, but she seemed much older
than her age as I watched her massage her wrists and rub her
knees. Life had been hard on her. She had been hard on herself. I
wondered why she just didn't go back to La Rosaleda, take me
with her, and accept help.

Because, I reminded myself, *she either really believes he won't
take her back or doesn't think she deserves it.* She would punish
herself by depriving herself of Blake's love, of her La Rosaleda,
where her heart now lived. And she would deprive me also
whether she meant to or not. I eventually stood up and headed
to my room.

"I'm sorry, Kitty. This is getting too hard."

I turned around. She was crying and so was I. The sharp words
died on the tip of my tongue. I took a breath.

"You say you want me to remember her, but you hold things
back that might make a difference to me."

"Only to protect you, Lucy. Some things will never make a difference, at least not one that matters. Believe me."

I looked away.

"Kitty. I know this is hard for you. I can see that you don't want to divulge every single thing, and you don't have to. Please understand that I want—I need—to know, but I'm not trying to hurt you."

"Yes. That's exactly it, dear. I don't want to divulge every single thing. I'm sorry, but you are going to be disappointed as you learn more. That is, if you aren't already." She sighed.

I already had my arms wrapped around her again. "I'm sorry. I would never judge you, Kitty. You are my grandmother."

"You just don't know. I have done terrible things. I've been part of horrible things." She was now shaking and losing control, not like my usual calm Kitty. I squeezed her to me momentarily, and when I pulled away to look into her face, I grasped her arms. I could feel the bones just under her skin. Surprised, I squeezed her tighter. I'd never felt that deeply into Kitty before.

"Kitty," I whispered. "You are too thin. You've lost an awful lot of weight!" I wondered how I hadn't noticed before.

"Oh," Kitty said. "Maybe. I guess that would explain why some of my clothes look sort of strange on me lately." She tried to laugh, but it fell, a choking noise in the silent room.

"You've been worrying yourself sick over all of this, haven't you?"

She laughed. "Dr. Larimer said losing a little weight would help my arthritis. Maybe it will keep it from getting worse before I really do get old."

I reached down and picked up her cane, which she'd dropped when I hugged her. Once again I thought of how young she was to suffer from rheumatoid arthritis. It wasn't all that bad now, but Dr. Larimer had said it would eventually get worse with age.

"I'm sorry I upset you, Kitty."

"Don't be. It's not your fault." She walked into the kitchen to start the tea.

While she puttered with breakfast, I took a long shower. This was the latest I'd slept in a long time, but I didn't feel refreshed, only more exhausted. At breakfast Kitty and I were both quiet. As I cut into the sunny face of my eggs, I tried to concentrate on planning my day. If only it could be as bright as the yolk running out over the white plate, maybe I'd get out of the mood I was in.

I knew Kitty would spend the day gardening, so I thought I'd offer her some help. I also thought about calling Dr. Larimer but wasn't sure if it would be appropriate to call his private cell number on a weekend when he was with his family. As I bit into my buttered toast, I decided against it.

I ended up spending the majority of Saturday and Sunday alternating between homework and gardening. By Sunday night I was so impatient about the loose ends of Ruby's story that I risked calling Susannah to vent about it.

"Lucy! What a surprise. I'm so glad you called." I could hear little Maria chattering in the background.

"I'm sorry," I said. "You don't have time to talk to me."

"Yes, I do! Just let me get Maria settled with her daddy. Troy will put her to bed while I sit out on the back porch and talk with you. It's such a nice night, and I need the fresh air anyway. Hold on."

I waited as she shuffled around and finally announced that she was alone.

"What's up with you?" she asked.

I told her about my conversation with Dr. Larimer and the pictures and quietly shared the things Kitty had told me. I was on my back porch too, and even though I knew Kitty was getting ready for bed, I didn't want her to hear me.

"Oh, my goodness," was all Susannah could say.

"I know," I said. "It's a lot to take in. Imagine if you were me."

"Oh, you poor thing," she said. "Well, just take some deep breaths, and know that this too shall pass."

"Huh?"

"The worry will all pass. And when it's over, it will all make sense."

I was silent, but I was thinking, Is that it? Is that the best advice she can give me?

"Lucy? Are you still there?"

"Yes. It's just not that easy to do. I can't just take a breath and wait for it to pass. It feels like I'm going crazy just thinking about it all."

"Do you want to come over?" she offered.

I was touched. "No, but thanks. It's nine. You have a family."

"Yes," she said. "But I can still be there for a friend. You can show up anytime."

"Maybe another time."

"Breakfast then?"

"That sounds great."

"At Martha's?"

"How about tomorrow?"

"Until then," Susannah said, "don't worry. Be excited! Just think, you're learning so much about Ruby. And now it looks like you might have known your grandfather at one time too. It gives me shivers to think that you might see him again someday, Lucy!"

"I guess you're right. Hey, Susannah. What about Mary? How is your mother?"

Susannah grew quiet. "Oh, she's okay. Did you know Kitty has visited her a few times recently?"

I was surprised. "No, she hadn't mentioned it." I felt bad realizing that I'd been so focused on digging through the past that I hadn't even thought to ask Kitty what she'd been doing with her time.

"Yes, and it's really cheered my mother. I'm thankful for Kitty."

"Well, I'm not surprised. She really spoke highly of Mary after they met."

"Hey, Lucy, I'm not going to fill you full of my dreadful thoughts. My mother is so positive, and I want to be positive for her too. I'm trying not to be too down about it."

"Okay," I said. "I understand. Your being positive probably helps her too. I've heard that when people are positive they live longer."

"Yeah," she said quietly, her tone hopeful. "That is what they say."

Hanging up the phone, I tried to be positive like Susannah. Even with all she was going through, she was still upbeat. And perhaps she was right about my learning about my grandfather. I should take some time to be excited about the new possibilities in my life, but it was Kitty's life that made me worry. My decisions would now be the ones affecting her life instead of how it had always been.

Breathing in the night air, I caught the fragrance of Kitty's roses. Actually they had been Ruby's roses. The entire garden had been Ruby's, and despite her problems with asthma, she had planted more and more. After hearing about La Rosaleda, I felt I knew why she had grown our garden to overabundance with roses and flowers. It was her way of having a piece of La Rosaleda in our backyard.

ood morning, dear! You're already dressed? My goodness, you are in a hurry today!"

I turned to see Kitty holding two cups of tea. She wore her yellow robe with orange flowers, and by the look on her face I could see she held no grudge against me. She was still my Kitty, just like always.

"Thank you!" I accepted the cup and breathed in the fragrance of Earl Grey. "This is exactly what I needed."

"It's what you need every morning, silly."

"This morning more than usual."

Kitty frowned as she slowly sat down beside me. I saw her shiver and realized the morning was especially cool. Before long we'd have to drink our tea inside during the short Sacramento winter.

"I'm sorry for being grumpy with you last night, Kitty."

"Oh," she said, "you need to be grumpier than that if you're going to bother me. Besides, I understand. You need to know, even if it's hard for me to dredge through it all."

"The more I know, the closer I get to remembering something. Isn't that what you've been trying to do for years, Kitty? Get me to remember?"

"Yes, but that doesn't mean we tear apart the good life we have now. Must we really dig so deep? Maybe some things are okay to forget."

I was hurt. Maybe she wasn't back to herself after all. I felt my cheery mood shifting.

"So it's okay for me to know things, just as long as I don't dig too deep into your secrets?" I accused.

I stood abruptly. I was angry, but I wanted to soften the blow. "I love you, Kitty. I have to go to school now."

I slid open the glass door, and when I glanced from inside out to the porch, I thought I saw tears on the side of her face. However it could have just been the rising sun reflecting off her earrings, so I didn't go back. I pushed my concern away and headed out the front door to join Susannah for breakfast at Martha's. I tried to ignore the guilt that swelled inside.

"How'd you manage to get away this morning?" I asked after we were seated. I glanced around; Martha herself wasn't at the restaurant that morning. *Too bad,* I thought. Service was always more pleasant when she was around.

"Troy has the morning off to run some personal errands, so he volunteered to take Maria to school."

"You are so lucky to have him."

She smiled as pink crept into her cheeks.

"I am. He is just the best, but I have to be honest with you. Marriage takes a lot of work. Even ours."

I nodded, not really knowing but believing her.

"I wonder what Kitty and Blake fought about?" I asked. "When and if they did, that is. It sounds like they didn't fight very often."

"Probably not until Ruby came along." Susannah laughed. "Kids always complicate things even though they're a joy to have around. How is Kitty today?"

I sighed. "Not well. She's worried sick about everything. I know I've been full of too many questions, but it's hard not to ask them."

Susannah patted my hand. "It is her story to tell or not tell, Lucy."

I tried not to roll my eyes as I listened to her explain why Kitty had a right to keep some parts of her life to herself.

"But that's not fair," I pointed out. "Those secrets affect me in very important ways."

"Life certainly hasn't been fair to Kitty, has it?"

I attempted a laugh to ease the sudden tension. "Whose side are you on anyway?"

Susannah didn't laugh. "I'm on both your sides, Lucy. Only you two can figure all of this out. I agree with you that it might be better for both of you if the truth comes out, but you can't force Kitty to tell you everything any more than she can force you to remember Ruby."

I bit my lip so I wouldn't say anything unkind. Her words were burrowing into just the right wounds.

"But even though you shouldn't force Kitty to tell you things about herself, that doesn't mean you can't find a way to meet your grandfather now that you know about him. I would even take you to La Rosaleda, Lucy, if you really want to go."

"Maybe," I said. "Perhaps someday."

She tried changing the subject. "So how are things with you and Max?"

Now it was my turn to blush. "Great," I said quietly.

"Well, from the way you both looked Friday night, I would say more than great."

"Oh, I don't know," I said. "I'm not starting out with much faith in the situation. Seems my family has a history of bad relationships with men."

"What about Blake? Isn't he a good example? He and Kitty had a great relationship."

"Mmm. I guess they did, but it didn't work out, did it?"

"Maybe it's not over."

"It's like you just said. It's her story, so it's her choice. I don't know. I already asked her to go back to La Rosaleda to see what might happen with my grandfather, and I thought she was going to throw her teacup into the air."

"That's so sad. I hope she changes her mind someday. But what about you? Seriously, Lucy. I would go with you! Let's go this weekend!"

"Now I'm going to throw my cup. Wow! Would you really go with me?"

"I would love to. Just sell me the rights to your story so I can handle the movie." We both laughed.

"Like I said. Someday."

I sat staring into the kitchen at the roses Max had given me. They were still fairly fresh, and I didn't have the heart to throw them out yet. They made me think of the roses Blake had planted around his and Kitty's house. I wondered if they were still growing over the porch like Ruby had once described to Kitty.

"Do you ever miss Blake?" I asked.

"Only every minute of my life."

"Do you think he misses you?"

"Yes, but he misses the Kitty he thought I was. If he knew who I really am now, he would know he hasn't missed anything at all."

"Oh, Kitty. I have a hard time believing that."

She stood. "Speaking of your grandfather, wait here. I have something to show you."

She disappeared for a few minutes before returning with two envelopes and a blue floral hatbox in her hand. As she handed one envelope to me, I noticed it was yellowed and creased. The handwriting on the envelope was addressed to Kitty in care of Ruby DiCamillo. The return address was from Frances-DiCamillo Vineyards, La Rosaleda, California.

I looked up at her wide eyed. "Is it from my grandfather?"

"Yes." The look in her eyes held an apology but was distant. She sat down and focused on her hands in her lap, massaging them like she did when they were in pain.

"I happen to know that Blake has no idea how I've changed or he wouldn't have written that letter. Open it."

I did, carefully so as not to tear the creased stationery. It was dated a few weeks before Ruby's death.

My Dearest Kitty,

I'm not sure what to write, but I don't dare miss another chance to tell you I miss you. I wish every day for you to come home.

There is nothing that could take my love from you. I realize this even more as the years go by. I have so many regrets about that night all those years ago. I would give anything to go back and make you feel safe instead of treating you so harshly.

As you now know, Ruby has been coming to see me for several years now. She is the one who gave me your phone number. I wish you wouldn't hang up because hearing your voice is wonderful. Ruby has explained that you don't want a reunion. I pray you will change your mind.

Ruby is lovelier than I even expected. When she arrived home the first time, she looked so much like you that I thought you'd come back. Then when I saw her smile, I knew she could only be our Ruby.

And little Lucy. She is a mix of all the best in you and Ruby. She loves to take long walks with me through the grapes, just like you did. I now understand how Isaac must have felt about Ruby when she was little. He used to say his granddaughter lit up everything. So does Lucy for me and for her mother.

Do you recall seeing me in San Francisco? You looked beautiful. Ruby said you thought I rejected you. I'm so sorry, Kitty. I thought you had gone on with your life and did not want me.

If you ever want to visit, you could stay in our loft. Yes, I finally bought it and it is ours, paid in full. I gave Ruby a key and am enclosing another one. I'll keep it ready for you just in case.

I'm also sending some money. Ruby says you won't take it, but please do something nice for yourself and the girls. Ruby says you've not touched the account I set up for you. As much as I long for you to come home, I want you and the girls to be provided for. I've enclosed the account information in case you've lost it. Please use it as you see fit.

The fruits of this vineyard are rightfully your inheritance, Kitty. Yours, Ruby's, and Lucy's. I'm just the caretaker.

I have prayed for you since the day you left. I can't explain in a letter how much I miss my wife.

Your husband,
Blake

I accepted the handkerchief Kitty offered and tried to keep the letter dry as I carefully placed it back in the envelope.

"What are these other things?" I croaked.

With a look of regret on her face, Kitty slowly handed me the other letter and the box. The letter was unopened and addressed to Lucy DiCamillo at the same address we still lived at now. It was also from Frances-DiCamillo with the name "Grandpa" scribbled over the preprinted stationery. I gasped as the room went white.

He'd known where we were all this time? Then why hadn't he come? Because Kitty kept him away, just like she hid these letters from me.

I sucked in great wafts of air and closed my eyes, an attempt to force myself to stay calm. My disease was exacerbated by stress, but Dr. Larimer had told me that the attacks wouldn't happen so often if I would just stay calm.

Kitty reached for the inhaler, but I lightly brushed her hand away.

"I can do it." I picked up the inhaler and breathed deeply. I hated it so much. It was like a drug I couldn't go without. If I didn't have my fix several times a day, I couldn't breathe. I could even die if I didn't get enough oxygen in time. It sounded extreme, but it had happened to Ruby. It could happen to me—the way the breath had left and her lungs hadn't let another breath back into her body. At that moment, feelings against Kitty I'd never experienced before piled up around me like bricks and mortar.

"Lucy, dear. I'm so sorry."

"You are wrong, Kitty. He says in this letter that there's nothing that could have happened that would change his love for you."

"He lives in a fantasy world if he thinks that."

"*He* lives in a fantasy world? His wife abandoned him and rejected him all over again when he tried to contact you!"

She looked surprised for a moment, like she hadn't considered how he felt.

"Why did you hide this letter from me? Are there more?"

"They're in that box, and I didn't really mean to hide them at first. That one must have come around the week Ruby died, and she wasn't able to give it to you. I kept my own letters tucked away too because I had made a choice to stay away from Blake. It was for his own good and for yours too. Nobody understands how important it is that I never go back there. Ruby never did either."

She shook her head as if we were all too daft to understand.

"So when you saw I'd lost my memories, you just decided to take advantage of it and not tell me I knew my grandfather?"

"Absolutely not, child," she said emphatically. "I wasn't taking advantage, Lucy. You were very fragile. I was protecting you!"

"No! You were protecting yourself!"

Kitty was silent. She lowered her head to hide the tears I could see pooling on her chin.

"And we have been living like we're poor! We didn't have to be poor! I could have gone to college even without a scholarship, so why did you make me study so hard? Why did you keep me sequestered in our home as if making me smarter was the only way I'd have a good life?"

She was silent, running her fingers in a circular motion around her knuckles.

"You were hiding me!" I exclaimed. "Weren't you, Grandmother? You were keeping me hidden just in case he showed up here! And I can't believe it. He gave us money. Your own money and you let us be poor!"

"Not poor, Lucy. We have earned our way and have had everything we needed. You go to a private school. Do you know how many people could never afford to go there or even hope to score high enough to have the scholarship you do?"

"But it didn't have to be so hard! You didn't have to worry about money so much when I was growing up! Why did you keep it a secret from me? Life could have been easier."

"It was, Lucy. Think about it. Your mother was a very young single woman, and she chose to live simple then, even though she could have taken you to the vineyard in La Rosaleda. After she left us, we still lived a very simple life, but we weren't destitute. I did use some of the money he gave to you girls. Where do you think I found the money to fill in the gaps? Her life insurance?"

"She didn't have life insurance?"

"Only about five thousand dollars. Enough to pay for the funeral. I used the money from the trust Blake set up for you but only when I needed it for you. I used my own money to take care of us, but yes, the money from his account was used to pay extra costs for your schooling, to fill in gaps when paying utilities as needed, and for many other things benefiting you that you don't even know about. Like violin and piano lessons—anything that benefited you primarily I didn't hesitate to pay for with Frances-DiCamillo money."

Her hands were now flying about her.

"The money that was in Ruby's separate account is still there. Ruby used it to live on when she was alive, but it became yours when you turned eighteen, and Blake has continued the monthly deposits. You can have it. It's yours, but I want to warn you, dear, money can be dangerous to have if you don't know what to do with it."

"You mean we could've lived a completely different life than we have?"

"It was good for you to learn what it's like to live in the real world, mija. I didn't want you to be like I was when I was young— naive and easily taken advantage of because I was sheltered by a life of ease at Frances-DiCamillo."

"But I didn't get to experience the real world," I said. "You kept me in a bubble of your own making!"

"I was only protecting you from what I knew was out there. There are lots of bad people out there, Lucy. Believe me, I know something about that!"

"But we had family," I said quietly. "They would have pro-tected us."

"We have a family right here, Lucy. Me and you. I always made sure of that."

I stood up from my place on the couch. "Just like you did with you and Ruby, right? You thought you could be her whole family then too! But she didn't like it, did she? She didn't want just you! We had family in La Rosaleda! I so much would've liked to have a grandfather!" I was scarcely aware that I was yelling. "What could be so bad besides what you've told me, Kitty, that you can't confess it and go back?"

She was silent, and I felt a touch of guilt. I had no doubt that her secrets were probably horrible, but whatever they were they'd taken so much from me too.

"Kitty," I implored. "I feel like your secrets are keeping us from something great. Something wonderful. I want to know my grandfather! And what of George Fields? My father! Who is he? Why don't you tell me more about him?"

I was standing now and waving my hands in the air too.

"Has he written me letters that you have hidden too? Are they in here?" I reached for the box.

She shook her head. "Lucy, I'm sorry but that is one thing I have not kept secret. The man is gone. He has never made an effort to find you, and according to Ruby, you should be glad about that. You want to know something? Not everyone has a father. There's nothing wrong with that!"

I shook my head. "That's easy for you to say. You had a wonderful father! But what of me? I have never had any male relative in my life! At least since Ruby died. And I can't even remember when he was there. I had a whole different life before she died, and I think you're glad I can't remember it!"

"And why is that so bad, dear? You're making friends now, and I've decided that it's okay for you to date Maxwell. I like the boy very much in fact."

"You've decided it's okay?" I asked incredulously. "You think it's okay to decide if I get to have a male friend or not? Just like you decided I didn't need a father or grandfather?"

Part of me was disgusted with myself for the things I was saying to Kitty, but who was she to keep me away from my grandfather?

"You took Ruby away from him, and then you took me too!"

I stood up with the letters and the box.

"Please be careful with those. I would like to have the ones back that are addressed to me."

I gasped again.

"Why? Why would you want them, Kitty? You don't want him!"

I knew I was yelling, and I vaguely thought of what Kitty had told me about daughters always pushing back against their mothers at some point in life. Why did she have to be my mother too?

Kitty suddenly stood up more quickly than she should have. I winced at the pain I knew she felt in her joints as she leaned heavily on her cane, but she didn't seem to care. She lifted her cane and pointed it at me.

"Don't talk to me about what you know nothing about. Do you hear me?"

We were both angry, and tears rolled down both our faces. I wanted to hug her and apologize, but at the moment I was too shocked. I'd never seen Kitty so mad at me, and it hurt.

After a moment, I did have the decency to whisper, "Yes ma'am."

"You think you know all about life just because you're already graduating from college when most kids your age are barely starting? Well, being educated doesn't make you wise, child. Yes, you've had a hard life. You and everyone else out there. Life just isn't fair, is it?"

I shook my head, holding back my emotions for now.

She continued. "Susannah's mother could die of cancer, right?"

I nodded my head, my sadness for Susannah renewed at the thought of her mother's having to endure cancer treatments. "But she might survive."

"Yes," Kitty said, choking up. "She might and she might not. Do you think that's fair?" Her voice was softening back to the tone she had used before.

I could see that Kitty was filled with grief for a friend she'd become close to so quickly. I wanted to hold her tight, but she wasn't finished.

"Do you think it's fair that Susannah can't bear her own children? Is it fair that she now has a greater risk of breast cancer?"

She took a deep breath. "Dear, your mother was ripped away from you and me, and that wasn't fair and was nobody's fault."

I shook my head in disbelief. "Mine," I croaked.

"No!" Kitty grasped my shoulder with her free hand. "Not

yours. Not mine. Not anyone's. But it is my fault that your grand-father and La Rosaleda got ripped from you and Ruby. It's entirely my fault. I accept full responsibility and I'm sorry. If you knew the truth, you might understand why I made the decisions I did. The one thing in my power I could've changed was to leave Ruby there. I admit it was my selfishness. I couldn't bear not to have her with me. I needed her so much that I didn't even let myself think about what she needed. Maybe your lives both would've been different had I left her there. I'm sorry my decisions have made life unfair for you."

I was sobbing, but Kitty wasn't pulling me into her arms. She turned and made her way around the coffee table and to her room. I wasn't sure what to do. I stood where she'd left me for several min-utes before I carefully placed the letters and the small hatbox in my backpack. I found a pen and wrote a note to Kitty saying I was going to the library.

I signed it my usual.

Love, Lucy.

25

The smell of espresso found its way out the screened window of Martha's. It was never too late to have a coffee in Sacramento, and besides, it was only a few blocks from our apartment, and I no longer felt like hiking clear across campus to the library. That had only been an excuse to escape from the house.

"Lucy DiCamillo! And how is your grandmother this lovely evening?"

I attempted a smile for Martha Schneider, who ran the shop. She had her hair in cornrows as usual and was dressed in a blue kimono-style dress that Kitty would have loved. In fact, Mrs. Schneider always reminded me of Kitty when I saw her dressed in her more casual, comfortable clothing made from rich, flowing fabrics, the same styles Kitty had chosen in recent years for their practical beauty.

"You know," I replied teasingly, "beautiful, bossy, compassionate. The usual." Then I sobered, thinking already of a peace offering to bring home. "Honestly? Kitty isn't feeling well today. Maybe you should make up a green tea I could take to her?"

"Just let me know a few minutes before you leave, and I'll have it ready. How about you, Lucy? What do you want?"

"Cappuccino with a double shot."

"Bad day?"

"Sort of."

I made my way to a corner seat where I could stare out at the American River flowing through the park in the distance. It meandered slowly as I watched a mother and her young daughter walking hand in hand alongside. I wondered if I'd walked those same steps once with Ruby. I felt an intense desire to tear open the letter from my grandfather but waited until I had my cappuccino.

Using the butter knife, I slit open the envelope and unfolded the letter.

Dear Lucy,

    I hope you had fun helping me press grapes last time you were here. I can't wait until you come back so you can help again. When you do, we'll drive over to Bodega Bay like I promised, and I'll show you the rocky cliffs and how to eat an oyster. They're kind of slimy, but if you get the ones with hot sauce, you might think they're tasty. And then we'll pick flowers for your mom. She loves roses, just like your Kitty, so we'll go over to the Rose House and pick a whole bunch. I can't wait to see you. I love you.

    Love,

    Grandpa

I felt the weight in the center of my chest growing heavier as each subsequent letter, before that moment unopened, spoke of his loving me and how everything would be okay even though Ruby had gone to heaven. He wrote the same words repeatedly:

…don't worry about your mom. She's in heaven now. Everything will be okay, Lucy girl. God is with you all the time, and that's who Ruby is with. She isn't far away! Call me if you need to talk.

His last letter to me was only dated three months earlier, asking how I was—and Kitty too.

"Call me if you need to talk," the last letter had said, like all the others before it. My hands felt heavy holding the letter as I realized that I'd been cheated of this by Kitty. I could've called him a thousand times had I known.

If Mrs. Schneider noticed my tears when she walked up to leave me another cappuccino I hadn't even ordered, she didn't let on. She just patted my shoulder and went on to the next table. It took a long time to make it through all the letters. The ones to me had been unopened, but each letter to Kitty from Blake had already been neatly opened, and the paper was worn and creased.

Every letter made me cry, just as Kitty must have each time she read them. Each one was filled with simple proclamations of love from Blake, details about what he had been up to, always ending with a plea for her to come home. Some contained pictures of Frances-DiCamillo, one in particular of the house Blake and Kitty had shared. The front porch of the Rose House was completely encased by the bush planted decades ago; its deep red blooms covered the sides and roof. I stared at this photo for a long time trying to picture Kitty and the child Ruby waving to my grandpa from the porch swing as he walked back from a day's work in the vines.

I'd made it through every letter and had gone back to the one Blake wrote about Ruby's funeral when I felt a hand on my shoulder. I looked up, surprised to see Dr. Larimer. "Oh." I fumbled to wipe away my tears.

"May I sit down?"

I sniffled and dabbed my eyes, but the compassion in his eyes caused fresh tears to well.

He didn't wait for my answer. "I've been meaning to call you. I was driving in the area and just thought I'd stop in, but I didn't expect you to be here."

I shrugged. "I'm supposed to be at the library."

"Your mother and I used to meet here sometimes for coffee before she passed away. Did you know that?"

"No." I shook my head. I knew Martha's had been here for a

long time, but I hadn't imagined it had been there when my own mother was alive.

"Seems like an answer to prayer to find you here."

I suddenly didn't feel like saying anything, so I busied myself putting the letters back in the hatbox. I noticed that he was looking at the envelopes. He reached over to help me stack them, and then a look of bewilderment shadowed his face as he studied one.

"What are all these?"

"Letters from Blake Birkirt."

"Your grandfather," he corrected.

"Yes. Grandpa."

He placed the letter on top of the stack and then studied my face. Embarrassed, I rubbed beneath my eyes and glanced out the window.

His voice was soft. "Have you been receiving these letters all along?"

"No, Kitty has been setting them aside. Tonight is the first time…"

He cleared his throat. "I came at a bad time after all. I can leave."

"No, please. Don't leave. You came at a good time. Maybe you can help me piece together some of the information from these letters."

He shrugged. "I can try."

I shuffled the letters and was surprised when a key tinkled from one of the envelopes onto the floor. Dr. Larimer leaned over and picked it up. Looking curiously at it, he handed it to me.

"I might be able to help you with this one. People don't use keys like this much anymore. It belongs to an old house I bet. Probably either the loft or the house Ruby lived in with her parents, their little cottage."

I somehow wasn't surprised that he seemed to know about the loft. Our eyes met, and I felt an inexplicable connection with him for the briefest moment. The knowledge of someone else besides Kitty sharing one small detail of my life engulfed me, and suddenly I was in tears again. I wished more than anything that Ruby hadn't died.

"You spent a lot of time with him, you know?"

"Were you with us?"

"During some visits, when you were between six months old and two. Sometimes when I visited my grandparents, I would stop by Frances-DiCamillo to see you and Ruby."

"You were there?"

He was silent for a while, staring at me in a way that didn't make me feel uncomfortable, only extremely sad as I noted the same grief in his eyes as my own. The words of Emily Dickinson were there again.

I measure every Grief I meet
        With narrow, probing, Eyes—
I wonder if It weighs like Mine—
        Or has an Easier size.

I knew its size wasn't easier for him, only different.

"You and Ruby weren't together?"

"We were friends then. Truly friends."

"What about before?"

"You look like you've had enough surprises for one night."

"What's one more?" I tried to laugh, but it came out as more of a guttural sob. "I need to know about my mother, Dr. Larimer."

He took a deep breath and leaned forward.

"Okay, but first it's Matt to you. Not Dr. Larimer."

I shook my head. "Kitty would never go for that kind of casual disrespect." This time I managed a real smile, and he chuckled in response.

"I'm sure of that, but still it's Matt from now on, okay?"

"Sure."

I stared at this man who'd always had a strange part in my world that I could never explain—remaining a stranger yet familiar in my life. He had a clean-cut look about him that reminded me somewhat of Susannah's husband, Troy, but Matt was older, probably late thirties or early forties. He had early gray hair in his brown sideburns and a hint of fine, branching lines crinkling at the corner of his eyes. I could easily see how Ruby's feelings toward him had turned from childhood friendship to something more. There was kindness in his eyes that was real despite the serious way in which he carried himself. I also finally understood why he had always been so personable with Kitty. He knew Kitty and me. He probably knew more about the culminating information of my life than I did but presumably had never been allowed to say anything.

"Did Kitty forbid you to tell me the nature of your friendship with Ruby?"

He sighed, staring out the window toward the river.

"Yes, and at first I agreed. Now I'm not sure I can keep my word anymore."

"What happened when Ruby died?"

"You know what happened, Lucy." He stared at me with his kind eyes again, and I felt small, like a little girl without any parents to keep me safe.

"I mean what else?"

"At the hospital?"

I nodded yes.

"I was only a resident at the same hospital I'm at now, but of course when I heard about Ruby, I wanted to help. I didn't tell the doctors I knew her so well, and they allowed me to assist. When they saw me get emotional during the consultations with the team about her chances of recovery, they knew. They tried to take me off the team, but when I refused to go home, they decided to let me stay. As you know, there was no chance of her recovery, Lucy. Her brain was no longer active. It was only the machines that kept her organs alive."

I swiped at the tear escaping down my cheek.

"I followed up with Kitty a few weeks afterward, and she let me see you. I knew it had been traumatic. You lost your memories really fast, and you were at a very fragile time in your life. The mind of a child is very sensitive, and I agreed with Kitty that you needed to have nothing but love and security."

The sudden memory of his presence on the day of Ruby's death flooded my mind with a brightness that pierced my consciousness. The lights had hurt my eyes; the gleaming floors, metallic and white, had been everywhere. Ruby was being rolled away down the hall. Remembering caused me to reach up and rub my forehead, the pain physical as well as emotional.

"Thank you for stopping the nurses so I could say good-bye to Ruby," I croaked.

He attempted a halfhearted grin. "You would've been hard to keep away."

He was right. I still felt the horrendous longing that had propelled me down the hallway in that awful moment. "I was afraid."

"I know," he said quietly. "And it's okay."

He made a movement with his hand to reach toward me when Mrs. Schneider quietly shuffled over to us. She placed her hand on Matt's shoulder.

"Matt, what will it be?"

I didn't miss the fact she called him Matt.

"Oh, the usual. Thanks."

"You come here often?" I was surprised.

"About once a week. It's a good place to get away from the demands of people. I like to do research while I'm here too; you know, read boring medical journals and so forth."

I nodded. It was a nice place to get away from everyday things.

I often came with Kitty, who liked the tea and Mrs. Schneider—
who was better known as Martha to most.

"But I've never seen you here."

"When I come, it's usually in the evening."

I shook my head in surprise. "All this time we've been hanging
out at the same coffee shop? Maybe we could have spoken about
things earlier."

"I couldn't have told you anything before now. At least I
wouldn't have felt right about it."

Mrs. Schneider set the tea in front of Matt and glanced at me.

"For a moment there you looked like your mother." She
winked and walked away.

I tried not to show my shock but couldn't help it. "Does everybody know about my past but me?"

"No, no. It's just that Martha's has been here for many years,
believe it or not. If you haven't noticed, things don't rotate so much
in this neighborhood. Ruby and I met here sometimes when she
was attending school. You did know she was a student at the university, right?"

"I've always known that." I motioned toward the hatbox. "And
one of these letters was congratulating me for being accepted into
Ruby's alma mater."

"That's why Ruby chose this location for an apartment, or
rather, why your grandpa encouraged her to live in this area. Anyway, we weren't together at that point. We could only meet as
friends. I was no longer available, a big mistake I regretted at the
time, but I'm at peace about it now."

He looked down at his tea as he slowly stirred sugar into it. His
eyebrows were knit together, and he looked sad. I didn't think he
was at peace at all.

"You cared about her?"

"I loved her."

He said this simply, as a fact, and looked back out the window at a houseboat maneuvering its way around the bend in the river. "I think it's the reason she was so sad sometimes."

"Sad?"

"I was terrible at sticking up for what I really wanted in life, so I let Ruby slip away from me. I think we both bumped into each other here on purpose. I know it was definitely wrong since I was attached to someone else, but we were only friends. That's the sad truth, but just being in the same room occasionally helped ease our pain."

His story was even sadder than Kitty's in some ways. I felt like reaching across to hold his hand but realized he might be offended. After all, I was just Ruby's little girl. How could I comfort him?

There were so many things I didn't know about Ruby that Kitty had been very adept at keeping under wraps. I could see how it had been easy for her to do in the beginning. I'd spent so much of my time with Kitty at home or at the museum that I was a virtual recluse, and I hadn't minded at all. I had always been a loner at heart, it seemed, and so I thrived in our world of solitude. It was becoming more and more apparent of late that the reclusive life had been purposeful.

"Stop me if I'm telling you something you already know."

I shook my head. "No, because it's your perspective I want to hear. Besides I hardly know anything about Ruby, as you can see. The only things that really make me feel closer to her are the paintings and her piano."

He nodded, and I knew he understood.

"She played beautifully. And her paintings were remarkable, in my opinion. I'm not an art critic, but there was always a search, a sort of desperation, in her paintings that I identified with."

"Yes." I nodded in agreement. "I guess...I guess she was desperate at times in her life. I've felt the same sometimes."

"Do you paint as well?"

"Yes."

"I never knew that."

I just smiled. I guess I had never mentioned it during our brief doctor appointments.

"What do you paint?"

"I paint Ruby."

He smiled, not surprised.

"I paint her and Kitty. I paint memories when I have them. That's why I have so many unfinished canvases. But music is different. I compose it, which I don't think she ever did. I love playing her piano. It makes me feel close to her."

"She always said that playing made her feel closer to La Rosaleda."

"Really?"

"But that was long after Kitty had taken her from there. By the time Kitty convinced Ruby to move from San Francisco to Sacramento, she was ready to try going to school, and that's when she started attending your university. Her grades had been wonderful, but she'd been to so many different schools, all public, that the university seemed reluctant to accept her transcripts. That's where your grandpa stepped in. I know it sounds like favoritism, but he knew the dean through some business investments, and it only took a phone call and maybe a donation to get the board to actually read Ruby's application. Once they read it, they saw the great potential she had."

I leaned closer to him across the table. "The reason we moved into our apartment is so she could go to school here?"

"Yes, and the apartments weren't easy to get either. Have you taken a look around? You might have a tiny, old apartment, but the historic location and the real estate value is phenomenal. And you and Kitty are living in a very smart investment. Your grandpa picked a good area for you and Ruby to live. He made sure you would be okay."

"Investment?" I was confused. Kitty had always talked about paying rent.

"Your grandpa owns your apartment."

"You still know Grandpa?"

He smiled. "He will want to see you now that you know."

My eyes smarted as I realized what Kitty had kept from me all these years. It's not that I thought she lied. If I knew Kitty, she had probably been sending Blake a check every month out of pure pride and pulling money out of the account he'd set up and sending it back to him when she couldn't make the payment with her own small wage. That must be the rent check I'd seen her write once a month for years. Now that I thought about it, she'd always left the "pay to the order of" line blank. She'd said it was for the landlord's stamp, but it must have been so I wouldn't see Blake's name.

I shook my head angrily.

"Kitty has kept so many things secret from me. How did she think she could continue to do this when I became an adult?"

"I doubt she thought she could keep it secret forever, and now you're asking questions. It's hard for her. She has tried to protect you for many years. I think you're ready to know the truth, but I think she's afraid of what it might do to you."

"She's afraid of what it might do to her!"

Matt sipped his tea, weighing his answer, perhaps wanting to be supportive of Kitty but not hurt my feelings. He knew more, I was sure of that.

"Maybe it's true that she's worried what it might do to her. That isn't such a surprising way for her to feel. At least if you knew everything, you might agree."

"That's the problem. She divulges a little bit at a time but leaves out details that are very important to my life!"

"Ah, Kitty does hope you will recall things."

"Only what she wants me to remember," I corrected.

"Lucy, your grandmother doesn't want your memories lost, but you need to give her some time. You don't have to know everything *now,* do you? There are some things that have to do with her encounter with my father that you might never know about."

I hadn't wanted to bring up Mike Larimer, Matt's dad, and how he had almost fathered a baby with Kitty, or that she had chosen to end that pregnancy.

"Does my grandpa talk about that?"

"Not anymore. I only see Blake every couple of months when I go visit my grandparents. All he ever wants to talk about has nothing to do with the past. He only wants to ask me about you and Kitty and how you both are now. He always asks if you've been in my office lately."

"You divulge our secret medical information?" I teased, trying to lighten up the conversation a little.

"Not exactly." He chuckled. "But I tell him what I can and what I think is appropriate so he knows how you both are doing. If you want, sue me. Everyone likes to sue doctors."

We both laughed.

"I'm not going to sue you," I assured him.

I was silent then, still trying to absorb that while I had lived a life under what I thought was Kitty's cautious protection, I'd been secretly cared for by my grandfather, who had known exactly where I was all these years. Why had he stayed away?

Blake Birkirt had written me letters that went unanswered, but he'd never shown up on our doorstep even when he could have. I knew what Kitty's pride was like, and I could respect his seeming desire to respect her need for separation, but I'd been denied a relationship with him in the process. And yet…how could I be mad at him? I was too tired to be mad anymore. This was all so confusing that I could scarcely even stay mad at Kitty. More and more I was finding myself swaying back and forth between anger and compassion for her.

"I imagine Kitty hasn't lived as easily as you think with all these secrets swimming around in her heart, Lucy. I don't know what her big fear is, but it's so big that her husband has been within reach for more than twenty years and she hasn't contacted him once."

"She has read every one of his letters," I said, pointing to the hatbox.

"She certainly hasn't picked you up and moved you to a secret location either, has she?"

I shook my head no.

"So what about you and Ruby? Why didn't you just marry my mother and take her to La Rosaleda to live since you were in love?"

His face looked pained. "Lucy, you know I have a wife and children now, right?"

"Yes."

"It wouldn't be appropriate for me to get into it all here, but my wife and I haven't always been as happy as we are now. There was a time when we were pushed together by people who were more worried about appearances than whether or not we were right for each other. That was when your mother was pushed out of my life, and I admit it's my own fault. I should have fought for her."

When I heard Matt Larimer's version of the story, I felt the closest to Ruby I had ever felt. He filled in details I'd only imagined about Ruby—what her dreams were, what she longed for, what she wanted in life, her joys, her pains. Most important to me, I finally learned about the man she'd loved: a sad story about unrequited passion that was more amazing to me than any fiction. And even more heartbreaking.

LOVE CAN'T BRING
BACK THE DEAD

26

Ruby used to say we were open canvases." Matt smiled at the memory of when he and Ruby were so very young at La Rosaleda. He could see the two of them, as if in one of Ruby's portraits: Ruby at his side, alive and beautiful, a friend to lean on in a life that had been constantly unstable. They were walking through a vineyard. It was Frances-DiCamillo. They were holding hands. "She said we could paint it however we wanted to."

Matt pulled Ruby along one row that angled up and over a hill, allowing a spectacular view of the valley before them. The vines stretched for miles, all fully leafed with only a glimpse of the grapes that would soon spring in full clusters.

"Lucy would love living here," Ruby said.

"She would."

"But I could never abandon Kitty."

Matt squeezed Ruby's hand. She smiled, and he was amazed that she still looked at him that way even after all he had put her through. *Are we destined for the same life of separation Ruby's parents led?* He felt a sudden rush of heaviness.

She must have sensed it, because she pulled away.

Matt stopped in the vines and pulled Ruby toward him, a quick embrace. They stood together for a moment, looking at the sweeping valley around them. It wasn't a happy, romantic moment. He had messed up everything.

Ruby's sudden tears jolted him. He pulled her tighter, and both of them slowly sank to their knees. Her breath came in soft gasps as a breeze rustled through the grape leaves. She struggled to find the inhaler in her pocket, and he helped her put it to her lips and breathe in just as when he'd found her in labor.

Blake had encouraged him then: "Go for me. Go for us."

Matt had gone for them but for himself too, and he had breathed with Ruby, worried about her asthma and the baby. He recalled the moment Lucy was born, crying and safe in her mother's arms as Ruby had been in her own mother's. There had been no earthquake then, as on the eve of Ruby's birth. All had been happy for a moment until the earth around them shook in different ways that were far more complicated than the falling balcony in La Rosaleda so many years before.

What have I done to Ruby? he thought. *How is it I've fallen into this trap of my stepfather's making?* He had never loved Leah for even one moment, and before he knew it he was engaged to her.

Leah. It had all started when he and Ruby had been reunited in San Francisco and before Ruby was pregnant with Lucy. The days had all run into each other, and while they hadn't proclaimed their love openly or to others, it was obvious…except to Matt's mother and stepfather. They had other plans to fix him up with their friends' daughter, Leah, a student at Berkeley and a sweet person.

"She's very pretty," his mother had said.

"She's beautiful, Mother, but she's not as pretty as Ruby."

"Ruby is a friend."

Matt hadn't answered.

"And she's Episcopalian. Not the same church as ours, but she is a believer at least."

"Mother, she doesn't like church. I don't think she believes what her parents do or even what we do for that matter."

"Your stepfather doesn't believe what I do, and does that matter?"

"It doesn't make things easy on you, Mother."

"No, but it's easier than it was before."

And the conversations had gone on like this, Matt believing he had made himself clear to his mother about Leah, and his mother going along with his stepfather to get Matt and Leah together.

Ruby had grown tired of it all early on, and she'd begun to hang out with George Fields, a man in his thirties who somehow convinced her that his so-called bohemian lifestyle was adventurous. Matt thought Ruby was just trying to make him mad and could see very well that George wasn't bohemian at all, but a lazy washout of a man who had no self-respect, let alone respect for a young woman like Ruby.

Ruby ended up pregnant.

She had lashed out angrily at Matt and claimed the baby was George's. She'd then demanded that Matt stay away from her.

When Matt ignored her wishes, showing up at her San Francisco apartment, Ruby had thrown herself in his arms and begged him to help her.

With her father's promise to help her pay for moving and for medical expenses, Ruby moved in with Kitty. At first Kitty protested Blake's money, but in the end Kitty silently accepted Ruby's choice to use Blake's assistance, even though somehow she managed to completely avoid Blake through the entire ordeal.

Matt's plan was to work through things with his parents and Leah before sharing his long-term plans with Ruby. Since she was in such a transition with the baby on the way, it would have been a bad time to talk to her about his parents' latest meddling escapade.

A ring. A simple but expensive ring had been placed under the tree at Christmastime. Matt, who was passing out the gifts, found it wrapped in iridescent pearl wrapping paper, buried under the gifts, with Leah's name on it. With blood rushing to his head, he recognized the box and started to tuck it into the pocket of his slacks, but Leah had already spotted her name on it. She'd shrieked with joy as she grabbed the box and ripped it open. The solitaire sparkled bright among the Christmas lights, its beauty thankfully pulling gazes toward it instead of Matt's glowering face.

Then his heart had sunk further at the sight of his mother smiling sweetly down at him. Leah jumped up and gave Matt a bear hug that felt heavier than it should have from such a little woman.

"Yes! I will. Of course, I will. I love you so much!"

Later, Matt and his mother, Charlotte, had a hushed but heated argument in her bedroom.

"Oh, I didn't know you were going to pop the question at Christmas. When I saw the little gift on your dresser alongside the other one for Leah, I went ahead and put them under the tree. I hope you don't mind that I put her name on it for you."

"Only the bigger gift was for Leah," Matt said tightly under his breath.

"The cashmere scarf? Is that all you were going to give your girlfriend for Christmas? But the ring…?"

Charlotte fell silent, and tears pooled in her eyes as the realization set in that she'd done something that disappointed her son very much.

Matt dropped his arms and softened when he saw that his mother had made a mistake, a big one to be sure, but a mistake nonetheless.

"What am I going to do, Mother? That ring was for Ruby. Didn't you notice that the paper was white, not holiday?"

She shook her head no and wiped away tears.

"I want to marry Ruby, but I was going to wait until the baby is born and we had time to work out some details. Things haven't exactly been very good between us lately, but we just need some time to sort things out."

"I'm sorry, so sorry. I didn't know. I saw the box, and you and Leah have seemed so happy, I just thought…" Charlotte sat down slowly on the bed. She stared out the window in silence for a while before asking, "Would marrying Leah be such a bad thing? Ruby has her father to help her now."

Feeling defeated, Matt walked out, mumbled something about going to work on a project, and Leah, confused but still happy, was left sitting with his stepfather and her parents in the kitchen.

They were happily chatting over coffee, planning his life, as he drove away.

He had to sweep all the trouble into the back of his mind when the baby was born. His chest had filled with overwhelming happiness when he'd taken the baby from her and stood at the window, cooing and talking to the small sleeping infant in his arms.

"Maria Lucero DiCamillo. My Lucy." Matt had leaned down and kissed Ruby on the cheek then.

"You're a tired mommy. Why don't you take a nap, and I'll hold Lucy for a little while. I promise I'll be careful."

But when Ruby was home and dealing with her emotions and a failed attempt to nurse her baby herself, Matt knew there was no going back.

"Your parents obviously have plans for you, and they aren't with me!" Ruby yelled. "They haven't even come to see my baby, not even your mother!"

"Ruby," Matt had implored. "You don't mean the things you're saying. I love you, and when things settle down around here, I want to be part of your life."

She'd paused for several minutes and Matt thought she was considering his offer, but then she began to cry and shout at him again.

"Matt Larimer, you are such a wimp! Why do you have to work so hard to get out of your silly entanglement with Leah? Don't act like I don't know. Why can't you just tell her you don't love her! Just tell your parents *no!* Just do what you know is right!"

"I'm trying, Ruby, but it's not as easy as you think. Can't you understand that?"

"No. No, I can't. Why is it me who has to wait around for you to make choices while you're going to fancy parties and balls with Little Miss Society Girl because you can't stand up to your parents? What about your mother? Why doesn't *she* stand up for you?" Her face had softened, but her eyes were still red, the anger pushing its way out at him.

"I don't know, Ruby!" Matt's voice rose. He bit his lip for a second before shouting, "Sometimes I think you're just like your mother. Maybe you want to be alone and bitter! "

His words died down when he saw the look on Ruby's face. She was staring past him toward the door, her face white. Before he even turned around, he knew that Kitty had come back from her walk with the baby. He felt like he'd just been hit with a wrecking ball. He hadn't meant for Kitty to overhear his words.

He held his head down. "I'm sorry, Mrs. DiCamillo."

"Matt Larimer, I think you should leave. "

Kitty seemed to be making the choice for Ruby, just as she had since the day she took her away. Ruby was ensnared, and maybe the only way she could break free from the tangled bits and pieces was to break free from him too.

"I miss you," Ruby breathed into the phone. "I miss my friend."

That's all he had needed to hear, and if all he ever had was Ruby's friendship, then it's what he would take.

They didn't talk about what had happened or what would eventually happen. For a while they met at Martha's for coffee and visited for hours. Kitty knew, but Ruby didn't listen to her when she complained.

"I promise we aren't trying to blindside you, Mother. We know you don't want Blake anymore," Ruby had said.

"That's not what I said," Kitty had protested.

"Mother, it isn't about you. For a change this is about me, okay? This is about my friendship with someone other than my mother. Am I allowed that?"

Everything was moving slowly, but Matt vowed to be patient, and the dragging time actually gave him more opportunity to deal with his stepdad and mom in a better way.

He'd planned in detail the moment he would break things off permanently with Leah, but it was between the invitation and his arrival in La Rosaleda that Leah had sprung the news on him. It was awful, devastating news that he would never from that moment forward understand the reason for. Life had foiled him.

So as he comforted Ruby in the vines, his world was blanketed with confusion. Her cries began to quiet, but they still racked her body heavily.

A car horn sounded from the direction of the main house, and he knew that Blake was calling them back for the snack they'd promised Lucy. Matt knew he was short on time and pulled Ruby up to her feet. He looked into her eyes.

"I love you, Ruby. Tell me what to do. Tell me to leave her and I will."

"How can you? She's pregnant!"

"Not with my child," he reminded her.

She said nothing. He turned her chin toward him.

"You do believe me, don't you? It's not my child."

"That is a very unbelievable story," she said.

But it was true. He'd never been intimate with Leah beyond kissing good-bye. She couldn't trap him by telling him that the baby was his because it was impossible. She hadn't even tried, but instead, in a fit of tears, she'd confessed to him the baby belonged to some guy she'd met at a fraternity party at Berkeley. She was ashamed to tell her parents that a stranger was the father of her baby.

He watched Ruby's face now for some indication of how she felt. She seemed to struggle with what she was about to say. He wasn't sure if he could believe her when she said, "I don't see how you have a choice. She is alone. Her parents would probably dis-own her or pressure her to get an abortion, which she doesn't want to do."

She paused as tears streamed down her cheeks. "Maybe you should just be responsible and help her. She has you trapped either way. Don't you see it's a trap?"

He swallowed, trying to keep his own tears at bay. He couldn't cry in front of her again. What kind of man was he? And why had she said that? Surely it wasn't what she felt. He wanted her to tell him to leave Leah, to be brave and do what was in his heart!

"Why would I be obligated to raise another man's child?"

"Why would you be obligated to me to raise another man's child, Matt?"

Matt stepped back a pace. It had been a long time since she'd said aloud that Lucy belonged to someone other than him.

"If that's true, about another man being her father, I don't care. What about you? I want to be responsible for you and for Lucy. It's you and Lucy I want, Ruby. Please, Ruby. Tell me what to do. I want to know if you want me. I've been praying every day, and I'm just so confused about how to get out of this thing with Leah the right way, but I want a life with you if you'll have me."

"I don't believe the baby isn't yours."

Matt's jaw dropped. He managed a deep breath. "It's not my child. I've never even been with her."

"How am I supposed to believe that? You were with me, weren't you? Isn't that how men are? Sleeping with all the different girls they can?"

"I don't want to be with anyone else. I want to do the right thing." He tried to pull Ruby close, but she pushed him away.

"I've learned my lesson. Men use you, and then they walk away."

"Let me ask you: were you really ever with George?"

She began to cry. "I can't do this. It's too hard. Love shouldn't be so hard."

"Maybe it is. Maybe that's why people give up on it so easily. Maybe it's something we have to fight for."

"I'm tired of fighting." He could see that Ruby wanted to run away. Instead she walked. Helplessly, he watched her heading back toward the big house, her figure growing smaller, eventually disappearing between the vines.

Defeated. Matt thought about how he'd been so wrong. He had waited for everything to work out perfectly, to let Leah go compassionately, to allow Ruby to express her desires for the future, to preserve his mom's happiness—and all for nothing. He should have spoken up for the woman who was waiting for him the whole time.

SOME RENEW THEIR SMILE

Lucy

27

Matt set down his coffee cup. He talked about when he held Sam in the delivery room, thoughts of me and Ruby filling his mind, and then how he pressed them back as he smiled down at the baby he would adopt in his heart even though he would never need to do so on paper.

Matt said he often reflected on Ruby's words in the vineyard: *I don't see how you have a choice.* He had never understood completely. He never believed that I wasn't his, only that Ruby was taking away his privilege to be my father because of what he had done, what he deserved.

Except for the happiness brought by Sam, Matt talked about being tortured with memories of Ruby every day. If not for Sam, he said, he would've picked up and left Leah, throwing himself on Ruby's doorstep, begging her to take him back, but he never did. Sam deserved more. He would always do right by Sam. If only he could do right by Leah someday too. But what he had wanted most, he said, his face serious, was to do right by me, by Ruby's daughter.

I stared at Dr. Larimer across the table. *Should I really call him Matt? Or...Father?* I searched his face for recollection. Recognition.

He gazed back, intent, perhaps searching for the same thing. I wondered if he saw anything in my face that said I was his. I studied his features, noting that his nose was similar to mine, which could explain the more European look I had compared to Kitty. But then again, maybe it was just my imagination.

"Am I…?" I paused. I didn't trust this moment. I'd been waiting forever to meet my father but had expected some time to prepare for it, to come on my own terms. I always thought it would be the result of research, and I could choose whether or not to initiate contact. Now here I was, and the moment was so simple, so anticlimactic. Everything seemed so obvious. I should have guessed it a long time ago. Still…

"Are you my father?"

As the words left my lips I felt like a giant impostor.

His eyes met mine with compassion and perhaps something that looked like parental longing. Maybe that was just wishful thinking on my part. He searched my face a long time, and when he did speak, he seemed to weigh his words before he said them.

"I think so."

"You think so?"

"I hope so."

I didn't know how to respond to that. I couldn't really jump up and give him a daughterly hug with an *I think so*. "Ruby never told you?" I asked.

"She never confirmed you were his."

I was silent a long while.

"Is there a way to find out?"

"Maybe," Matt said. "I know where George Fields is."

My heart jumped…but more in dread than anticipation.

"He owns a record store in San Francisco and has made quite a name for himself in the music industry. If you were into rock music, you'd probably recognize his store. You could visit it, I guess, tell him who you are, and see if he can confirm his relationship with Ruby."

I frowned. *Hey, Mr. Fields. Did you have sexual relations with my mother?* I shook my head and said with raised brows, "Talk about uncomfortable."

"Yeah," Matt said, "especially if he's not really your father."

"I hope he isn't."

Matt nodded. I had a feeling he had lots more he wanted to say about George Fields. Matt cleared his throat. "Are you sure you want to dig into all this?"

"I have to."

"Then you could come to the hospital and submit to a blood test."

"Not very sentimental, is it?" I asked. "Sounds like a really bad soap opera."

"Are there any good soaps?" he teased. "I've always hated the way they portray doctors as slime balls."

He finally smiled a crooked grin, and I realized he felt awkward and nervous too. I watched as he clicked his spoon over and over on his mug. It was hard to believe that this man was the same family doctor who'd always known what to do and say. I wished I could do something to bridge the gap.

I reached across the table, and he clasped my hand.

"I want to know," I said quietly.

His sigh was huge as he placed his other hand firmly on top of mine. "I do too. You have no idea how much."

"What about Leah?" I didn't want to hurt her.

"She wants to know too. We've both gone through a lot of changes since Ruby died." He paused. "When Ruby died, I felt my life fall apart; the regret I felt consumed me. Then, in the middle of all that, I almost lost Leah and my son too."

I waited.

"For many years things weren't good," he said. "But she had been innocent about all my parents' matchmaking and interference. Over time I saw that, and I did fall in love with her. I wanted to make her happy. I wanted that for Sam. If not for Sam, I might not have made it."

"He must be a good son."

"He is. And I have two girls too—nine and twelve."

My heart leapt. Little sisters? The thought of having sisters to look out for touched me. But that was a maybe. We needed tests first to confirm things. "Do you think anyone else knows the truth?"

He seemed to mull that one over in his mind. "Your grandfather maybe, but I can't be sure. He would be the only one, I think." Then he shook his head, like he was going to say something but changed his mind.

"What is it?"

"Nah, talk about a soap. It would be too simple to be possible."

"What?"

"Well, maybe in the drama of it all we're overlooking the obvious."

"What could be more obvious than my doctor being my father?" I asked jokingly.

He laughed. "I don't suppose you've ever seen your birth certificate, have you?"

"Yes, according to it there must have been an immaculate conception, but we know that only happened once in history, right?"

He laughed good-naturedly at my joke. "It is true—only once."

I smiled, wondering what he knew about Ruby's faith. I had a feeling he might be the person to explain some unanswered questions, but I tucked away those thoughts for another time.

"What about Kitty? I can't believe Ruby didn't tell her. For all their disagreements, they were so close." It was my turn to sigh. "I wish Kitty would set her pride aside and just tell me everything she knows."

Matt looked kindly at me. "She may not know everything you think she does. Don't put your whole world on her shoulders. If you do, she won't be able to help but will only fail you."

Part of me felt as if he'd taken her side. "But all this time I thought it was just my mind blocking the truth. Now I know it wasn't just me; it was Kitty too."

"It was your mind," he said, reaching over to clasp my hand again. "I'm still your doctor, you know. I recorded many of these observations in your record. The things Kitty has kept from you affect you, of course, but many of the things she keeps secret are hers to keep. Maybe you need to accept that there are some things you'll never know."

I busied myself with straightening the tablecloth.

"Give her time."

I looked down at my cup, long empty. Even after the four shots of espresso, unusual for me, I felt exhausted.

Matt walked over to the counter and paid for our drinks. While I waited for them to make Kitty's green tea to go, I wished that Matt and Ruby hadn't wasted so much time with their silly misunderstandings. What had resulted from their drama was a lost chance to have a life together—a life I could have been part of. Maybe if Ruby and Matt had married, she would have had someone to keep a closer watch over her asthma, I would have had a father, biological or not, and she would have been happier.

That last thought oozed out as Matt returned with the tea for Kitty.

"Lucy, she was happy. You were her world. You made her happy."

"It's my fault," I said.

"What?"

I thought about confessing, telling him I'd been too slow when she'd called for me that day, but suddenly I was unsure if I could trust him. After all, I didn't even know if he was my father or my doctor. Plus, he was the son of my grandmother's only enemy, the one who ruined the marriage between Kitty and Blake. *Be careful,* I thought. "Oh, nothing."

"I think you need to go home and get some sleep. Have you been taking care of yourself? Do you carry your inhaler with you at all times?"

I laughed. "Boy, you sound like a father. And yes, I do and I'm fine."

He reached out and tousled my hair. It was a familiar gesture, and I caught a glimpse of the Dr. Matt Larimer I actually knew. It brought a sense of normalcy back.

"Call me tomorrow, and we'll make an appointment for the tests. Are you going to tell Kitty?"

"I don't know."

He stopped as we walked toward the door. "Listen, Lucy, if we have the tests done and can't confirm anything, I'd still like us to be friends. I feel I owe it to your mother, you know, to look out for you."

"Is that the only reason? Obligation?"

He stopped walking and touched my shoulder in what my heart hoped was a fatherly gesture.

"Not obligation. Responsibility."

He gazed down at me with the same affection I'd seen before in the doctor's office.

"I was immature back then," he continued. "I didn't listen to my heart, and I sure didn't listen to Ruby. I did what made everyone else happy except for your mother."

I looked into his brown eyes, seeking the person who'd loved my mother so much, who'd held me when I was only an infant to a lost, unmarried mother. I really liked this man and realized that the affection I felt for him could easily morph into that of a daughter toward her father. After all, he'd been the closest thing to a father in my life already, even if he'd only been my doctor.

The realization suddenly seemed pathetic and made me sad.

He reached over to give me a hug that was awkward but desperately warm. I pulled away and turned to walk the block home but before reaching the curb turned back.

"Dr. Larimer? I mean...Matt?"

"Yeah?"

I noticed he hadn't moved.

"When did my grandmother forgive you? I mean, she can really hold a grudge, but she must have forgiven you since we've been coming to you for appointments all these years."

"When Ruby died," he answered softly.

I was surprised.

"What about Ruby? When did she forgive you?"

"I don't know if she ever did. Would you have?"

I shrugged. "I don't know."

He waved at me with a lost look on his face. For one more moment I wished everything had been different, that Ruby had married him and we'd been a family, but that was all a fantasy that could never come true now. I momentarily wondered about Leah, if I would get to meet her.

I was glad Matt had found happiness in his life, and then I knew that I too, like Kitty, had chosen to forgive him even if Ruby hadn't. I didn't say so out loud, but I smiled and gave him a small wave before turning and crossing the road.

28

I sat with Susannah and Max beneath a sprawling oak in the university square, both of them staring back at me in shock.

"It's amazing!" Susannah leaned toward me and affectionately patted my leg. "You might get a father and a grandfather before you know it!"

Max hadn't said anything, and the conversation drifted to Maria and to Susannah's latest proud mommy story.

"How is Mary?" he asked at one pause.

Susannah's mood shifted. "Not well. She isn't responding well to the treatments. They take a lot out of her. Plus we're now waiting for another test to come back to see how much the cancer has spread, if any. Of course, my dad never leaves her side, and I go to be with her every day. Kitty's there a lot too." She turned to me. "Did you know she and Kitty have become fast friends?"

I smiled. Kitty didn't reach out to many people, but if she did, it meant she really cared. "It's good for Kitty to get out," I said. "She loves sewing with your mom. Did you know they're making a quilt together?"

Susannah smiled, but her voice trembled. "Mom is so excited. She says if she lives, she's going to hang that quilt on the wall, and if she dies, then it's for Maria."

I reached over and gave Susannah's shoulders a little hug, and it seemed to trigger all the tears she'd been fighting.

Max laid his hand on her shoulder. He whispered a prayer

"for healing…for strength." I didn't know whether to be embarrassed or moved. I glanced nervously over at the sidewalk, then turned back to lean closer to Susannah, a little ashamed for being embarrassed.

Susannah squeezed Max's hand. "Thank you so much." She thanked me too, but I knew the only comfort I could offer was somehow different, on a level of caring and maybe not—what was it I'd heard her say her faith gave?—peace.

"Let's talk about you, Lucy!" I recognized the effort for diversion when the pain reached too deep. "When are you going to make a trip to La Rosaleda?"

"I would go for the day," I announced. "What about this weekend?"

Susannah frowned. "Unfortunately, Troy and I have plans, but you should go anyway. The drive isn't all that long."

"But I don't drive," I reminded her.

"I could take you." Max looked at me and shrugged. "I'm free."

"Are you sure?"

"Positive."

"Great!" Susannah hopped up. "Now I really need to pick up Maria." She slung her backpack over her shoulder and said good-bye.

"I don't want to be a bother. It's a long drive to impose on you."

"Not at all," he said. "I drive to San Francisco a couple times a month, so I'm used to it."

"To visit your parents?"

"Yeah, sometimes to go out on my dad's boat."

"Do you like it?"

Max leaned back in mock offense. "A thousand questions, is this?" He winked. "I do. I love my dad's boat. Life on a ship really gets into a person's blood, and it will always call me back. There's nothing like the wind in your face and the smell of the salty air when you're on a ship."

"And smelly fish?" I teased.

"That too." He laughed. "But you get used to it. What about you? Do you like the ocean?"

"I've never been on a ship."

He looked surprised. "You haven't been on a ship, and you don't drive?"

"No."

"Neither you nor Kitty drives at all?"

"No, we don't even have a car."

"Driving can be fun," he said.

"And deadly."

"True, but when it's your time to go, it's your time."

"You think so?"

He nodded.

I hesitated, thinking of Ruby. It couldn't have been her time. I said as much to him, and he didn't respond, just reached over and briefly squeezed my shoulder.

"I think I could have stopped it." I recounted the details of the day Ruby died, the things I'd never mentioned to Kitty: lingering to smell the roses, the mess I'd made and stopped to clean up, the poking around the house looking for Ruby's inhaler.

I couldn't look him in the eye anymore. "I was always getting into trouble as a kid for being slow; I've always known it was my fault." I finished, filled with fresh shame once again and hopelessness and guilt for messing up Ruby's and Kitty's lives. I felt suddenly stressed and breathless, a reminder of my asthma, one more thing Kitty hadn't needed to deal with but did.

Max sat quiet. Finally he said, "That's quite a burden you've been carrying around all these years."

I stared at our sandals, both stretched straight in front of us, and noticed how the light shone through the oak branches to dapple our legs and arms. Max laid his hand over mine, and I turned my palm to face his, watching the light and shadows of the leaves dance over our fingers, now woven together.

I took a deep breath and noticed how loud my breathing seemed. All other sound seemed muted: the chatter of other students walking past, the birds singing in the trees, the distant sound of cars in a nearby parking lot. Max clasped both my hands, and the sounds of the campus suddenly poured around me again and I could breathe normally.

Max's voice was tender. "You were just a little girl." He squeezed my hand tighter. "You definitely aren't a little girl anymore."

I stared at him. So often I did feel like Ruby and Kitty's little girl, but hadn't Kitty even said something recently about needing to let me grow up? I looked down at our hands. I didn't want my backward, reclusive ways preventing me from getting to know Max better, but I wondered how I could let the past go when I was in the middle of chasing it. I wasn't sure what parts to release and what to seek.

"Thank you for being a friend." I smiled when I noticed color creeping up into his cheeks this time. *So Maxwell Sheffield is human after all.*

"Thank you," he said. "That will be enough to carry me through the whole day."

"Just the day?" I teased.

29

The morning was warm, and the breeze swept the hem of Kitty's kimono around her legs as we walked. She was wearing the red one today. Her bleached blond look had begun to fade to silvery brown, and she'd swept her hair back into a red scarf like a distinguished traveler from a destination magazine.

Kitty is still every bit as lovely as in her younger pictures, I thought. Only softer, more wizened.

"Ready?" I asked as we headed to the hospital. It was obvious to me that everything wasn't going to work out well for Mary. She looked gaunt, and her long gray hair fanned over her pillow gave me the sickening feeling that she was already dead.

"Things don't look good," Troy whispered to me as I greeted Susannah with a hug.

"Mary?" Kitty whispered. She'd taken a seat next to the bed, and I tiptoed beside her hoping Mary would wake even for a moment. How had this gone so fast? Mary's immune system was low, and the surgery and chemo had failed. She looked frail, and I was tender when I reached over to caress her hand.

Mary's hand moved beneath mine.

Kitty brushed away a tear as Mary strained to open her eyes.

"Kitty," Mary said in a whisper. "I'm so glad to see you." She looked over at me as I gently patted her hand. "And Lucy. You are so beautiful. Like Kitty."

I gave Mary a gentle hug and told Susannah I would be right back. With Mary there seemed to be no more unknowns, and the thought filled me with fear. Memories of Ruby's death crushed my lungs, making me gasp for air. I left the room, searching my purse for an inhaler.

I needed escape, and the arrangement I'd made earlier that day with Matt gave me a reason to leave Mary's room. The blood tests. I turned toward the lab.

A beeping noise called me down the hallway, where the gleaming floors and severe lighting washed out everything. I felt like I was in a world of white and light. Is this what so many people experienced when they reported a desire to go toward the light during a near-death experience? What if people who felt pulled by some heavenly brightness and claimed to see the other side were simply delirious and blinded by hospital lights and machines? What if there was no God at all?

I thought of Susannah and her mother. Susannah believed in God with all her heart. That was it. No explanations, she'd say. "It's simply faith. You just have faith. I feel it in my heart that God is real and there and loving us all the time, and that's enough for me, never mind that I believe that the Bible is evidence whether scholars do or not."

Faith in what? I often wondered. How could someone be expected to have faith when people everywhere, even in this very hospital, were dying painful, horrible deaths—and some maybe too soon? People's lives were being ruined every day. People were making the agonizing decision to turn off machines. Babies were lost. Little girls were orphaned, their mommies taken away from them when they were too young to even know what dead was.

I walked faster into the bright lights, lost in unanswerable questions, until I found myself at a desk. The woman sitting there in blue scrubs smiled at me with shining, bright white teeth. I watched her mouth move, her teeth gleaming beneath pink lips, but I heard nothing. She must have been waiting for me to arrive because she ignored my lost look and turned toward the phone.

Within seconds Dr. Larimer—Matt—was at my side. He

guided me by the elbow through a maze of doors; I had a feeling
we were getting special treatment. Technicians slapped him on the
back and smiled warmly. Did they know? Well, of course they did.
They were doing tests to see if I was the man's daughter.

I wasn't sure if I could trust the tests. I'd heard too much about
these kinds of things in bad movies and on daytime television. I
remembered seeing some episode on TV. A man who was told that
the child he'd raised wasn't his tried to leave the talk-show stage;
the camera crew followed him, cameras in his face, to catch every
agonizing grimace and cry. Finally the man had cowered in a corner and covered his head.

How disappointed would Matt be if the tests came back that I
wasn't his daughter? And how would I feel and react?

Matt smiled at me and gently patted my back as he admonished
the poor lab technician not to poke me too badly when drawing
the blood.

The technician winked at me. "If the level of his overprotec-
tiveness says anything, I know how these tests will come back." I
laughed and let my arms and shoulders relax so he could do his
work.

"Good girl," he'd said. "Now your turn, Doc. I might not be
as easy on you if you don't behave." He slapped Matt on the shoulder. "Loosen up or this is going to hurt."

Matt didn't laugh but took a deep breath. I hadn't imagined he
would be nervous too, not about the pain, but about the knowing…or not.

And that was it.

The technician said he'd call each of us individually.

Matt's beeper sounded, we shuffled out of the office, and he
reached out and grabbed my hands before turning down the hall.
"Whatever the tests say, let's stay close."

My guard dissolved, and I squeezed his hand back.

"I'd like that."

I stood alone in the hall when my cell phone buzzed. Alone and feeling a little bit of peace about the situation, which I hadn't felt beforehand.

The vibrating of my cell phone interrupted my thoughts, and I felt guilty for not having turned it off, being in a hospital and all. I moved to shut it off, but then answered when I saw that it was Kitty. I thought she must be ready to go home.

"Lucy," Kitty said.

Kitty's voice over the phone sounded stilted. I knew she had been crying. "They are saying there isn't much hope for Mary. Come down and tell her good-bye before we go. She might be much worse next time we see her."

That place in my chest that'd been so full a moment ago emptied as I hurried down the hallway to offer my condolences to Susannah. Or whatever one would call it. What does one say when death is imminent but hasn't yet arrived?

I sat in the waiting room, next to Susannah, struggling for the right words of comfort. I'd only been a little girl when Ruby left, but surely some things between mothers and daughters were the same no matter what age. I clasped Susannah's hand, and she was quiet for a while.

"Lucy, I feel that God brought you and Kitty into my life just when he knew I was losing my mother."

"I'm so sorry."

"We should pray."

Susannah said that as a statement, but I felt like it was a question.

"Anything is possible," she reaffirmed. "Anything is possible through God."

I felt the hole in my chest expand and tried to breathe deeply enough to fill it.

Susannah looked at me and whispered, "Will you say a prayer with me for her?"

Shame filled me as I felt my cheeks flush with embarrassment and doubt. I looked across the floor and slowly shook my head, at a loss. "Susannah, I—"

My eyes fixed on the Jesus sandals coming toward me.

I felt glad and relieved that Max was there and could share reassurances with Susannah in place of my absent faith.

He smiled at me, and I croaked, "She wanted me to pray." I was embarrassed how the words came out like an accusation or a plea for help.

Max sat beside me and his hand briefly brushed my knee, a reassurance I felt so inadequate to receive.

Troy sat on the other side of Susannah; then Max swiftly moved to a knee in front of me. He laid one hand on my arm and one on Susannah's knee. Troy knelt also, and this time I was filled with respect.

As Max's words of Christ, joined by Troy's, were whispered into the small space between us, I began to get a sense that I was part of something at that moment that was bigger than me, something bigger than my search for Ruby or my father. I felt warm and safe then, like I was wrapped in one of Kitty's quilts. And I felt renewed, like the moment when I breathed in the medicine from my inhaler. The whispers were like oxygen. Susannah grasped my hand tightly. I tried to send her the little strength I had and I listened. I was amazed at Max's simple request, that Mary be healed "if it be your will." Such a simple request, just a few words, but so big. And even more astonishing to me was the acceptance each person, save myself, voiced that whatever the answer was, it would be welcomed as his plan, his mystery.

His mystery, I repeated silently. Thoughts of Ruby flooded me: watching her through the glass when she died. Kissing her goodbye, her skin already almost cool. The way I carried and searched for her memory, knowing that she was somehow not fully lost to me. *His mystery.*

When it was over, Max sat beside me and held my hand as I leaned away from him toward Susannah. She curled one hand in her husband's and one hand in mine, her head bowed forward. We all waited, I knew, to see if her father would come out of Mary's room and what his news would be.

Time passed slowly, and I wished I could read Susannah's thoughts. And in a way I could almost guess that she was thinking of the last time she spent time with her mother, maybe a walk or an outing to the park with Maria. That's what I always thought of with Ruby—our last time together. I hoped they would have more...

Kitty walked in with a tray of snacks, coffee, and tea. Even though nobody could eat, the idea of normalcy was comforting. Having a warm plate, even of hospital food, meant Mary was still with us.

Max stood, needing to be useful I was sure, and I watched him move from Susannah to each of her family members gathered in the waiting room. He was quiet and sure, his worn leather Bible in his hand. They reached out to him in gratitude. I knew he had a gift that I could never interfere with if I truly cared about him. Max would never, should never, give up his religion for me, I decided. And if he could never permanently choose someone who didn't share his faith, I would either need to convert or let him be.

His calling was bigger than me.

INTO THE VINEYARD

Lucy and Kitty

30

Kitty," I said, standing helpless in our living room. She was already on her way to the kitchen, where she prepared her remedy for every sorrow. Tea.

"What are your biggest regrets?" I asked, finally breaking our silence.

"Besides the obvious?

The teapot whistled, and she turned to remove it from the stove.

She poured the tea carefully. "There is one thing," she said, taking the chair opposite mine. "I've never told it to anyone, Lucy."

She took a deep breath as I held mine.

I was silent, afraid that if I said anything, she might lose her confidence and not tell me.

"I know," she continued, "that I've been really awful lately. I've been trying so hard to hide things, but there's one thing I do feel I need to tell."

Matt's words came back to me. *Don't put your whole world on her shoulders.* I looked Kitty in the eye. I reached across and held her hand, now getting worried about what the news could be. *What more could she be carrying?*

"You haven't been awful to me, Kitty. I have been the one pushing you."

"No. You're as you should be—you have a desire to know things I've kept from you. I'm the one who is sorry." The tears stopped her.

"What is it, Kitty?"

"About the abortion...I..." She placed her hand on her chest. "It's true that it was Mike Larimer's baby—Matt's father's baby. Blake was right about that."

I felt sick to my stomach and struggled to maintain a non-judgmental look, but I wasn't sure I wanted to hear about her affair with that man or how she might have been in love with anyone besides my grandfather. I had woven a beautiful fantasy in my mind of the relationship I was so sure they'd had.

"What Blake didn't know—and I've never told another soul—is that there was never an affair."

I crinkled my eyebrows, not wanting to hear the truth I thought I somehow already knew.

"Not an affair? Then how could...?" Realization finally dawned on me with a horrific thud.

"Are you saying...?"

Kitty nodded and stared into her cup, the shame blanketing the space around.

"He..." She couldn't say the word. "It's what I tried to tell you before, but I don't think you understood, not really."

"He *raped* you?"

It all made sense suddenly. I had misjudged her story, just as Blake had. Because the truth nudging at me had been too dark to believe. How does one comfort such a wounded person?

Unsure, I just stayed with Kitty all evening. We were spent—each of us—and there was nothing else to talk about. Moving to the back porch, we watched the sunset behind our garden in silence. The roses turned their antique color, which seemed so much what I imagined as La Rosaleda.

But could the vineyard of my dreams still be that way?

Beauty was replaced by fear—I was afraid for Kitty for the

first time. Maybe I shouldn't try to get her to go back. How would Blake feel if he learned of the rape? He was, after all, a part of a different generation that was not as accepting. How could Kitty ever tell him when she could barely tell me? Maybe it really would be too much.

We watched the sunset long after it had dulled, and when Kitty refused to go in the house, I entered alone, opened the back window, and sat down at the piano.

I played my favorite tunes from *When Harry Met Sally* because they were happy songs and all I could think of at the moment and Kitty loved them. I played them with passion, hoping that in some way they would speak to her, because I didn't know what to say.

"Are you nervous?"

I considered Max's question as I stared out the window of his van. It was my first time riding through the Sonoma Valley, and I was amazed at the layers of hills. Max was shocked that I'd never been in this direction, but of course Kitty never would have suggested that we go anywhere near La Rosaleda.

The acre upon acre of grapevines amazed me, a multitude of colorful leaves. *Like the trees in the Sacramento parks,* I thought. I could smell the sweet grapes hanging in the warm sun in bright purple clusters. The towns we passed through seemed relaxed, but I couldn't help thinking how they betrayed what the shops and restaurants clearly spoke of as upscale and exclusive.

Susannah had told me that the Valley, while frequented by the affluent, was known for not being as pretentious as its neighboring county, also known for grapes. I didn't have any idea if that was true, but when we stopped for lunch at a roadside café, I did feel at home, even beside the man hopping out of his BMW. I smiled to myself. High-end cars were zooming past us, but I was seeing just as many run-down-looking Jeeps too.

The Jeeps probably belonged to the locals, Max said, the BMWs to the businesspeople from just out of town, and all the other sedans to the tourists.

"What about those in minivans?"

He was serious. "Those are carrying pretty girls who can't drive, the girls compelled to date poor but trustworthy youth ministers so they can hitch rides when needed."

"Smart girls," I'd responded, and it had felt good to laugh together.

"I'm very nervous," I said, finally answering his question.

"You should be."

"Excuse me? That was hardly the reassurance I wanted."

"I just mean it's good that you know how serious this is. It's going to be a big deal to you and to Blake. Who knows? It might open the doors for Kitty to walk through."

"Maybe." I shrugged. I didn't tell him why I would no longer pressure Kitty to go to La Rosaleda. I felt in my heart that Blake would understand, but it was truly up to Kitty, her choice, and there would be no more pressure from me.

Signs announcing La Rosaleda began to appear, and my stomach grew queasy. I closed my eyes and tried to focus, but my mind jumped around, not landing anywhere safe. When I felt the van roll to a stop, I discovered that Max had parked along the town square in La Rosaleda. I didn't look around but instead looked down at my hands.

"How about we just walk around a bit?" he suggested. "We have plenty of time."

I felt in my pocket for the key Kitty had handed me that morning. I'd told her that Max and I were just going for a drive to the wine valley. She'd nodded her head knowingly and handed me the key to her loft.

"Just check on it for me," she'd said. "Come back this evening, and tell me how it looks."

"Sure." I was grateful she had given me her blessing to go.

"But behave yourself. The place is very romantic. You should learn from your grandmother's blunders." She laughed softly.

I was comforted by her attempt to joke. "Don't worry, Kitty. Nothing is going to happen. Besides, Susannah has already warned me."

Kitty smiled. "I really like that girl; I just wanted to remind you is all." She'd reached out then and hugged me close, and I couldn't tell if she was happy or worried about me going to La Rosaleda.

"Kitty, please come with me. It would mean so much if you could be beside me when I first see La Rosaleda," I pleaded. "I know you want to go with me."

She'd shaken her head and squeezed my hand. "No, dear. I simply cannot."

"Please," I implored softly.

She held out a pretty handkerchief and dabbed at my cheeks. "Not this time, dear. But you go. Be a good girl and..." She paused for a moment, struggling for the right words. "Tell him...tell your grandfather I said..." She bit her lip and reached for the words I knew she wanted to say, but in the end she chose safety. "Tell him hello, will you?"

I nodded as I pressed close to her. This woman was my grandmother, my mother, and my best friend; I knew that no matter what she decided about Blake now or in the future, I would always stand beside her, even if I hoped with everything in me that she wouldn't choose the safe way out.

"If you call and I'm not here, I'll be over at Mary's house."

My heart soared at the mention of Mary. I could hardly believe she had lived through not only that one night at the hospital, but through the weeks since she had been moved back home. She wasn't cancer-free, but suddenly there was hope. "The important part," Susannah had said, "is that God let her stay a little longer."

Kitty shook her head. "It's a strange twist of fate, isn't it, that Mary is alive? But as long as she is, I want to help her."

"Do you really believe that, Kitty?"

"What, that it's strange?"

"No, that it's fate."

"Oh, I don't know what I believe anymore, dear. I thought I did."

"But Susannah, Troy, and Max—they all held hands and prayed for this. "

Kitty reached out and patted my hand. "I know it meant a lot to Susannah."

"Yes." I nodded. "But I think it might have meant more."

She ran her hand along the edge of the handkerchief. "I don't know. Maybe it did, dear."

"I hope so," I said and though Kitty nodded in agreement I knew she was having a hard time getting past her pride. How could she admit now that the prayer for Mary might have been answered?

"Ready?" Max nudged gently, opening the van door.

"Walking around sounds like a good idea," I said nervously.

I waited for him to come around and open the door for me, remembering something Kitty had instructed before our first date: "Expect him to open doors, dear. It's okay to let him treat you special. Too many men miss out on opportunities to respect women because women are always rushing to do every little thing themselves."

I gazed around the small, noisy square. The concrete fountain of grapes in the center was surrounded by mimosa trees, their shriveling blossoms dropping in the breeze. Ducks huddled together beneath every color of rosebush one could imagine, and some of the roses rambled over archways and down winding paths. Shorter varieties edged the sloping sidewalks. *Kitty's roses.*

Each street around the square was lined with nineteenth-century mission-style buildings, and it was easy to imagine elegantly dressed women in long gowns from the 1800s on the arms of gentlemen in suits and hats. Of course, maybe the square of La Rosaleda would have only been populated by roughened, hard-working people dressed in practical fabrics—I didn't know—but I liked imagining the refined ladies.

I was struck with regret that I hadn't done more research about La Rosaleda before showing up on its streets. Because despite my imaginings, there were people from all over the place. Professional types in business suits, older ladies in Chanel skirts and jackets, California girls in flowing rayon skirts with their hair in braids.

My eyes swept around the square, and I tried to imagine Kitty walking these same sidewalks years earlier, perhaps pushing Ruby in a stroller like so many women were doing this day. I wondered if I could be standing right where Kitty had walked hand in hand some summer evening with my grandpa as a young man.

Somewhere a baby cried, a car door slammed beside us, and I jumped.

"You okay, Lucy?" Max tucked his arm around my waist, and we continued our stroll.

"Just wondering what La Rosaleda was like when Blake and Kitty were young."

We strolled past wine and cheese shops, bistros, boutiques, gift stores, classy restaurants, and an old movie theater still in operation. Eventually we came to a bed-and-breakfast on the corner of the northeast side of the square. A little sign in the window caught my eye. I looked at Max, surprised.

LA ROSALEDA BED-AND-BREAKFAST
HOME OF FRANCES-DICAMILLO WINES
THE ONLY PLACE YOU CAN SAMPLE THE FINEST WINE
IN THE SONOMA VALLEY

The door creaked as we stepped inside. Antique walnut floors. Large paintings. Bistro-style tables and chairs. A large brick fire-place at one end and at the other a spiral staircase with an ornate steel banister leading up to the next floor. Along the wall opposite the fireplace was a dark mahogany counter with a soda fountain, old-fashioned jars of candy, and a bistro menu. In the corner sat a small lady, bent over a guest book.

She glanced up, her wrinkled dark skin a stark contrast to the white tablecloth over the desk. Her sparkling brown eyes caught me off guard, and I saw the same dark coloring in her as in Kitty and in all the pictures of Freda and Ruby.

Her accent was strong as she said, "One moment please. I just need to check on the progress of my guests. I have slow ones today, but as soon as they check out I can tell you about the rooms available."

"That won't be necessary," I said quickly. "We're just visiting."

She studied my face. "You look familiar."

I shook my head as Max lightly rested his hand on my shoulder, reassuring me.

The woman's eyes flashed across the room to a painting I hadn't noticed before.

I knew immediately from the dark eyes and hair, the old-fashioned-looking clothing, and the resemblance to Kitty—and all the paintings in my room at home—that the woman in the portrait was Freda DiCamillo. I caught Max's eyes, and he shook his head slightly *no*. Feeling his caution, I didn't say anything, but the lady in front of me must have thought I was a ghost.

I wasn't as dark as Freda had been, though I supposed the family resemblance ran pretty strong between Freda, Kitty, Ruby, and me. The lady glanced back at me again, narrowed her eyes, and sat back down.

"Then how may I help you, Miss, uh…"

"Lucy. My name is Lucy."

Max offered his hand. "Maxwell Sheffield, ma'am. We just wanted to look around. Do you give tours?"

"Yes, but not until two. Could you come back then?"

"Yes," we both said in unison. I smiled back at her, but she still looked surprised and uncomfortable with my presence.

I waited until we'd exited the B&B and walked a few paces before asking Max, "Were you trying to warn me about something back there?"

"Yes!"

"Why? That portrait was obviously my great-grandmother, and that's obviously the only tasting room in town that has my grandfather's wine."

Max took my hand and escorted me across the street toward a bench overlooking the duck pond. "I don't think you should go around advertising to these strangers who you are just yet."

"The locals probably aren't strangers to my grandfather," I protested. "They can give me information."

"Yes, I'm sure they could." He looked evenly at me. "Listen, I just want to help you. I don't know why, but I feel like something's not right…like Rosaleda has been waiting for Kitty's and your return for a long time, and if you reveal yourself too soon something bad could happen."

"Don't you think you're being a little paranoid?"

"I hope so," he said calmly. "But I was just thinking about a few things in there. For one, you don't want someone to run off and tell Blake that you're in town before you're ready to see him."

I nodded. He was right.

"And, well, one thing you haven't talked about much is the fact that Kitty is an heiress."

"What are you saying?" I sounded more defensive than I meant to. "That someone is going to know who I am and try to rob me?"

"I don't know." He shrugged. "Anything's possible. There are scam artists everywhere."

"True. I see what you're saying. Money and prestige might not be a big deal to Kitty, but around here it might be big news."

"Especially if Ruby walked these streets when she was an adult.

With your grandfather's status so obviously high in this community, Ruby's homecoming and then death would have sent more than a ripple through the community, I'm sure."

I suddenly felt taken aback. I hadn't realized that my family history would bombard me as soon as I stepped out of the van.

"This is overwhelming, isn't it?"

"Yes."

"Do you want to go home? La Rosaleda isn't going away."

"But it's been this secret for so long, you know? I'm tired of waiting."

"And it has been here all along. It'll still be here next week or next month."

I took a deep breath and was unable to fill my lungs. After a few tries I reached into my purse for my inhaler, shooting the medicine deeply into my throat. I closed my eyes and thought of Kitty's remedies.

"I need some tea. Then we can decide what to do next."

"Fair enough," he said. "But now you have to choose a place to have tea." He motioned around the square at its array of shops. There were so many.

We stood to go, but I tugged at Max's hand and led him to the center of the square.

"Let's look at the fountain first."

Several paths twisted around the fountain and through the square, and we walked along one. At the fountain's edge, the fragrance of fresh rose petals floating in and about the monument filled my senses.

"Wow," Max said. "I wonder if they throw the petals in the fountain on purpose or if they just fall in."

What an interesting observation. I walked around the fountain wondering the same thing. On the other side Max had paused, his head cocked to the right. I wasn't sure, but his lips moved slowly as if he was reading something. I shuffled around as he was push-

ing aside petals floating on the water's surface. We leaned in and
stared into the depths of the rippling pool.

A large brass-looking plaque glittered at the bottom: IN MEMORY
OF ISAAC AND FREDA DICAMILLO.

The connection I felt to this town was suddenly magnified, and
I realized I couldn't sit down for tea if I wanted.

Max clasped my hands.

"I am part of here! This place!"

Max smiled wryly. "Lucy, I think your family *is* this town."

The idea was heady. "I've never been, you know, connected to
anything significant at all."

"Wait a minute. I disagree."

I raised my eyebrows at him.

"You are significant, more than you know, and you've always
had Kitty. That's significant."

He was right. I needed to give Kitty the credit she was due. A
pang stabbed my chest. "Yes," I agreed. I thought about all Kitty's
losses, all she had left behind or had taken from her. "Surely she
must miss this."

I reached over and ran my fingers through the fountain pool.
The fragrance of the roses filled the air around me as I watched the
petals swirl around my fingertips. I stared directly into the fountain, pretending I didn't feel Max staring at me. For a while I didn't
turn back, and when I did, his eyes locked on mine.

"What?"

"Nothing. Just you."

"Just me?"

"You are so amazing, Lucy. Not just beautiful, but you have a
delightful heart."

"How do you know?"

"I can see it in how you live your life. You search for truth.
That's noble."

But I knew that I wasn't noble at all. I was a coward, and I'd spent way too much time disrespecting Kitty and way too much energy on my own selfish needs and wants.

"What about you?" I asked. "What do you search for?"

He looked upward, contemplating his answer, then feigned nonchalance. "Besides the chance to spend more time with you?" I blushed as he winked. "Besides the obvious? I'm looking to feel peace with who I am and with who my parents think I am. My mom really has a hard time with my choice to be a youth minister."

I wondered how Max's mom could ever be disappointed in him. "Talk about noble—I would think your parents would be proud that their son works to help children."

Max looked down at his shoes and picked up a stray rose petal. "I was thinking about all the time your grandmother has lost with her family," he said, twirling the petal in his fingers. "It makes me want to make things right with my mom—not that we're estranged, but I just want her to understand and know that I accept her disappointment too."

"Her disappointment?"

"That I didn't decide to be a lawyer like her."

Max—a lawyer? I couldn't imagine.

"For a long time she's been disappointed, and I've just avoided the subject. I need to make it right."

"Well, you can't have it as bad as Kitty. She has about thirty years to make up for."

"Yes." He looked serious. "But I don't ever want my life to get to that point of regret. I feel a lot of anger with my mom right now, and I don't like that."

"Then go home and talk to her. San Francisco is right down the road from here. You say you go out on the boat with your dad all the time. Go this evening. Let's go now."

"You'd do that?" His eyebrows crinkled in surprise. "When you have such an important day ahead of you?"

"My day can wait until tomorrow. You've been so supportive

of me. I owe you that. Plus, I'm scared half out of my wits of what's going to happen next. Maybe if I go to San Francisco, then I can get another day to think."

He laughed loudly. "Well, I'm not going to let you get away with that. Today is yours, and I'm staying with you."

Our hands tightened as we stared through the fountain pool at Freda and Isaac's names on the bottom. I was reminded that my life could have been so different, and I wasn't thinking of vineyards, estate houses, or fortunes. I was thinking about having a father, grandparents, and great-grandparents.

I wondered, what would it have been like to live on soil that had been worked by my own ancestors for generations? What would it have been like for me to receive love from someone other than Kitty? What would it have been like to see Kitty grow older with the one she'd always loved instead of alone? Would she have been more cheerful, like she'd been during our picnic with Max? Would she have dressed the same? Would we have gone to church on Sundays? Or the local quilting bee? Would we have worked together at Frances-DiCamillo?

I could have asked more questions, but there were no answers. Those things were lost. Gone. Not even possibilities, thanks to Kitty's decision to leave and Ruby's death and the enormous space between Kitty and Blake…

At that moment someone jostled me.

"Excuse me," the stranger said.

"Sure." Max gently tugged me back into him a little. A young couple were mischievously splashing each other in the fountain. Half smiling at their playfulness, I put up my hands to shield myself from the water and backed up a few paces.

"Hey!" the girl exclaimed. "There's the name of that lady whose picture we saw in the hotel."

"Yeah? It's sad her winery closed down."

"It's not closed." Another couple had joined the first, and the second man explained, "It's just closed to the public. My wife heard that after the daughter of the matriarch's son-in-law died, the son-in-law stopped entertaining visitors."

Max and I backed away a little, like we were studying some roses.

"I heard one of the locals say he has a broken heart."

"It's a sad story," her husband interjected. "The lady at the hotel over there said the son-in-law has become a recluse. His wife has been missing for so many years, and his in-laws have died, and then there was the tragic loss of his daughter."

"A broken heart." His wife nodded, reaffirmed. Her tone was one of wonder. "The hotel clerk said something else intriguing too. The son-in-law's granddaughter has been missing or something for years until today. The clerk thought she saw the granddaughter in town today!"

Max gently placed his hand on my elbow in warning.

"I didn't believe that part," the wife was telling her husband. She turned to the other couple still playing in the fountain. "I'm sure she was sensationalizing because we're tourists."

Her husband winked. "Same as the haunted winery we toured yesterday?"

I winced at their laughter.

"Well," the young woman said, "*I* heard that same hotel clerk say that rumor has it the old man might have killed his wife and daughter. That would explain why his granddaughter doesn't come back."

Tears of anger sprang to my eyes. I wanted to shake these strangers and tell them that Blake didn't kill anyone, and he does too know where I am, and he's waiting for me! I could barely catch my breath, and Max helped me fumble through my bag for my inhaler.

The wife shook her head in disgust at the young couple.

"You guys are ridiculous. That clerk is obviously using the poor man to promote her business. She's practically taken over the Frances-DiCamillo name. She claims that she is the only one who offers tastings of the wine, but we tasted a glass of Frances-DiCamillo just yesterday at that little wine store over there."

I wanted to hug that woman as she and her husband and their young friends left the fountain and walked toward the shops.

As they moved away from us into the square I saw one of the men shrug and heard him mutter, "Let them think what they want. They're probably just scared. I heard the vineyard gate is literally chained shut with a handmade sign that says KEEP OUT. I'm telling you, the man is crazy."

I wanted to run behind and shout at him, but Max reached over and grabbed my hand.

"How dare they say such mean things about my grandfather!"

"It sounds like the woman who runs that B&B is the one who's crazy. If we go back for a tour, she's liable to kidnap you and post signs for all to come see the crazy man's long-lost granddaughter." His face filled with drama.

I shook my head and tried to laugh at his effort to relax me.

"I wonder why my grandfather allows her to do all that stuff with the vineyard name."

"If he's withdrawn from the public eye, he might not know what she's saying," Max offered. "But that doesn't mean he's crazy. The first thing you can do after you reunite with your grandfather is put a stop to that nonsense."

I was grateful for Max's faith in Blake when he'd never even met him. "Do you think it's true?" I asked.

"What?"

"That maybe Blake has become a recluse?" The very idea made me sad.

"We can see. It's a close walk, right?"

I nodded. "But let's—I mean you—drive."

31

We crested a hill, and I caught sight of the vineyards—acres of them spilling over an enormous portion of the valley. I sucked in my breath when I saw the large iron gate decorated artistically with iron grapes and roses. It really was padlocked shut with a KEEP OUT sign. But the estate didn't look neglected, and the gates were edged with beds of carnations and more roses. Beyond the gates, nestled between vine-covered hills, was the estate house. The late afternoon sun bounced off the huge, white mission-style house with its spectacular columns and a very large bell encased in one section. An abundance of windows sparkled. No. La Rosaleda had not been abandoned.

Max pulled to a stop in front of the gate, and I looked out the window at the heavy lock and chain. I could see how people might think the whole scene was odd, but for tourists to repeat some rumor they'd heard without knowing the truth just wasn't right.

"It's beautiful," Max remarked.

"I never could have imagined this. It's so well kept."

"I guess we can't exactly go in and see Blake now, can we?"

I shook my head. "That's okay. I need a little time."

Max began to inch the van away.

"Hold up!" I pointed toward a structure close to the main house and grabbed the door handle to step out for a closer look.

The Rose House.

I stared through the gate at a structure half covered by a blanket of red. It was too far away to see clearly, but I knew those were the rosebushes Ruby had described to Kitty—the roses that had taken over the entire front porch and crept over the top of the house from the front two corners.

Over the years I'd seen Kitty spend mornings and afternoons, evenings and weekends, training her favorite climbing rosebushes over the large trellis in our garden. She told me that trellises could be attached to roofs to help the flowers climb up and that with time the right kinds of climbing roses, well cared for, could cover a small structure. But I knew the work was painstaking and required great persistence. Eying the spectacular result in the distance, I also knew that my grandfather had to have spent a lifetime getting the roses trained over the house like that.

I tried to imagine Ruby when she had gone back to La Rosaleda and seen the house my grandpa said he'd saved for her return—and Kitty's. Had Ruby's heart swelled too when she was finally home?

I marveled that she had brought me here. Had I run across these grasses and touched those roses to my own cheek like any little girl would have who had such a playground as Frances-DiCamillo? I had no memory of this, of course, but I was sure we'd walked up and down those rows of vines, played in the gardens. I suddenly had an image of rose petals clasped in my fists, taken from a large rose near the big house. Was it me who had run up to the big porch and dropped the petals at my mother's feet, bare with red-painted toenails?

Another image flashed in my mind: clasping and unclasping hands, one a woman's and the other a child's. I could feel the woman's breath on my cheek as she leaned over, exhaling from the effort and inhaling as she lifted me onto her lap to sail back and forth in the white swing. I couldn't remember her face, only her feet and the feel of her arms around me and the warmth of her breath as we stared ahead toward the driveway, the town of La Rosaleda stretching in the distance.

These were memories, I knew, and suddenly I wished for my

paints and canvas to record them. *A memory canvas that could be filled in.*

I climbed into the van, glancing back at the estate, searching the yard and the porch, hoping for a glance of my grandfather. Stillness. Nothing.

"I'm so sad that he's shut himself away from the world."

"Maybe it's just the tourists he doesn't want to talk to."

But I knew that wasn't true. All the other vineyards and wineries we'd driven past advertised tasting rooms and tours, and their gates were flung open wide.

Why not Frances-DiCamillo's?

A van of tourists passed us, cruising slowly past the estate, the driver pointing and talking to his passengers. I felt sick inside as I imagined the rumors he might be passing to voyeurs and strangers.

And I felt scared.

I was scared that the locked gates meant my grandfather wouldn't want to see me. The property was practically barricaded; it didn't look like he was awaiting anyone's return. I leaned back on the seat and closed my eyes. I only wanted a short nap and Max's strong fingers occasionally massaging my hand.

So when my phone rang I nearly hit the top of the van. It had to be Kitty, and the growing protective tenderness I felt for her made me frantic. I searched around the seat as Max calmly pulled my phone out of the cup holder and handed it to me.

"Thanks."

"Lucy?"

It was Dr. Larimer—Matt.

"Lucy?" he asked again.

"Hi." The word caught in my throat. I knew what this call was about. The rest of my life hinged on the answer. I would either have a father, or he'd been lost to me because I'd already decided I would never contact George Fields. It was either Matt Larimer or I didn't want to know.

"Lucy." Matt's voice was gentle. "The results were inconclusive."

"Inconclusive?" I never imagined this. "Does that mean yes or no?"

"Yes and no. What it means is that our tests didn't prove or disprove anything. We can have the tests run again if we want. Maybe by a private agency with technicians who specialize—"

He paused, but I kept quiet. My head was spinning, and more tears began to surface. The new emptiness in my chest was so barren that I felt another asthma attack coming on, and I fumbled once more for the inhaler. "I so wanted to have a father," I whispered.

"Lucy?" Matt was concerned.

"I'm sorry."

"You expected the results to be positive?" He sounded hopeful.

"I was hoping for a yes."

I heard him sigh. "Me too."

"You said we can have them taken again?"

"Yes, if you want. So…how is your day?"

Now it was I who took a deep breath before answering.

"I'm in La Rosaleda."

"Lucy, that's great! Is Kitty with you?"

"No. She knows I'm here, but she didn't want to come."

"That doesn't surprise me. I'm sure she's terrified if you're there."

"I wish she wouldn't be that way. She's usually the bravest person I know."

"Me too," he said, and I smiled at how well we knew her.

"What's she doing today? Do you know?"

"Gardening."

"Ha! Why did I even ask? Are you coming back tonight?"

"I'm not sure yet. It was our plan, but I don't know. I haven't exactly felt like knocking on my grandfather's door. In fact, the gate is locked."

"I should have warned you. Blake got tired of the tourists. And some tour guides have been making up sensational stories in order to get the tourists excited, so he was definitely tired of dealing with that."

"We heard firsthand the rumors being passed around town," I said dully.

"Ignore those. As for Kitty, maybe I'll stop by and see if she'd like to take a walk this evening, just in case you aren't home by then. I don't think she's spent a night without you since you were little. She must be lonely."

"I'm sure that would be nice."

"Lucy," he said softly.

I pressed my ear into the phone.

"I'm sorry the results didn't come back the way we wanted."

My heart stretched toward his. I'd never wanted a father more, and Matt was the one I wanted, the man who had loved my mother even after death, someone who could share who she really was with me. Someone who knew her as Kitty never did—not as a daughter but as a woman with dreams and plans. I breathed deeply, trying to fill that place in my lungs that would never be full no matter how many inhalers I tried.

"Me too."

I hung up. Max couldn't help but hear, and I whispered apologies as we pulled back up to the square.

I covered my eyes with my hands, embarrassed to be crying. Again. But Max leaned across the gearshift and pulled me into an embrace.

Max pulled away and looked me over. I was a mess, like a child with a teary face and mussed hair.

Again he asked if I would like to go home. His voice was filled with compassion, and for a moment it made me feel angry. Tears didn't make me an idiot or some breakable thing. Why did everyone think I was too weak to handle the truth?

"No," I said, a speck of the irritability in my voice.

He frowned.

"I really don't."

"I just thought it might help you to be with Kitty right now."

"It would help me tremendously," I agreed, my voice softening. "But it wouldn't help Kitty at all. I haven't even told her about the blood tests yet."

She would react with anger pure and simple. She would feel betrayed, and we would argue. A stab of guilt hit me again at the thought of our recent unkind words. I was so ashamed of some of the things I'd said to her out of my desperation to dig up the past.

"Do you want to stay all night in La Rosaleda?" Max blushed, suddenly aware that he might have sounded inappropriate.

"We could," I said. "But...in two rooms."

"Of course." He let out a relieved breath. "We could drive to Santa Rosa, get a couple of hotel rooms, and come back tomorrow morning. That way you can take a little break from all this."

"But..." I reached into my pocket and pulled out the key Kitty had given me. "We haven't seen the loft yet. I'd really like to take a look at Kitty's first home, where Ruby lived when she was a baby."

Suddenly I was sweating and panicky. I surprised myself at how afraid I felt to walk into that loft. I couldn't explain it, but the thought nagged at me that there might be something in there to cause Kitty or me more pain. And I had a very strong feeling that once I stepped into that world, where pieces of Ruby surely would surround me, there would be no turning back. Unlocking that loft meant no more secrets and no more feeling lost, and I was surprised at how I'd become so used to living with both.

"Whatever you want to do, dear."

Was he teasing me by calling me *dear* like Kitty?

"I'm just the chauffeur," he added.

I laughed softly, and then we both were laughing together, neither one of us sure what was so funny. By the time we took deep
breaths and tried to quiet ourselves, the world seemed better. It had
felt good to laugh instead of cry. Max reached out and tousled my
hair as if I were his kid sister instead of the girl he had a crush on,
and I realized I'd laughed more since I'd met him and Susannah
than I'd laughed my whole life. Kitty and I had plenty of fun, but
we'd found our joy in music, art, her feeble attempts at teaching me
to quilt, summer walks, and old movies. We weren't chucklers or
belly laughers like Max and Susannah.

And like Ruby. I remembered my mother's laughter on the last
day she and I were together. Ruby laughed loud, a laugh that rang
through the house and still filled my mind. I grinned, wishing I
could go back and be little again, hanging out in my Barbie nightgown until late morning, playing in Ruby's things, giggling and
laughing so hard as she tickled me that I couldn't handle the happiness in my belly anymore.

"A nice memory?" Max asked. He'd grown quiet and was staring at me inquisitively.

"Yes. A really good one."

We shared a smile, and I took a mental picture of the way his
thick eyebrows raised and lowered. Another really good memory I
wanted to keep.

"So shall we go up now? Or tomorrow?"

I wasn't afraid anymore. But I also didn't feel the need to rush
to the loft all of a sudden. What could be so scary about visiting an
old, dusty loft anyway? I wanted to see where my mother had lived
once and why Kitty had loved it so much.

"You know, I really want to go up now, but let's wait. I think
I've had enough surprises."

I didn't say it aloud, but I also wanted to be able to savor the
moment when I walked into the loft, whether I'd meet gloom or
joy. It would be like on Christmas morning, when I would go

straight to Kitty's bedroom and wake her up instead of going to the Christmas tree like most children.

I'd ask, "What do you think is in there?"

And she'd sleepily smile, get into her fuzzy blue robe, and join in the game. "I don't know, dear. What do you think is under that tree?"

"Maybe a doll with clothes and a stroller."

"You think?"

I'd nod my head vigorously, and she'd take my hand in hers. "Well, let's go see!"

And after five or so minutes of savoring what was to come, we'd shuffle into the living room where the tree stood lit. The lights would brighten with what seemed a glowing orb around each one and where I imagined the Christmas fairies themselves lived.

Kitty never got to sleep in on Christmas morning like some parents did. She was my only playmate, my best friend; she'd always been so patient about my need to savor the moment before I jumped in, and I'd wanted her to share every special moment with me.

If only Kitty could be here too when we first go into the loft. It was hers. She should be able to experience her homecoming before I made my own entrance into the past.

"Well," I said finally. "I think I want to wait until tomorrow to be fresh and awake when I experience this place for the first time."

Max nodded. "I agree. Besides," he grinned widely, "I know this great Mexican restaurant in Santa Rosa that would cheer up any *senorita.* You've never had enchiladas like theirs. I guarantee it."

"Oh really?" I countered. "Is this a place where you take all your senoritas?"

"Absolutely!"

I raised my eyebrows at him.

"No, just the worthy ones, like you and my mother."

I chuckled, wondering if I should believe him but not really caring in the least. I was, after all, the only senorita holding his hand at the moment.

After dinner, clutching our bags of hurriedly purchased toiletries and clean shirts, we said good night to settle into our own rooms at the hotel in Santa Rosa.

"Thanks for driving me around," I whispered. "Thanks so much for bringing me here and spending the day with me."

"I know this is an important weekend for you."

"Maybe the most important weekend in my life."

"So far." He grinned.

I blushed. I couldn't pretend anymore that he wasn't alluding to some kind of a future together; it made me feel elated and nervous at the same time.

"Will you be scared by yourself? Have you ever spent the evening alone before?"

"No, but I do sleep in my own room now instead of Kitty's," I joked.

He leaned forward.

I found myself hoping this would be the moment, but I think the whole hotel room atmosphere made him nervous. Instead of the kiss I expected, an end to the evening like in one of Kitty's old movies, Max gave me a quick peck on the cheek.

Nervous myself, I backed up a few inches.

Max smiled wryly. "Lucy, I really care about you a lot. But if I stay in your room another moment, I'm afraid I'll open doors that will be impossible to shut."

He tried to laugh nervously as he swallowed hard and looked down at me.

"How do you know the doors are unlocked?" I surprised him by saying.

He grinned, looking put in his place.

"I see what you're saying. I'm sorry. I didn't mean that you…"
He shook his head as if he realized at that moment that he'd blown
it. But he hadn't.

Max leaned forward and pressed his forehead against mine. I
noticed that his breathing was warm and shaky, the moisture of it
floating around my face, and I realized I was sharing his air when I
took a shaky breath of my own. He leaned even closer and brushed
his lips on my cheek, and I felt what it meant when romance nov-
elists said people could sprout wings and fly straight to the heaven
that Max was so sure was up there.

How in the world could I fall for this Cinderella fairy tale stuff?

Kitty had always called it silly, but now I think she had been
dishonest. Surely she'd felt like this with Blake.

I never knew a kiss could be so awkward and flawless at the
same time, his lips so warm and light on mine.

He held me at arm's length.

"Not bad for a youth pastor."

He laughed, that loud belly laugh I so loved, and pulled me
into a bear hug.

"Good night." He pecked me on the nose.

"Good night." The door clicked shut; I turned and threw
myself across the bed, my heart bursting with a sudden happiness I
hadn't felt since…well…never.

32

We'd agreed to wait on breakfast until we were in La Rosaleda the next morning. Nothing was open around the square when we got there except the B&B we'd visited the day before and a small breakfast café sandwiched between two souvenir shops: Carlos's diner.

I looked through the windows at the folks seated around the room, and it was obvious from the casual atmosphere that we were at a joint for locals. A bell above the door jingled as we walked in, and everyone glanced up from behind newspapers and over steaming cups of coffee. Some folks were dressed in what I presumed to be church clothes, and a few of the men looked ready for work with wrinkled, faded blue jeans and baseball caps lying beside their plates of half-eaten eggs and bacon. I smiled to myself as Max quickly pulled off his own baseball cap.

A man behind the counter nodded and pointed to a table near the window. Conversation soon resumed, and a perky waitress dressed in a blue dress uniform and an old-fashioned lacy apron approached us.

"I'm ravenous," Max said to me. "Will you think I'm a pig if I order the big enchilada breakfast?"

"No. But I will think you're a Mexican food fanatic since we just had it last night."

"I am," he confessed.

The waitress winked. "There's no better Mexican food in the Valley than here."

I had to smile at the faith she had in the little restaurant with its fifties-style furniture, sparse décor, and mustard-colored seat cushions.

"I'll just have the buckwheat pancakes and fruit," I said.

Max peered at the menu. "And they're made with organic ingredients. Kitty would be proud."

I grinned. "Do you have something against organic food?"

"No," he teased. "I'm just jealous of you and Kitty's discipline. You'd think as a youth minister, I'd be the one worried about taking better care of my body, a temple of God, you know." He winked.

I rolled my eyes and snickered at him, starting to get used to his wry sense of humor. The waitress was laughing, so somehow she got it.

"You probably shouldn't encourage him."

The man behind the counter, who I guessed was Carlos, delivered our food a few minutes later.

"What brings you around these parts?"

I let Max answer for us.

"Oh, just bringing my friend here to show her the roses."

The man, an elderly gentleman who looked to be of Latino heritage, said with an accent, "This is why we call it La Rosaleda. We are a city of roses! A beautiful place to bring your senorita."

I blushed.

"Yes," he continued, "a wonderful place to bring your sweetheart." He must have noticed the way I was staring down at my plate because he said, "You are sweethearts, no?"

I looked up and smiled. "Yes."

Max's hand slipped across the table and squeezed mine.

"A nice couple. I'll leave you two to enjoy your breakfast then. Enjoy your day in La Rosaleda too."

"Oh, we will, won't we, Maria?"

"I'm sure of it," I said, smiling at Max's use of my first name. It sounded familiar on his tongue.

The man turned back around. "Your name is Maria?"

"Yes," I said, a warning signal suddenly going off.

"Ah," he said. "The name Maria brings back so many memories. There used to be a little girl who would come here with her *abuelo* and mama, a young single mother."

My heart leapt.

"You don't say?" Max said.

"*Sí!*" said the man. He smiled to himself. "And they usually sat at this very table so the little girl could see the ducks. Precious child. But that was before the poor *niña's* mother passed away. We called her little Lucy."

A scene began to unfold in my mind. Ruby's laughter. The bell at the door tinkling when we walked in. My grandfather waiting for us at our table. Grandpa's lap, his kind face and gentle smile.

"The little girl and her abuelo always had the same," the man was saying. "Pancakes and strawberries. Same as you're having now, miss."

I looked up at him, and for a moment I thought there was recognition. He gazed out the window toward the fountain. "Sí...Lucy made everyone in La Rosaleda smile."

"What was the grandfather's name?" Max asked.

The man pulled his gaze away from mine. "Oh," he said. "The gentleman still comes in here occasionally. I don't want to spread his business to out-of-towners. You understand?"

"Definitely," Max said.

He looked back at me. "The little girl always looked like her mama. You kind of have the same look, senorita. Are you Mexican?"

"Somewhere back in my history, I am." I nodded, hoping he wouldn't ask too many questions. "It runs through my maternal side."

"I can see that. Anyway," he said quickly. "I'm holding you up from your breakfast."

"It's fine," I said.

He nodded and walked away.

Max and I leaned toward each other.

"I think maybe he recognized you. Or at least he might have been thinking something."

"I do look like my mother and Kitty, though not quite as dark in coloring."

He reached out and brushed one of my stray curls out of my eyes.

"What should we do?" I asked.

"We can't be paranoid. You aren't a criminal, and we aren't exactly in hiding. I just don't want you to be forced into being the lost granddaughter until you're ready. Let's just enjoy our breakfast."

Max didn't look as relaxed as he sounded. I followed his eyes across the room, where the man was on the phone.

"He could be on the phone to anyone, right?" I asked.

"Sure."

But I thought about what Max had said the day before, about possibly stirring up the town and those who might want to exploit my arrival. Or maybe those who might just want to let my grandfather know I was in La Rosaleda, especially if they thought I had been lost. Maybe the man knew my grandfather personally; if so maybe he would call.

"I remember coming here." I was so busy grinning with the joy that I didn't notice some of the other patrons staring at me. When I did, I looked down and focused on eating my pancakes.

"We must have come to La Rosaleda on weekends," I told Max as we walked down the sidewalk. "I remember now. I couldn't have been very old, but I remember!"

Just the very thought that my memories could come back one by one lifted my spirits, and I couldn't mask my grin any longer.

"I like seeing that smile. I hope I see it more often." Max ducked into a gift shop for some gum while I made a quick call to Susannah on my cell phone.

"I'm ecstatic for you!" she said when I told her about some memories returning, the fountain, and seeing the Rose House.

I brightened at her cheery voice. She could always be depended on to noisily and giddily share in anything good that happened to me. "And how is Mary?"

"Oh, Lucy, you would not believe it. She is out in my backyard sitting in a lawn chair with Maria, who keeps bringing her flowers."

A miracle.

"Lucy, I'm so glad I have you to share this with. You seem like a gift from God, girl!"

"I'm glad too."

"Oh, and Lucy…"

"Yes?"

"Savor this day. I haven't been able to get you off my mind this weekend, and I've been praying so hard for you. I just have this feeling that this day is going to be big."

I felt tenderness toward Susannah. "Thank you," I said quietly. "And thanks for praying. Between Ruby and you, I should be covered in prayer, huh? Do prayers carry through from the dead?"

I glanced over at Max, who was offering me a stick of gum and interested in what he'd just heard.

"Some people believe prayer transcends time," Susannah said. "All I know is that God can do anything."

"You people are either fanatics or fantastic," I said. "I wish I had your optimism."

"Don't admire us. Join us."

"We'll see." I laughed, knowing she was only half teasing.

We said good-bye, and I admitted to Max that I'd needed to hear Susannah's voice because I was nervous about the day ahead.

"Don't have doubts, Lucy. Be brave. You've got all the courage you'll need."

"What makes you think that?"

"I can't think of a better reason than the simple fact you're Kitty's granddaughter."

I smiled. Nothing could be truer. I linked my arm through his, and we walked toward the alley leading to the loft.

33

Lucy?" I was taken aback by the voice on the other end of the line.

"Kitty?" The number showing was from Dr. Larimer's cell. "What's wrong?"

Max and I stood outside the door we thought led up to the loft. We hadn't tried the key yet and stood staring up at the balcony fire escape. It was exactly as Kitty had described in her story, covered with flowers in shades of orange, yellow, pink, and purple spilling through the railings. The flowers looked amazingly well-kept, and I wondered if Blake was the one keeping them looking so lush.

"I'm fine," Kitty said, but her voice filled me with doubt. "Lucy, I am sorry. I'm so sorry for the horrid words I've said to you lately. I was just scared. I'm sorry for all my secrets."

Suddenly I couldn't think of a thing that Kitty should be sorry for. She had said nothing horrid to me, and after all she was my grandmother and a mother—the only one I had now. She could say what she felt, and what could she ever really do wrong when I knew it was from her heart? I missed Kitty, and the realization forced me to sink down to the stoop. Not having her here to do this, this reunion, filled me with a sick feeling in my gut.

"Lucy?" Her voice was worried.

"Oh, Kitty. Don't. You should know…"

She finished the thread. "…that you are my Lucy. Nothing can be between us, right? Not really."

I smiled to myself, wishing she wasn't so far away. "Never, Kitty."

"Lucy, I need to talk to you, dear. Not over the phone, but at length. I've kept so much of your heritage from you. I'm ready to let go."

"Kitty," I assured her, "I don't care about the estate if that's what you're thinking—I just want my family. And you are my family."

"Your heritage of family is exactly what I'm talking about. The Frances-DiCamillo heritage. Not the money, not the grapes, but the way of life, the family." She paused, and then her voice came as a whisper crackling across the phone. "The love and even the faith."

Kitty wants her faith back?

"Dear," she said. "I want you to know about your history. Maybe you will hate the vineyard, maybe La Rosaleda is too small for you, maybe you won't want the faith of our family, but you deserve the choice."

"La Rosaleda is not too small for me," I told her. "And, Kitty, I remember it. Not all of it yet, but it's a start. I knew the roses in the square and the ducks Grandpa and I fed, and I even remember the pancakes."

I heard a man's voice and a shuffle. Then Matt's voice came across the line.

"Lucy?"

"Matt! Is she okay? What are you doing with her? Is she crying?"

"Tears of joy, sweetheart. Tears of joy. No, she's with me in my car. Where are you?"

I took a deep breath, my head spinning. *Where do I begin?*

"I'm sitting outside what I think is the loft."

I heard him mumble something to Kitty, who told Matt loud and clear, "Where it all began."

"Lucy," Matt said, coming back on the phone. "We'll be in La Rosaleda in two hours. Kitty asked for you not to go in yet. She needs to go in first. Can you wait that long?"

"Tell her I can wait."

Max and I stood, and I started to hang up.

"One more thing. Kitty wants to know if the Irish restaurant is still there."

I glanced around. "No, I see only an antique store."

"That's too bad." Matt sounded truly sorry at this news.

"But there are fresh flowers growing on the balcony. Tell her."

Max and I walked through the passageway of alley shops in La Rosaleda, and I tried to imagine Kitty and Blake walking the same steps across these old cobblestones. We passed small residential homes surrounded with flower gardens showing off fall colors of gold, orange, red, and purple; I thought about how this was where Ruby and Kitty had each learned their love of gardening. La Rosaleda was like a vast garden really. In hanging baskets, petunias still bloomed wildly in pink, white, and purple; impatiens crept beneath trees and corners of the gardens, hugging the shade and endeavoring to bloom until winter would finally force them out.

As we left the neighborhoods behind, we found ourselves walking past fields of grapes. My thoughts were gliding along those grapes, wondering if these were Frances-DiCamillo vines. I was reminded of how much Kitty had once loved the grapes and wondered how she would feel when she saw them again. She had told me that she loved seeing the seasons until it was time for harvest; I wondered if she had marked all these years away by the seasons in her mind.

We found ourselves back in front of the Frances-DiCamillo vineyard gate. I stared toward the house. I marveled again at the stately trees and manicured lawn. Did my grandfather hire help to do this, or did he care for it all himself?

"It's hard to make out the detail from here," Max said, "but it's a beautiful house, isn't it? I love the front porch."

"What do you mean it's hard to make out the detail?"

"It's just so hard to make out from this distance."

Funny, I thought, then found myself filling in the gaps for Max. "The railing is painted white, with diamond-shaped gables. The doorbell is copper and shaped like a rose. I know I can count every little petal of that rose. And the door—the big door is dark red with a stained-glass window of grapes and vines in purple, red, and green. There's a big flowerpot in the corner filled with pink impatiens. Can you see them? They're always overflowing from that porch. The steps are painted gray with roses and grapes carved and painted along the edges, and the white columns have scenes of vineyard workers and fields carved into them. The floor of the porch is terra cotta with painted tile around the doorway and in each corner of the porch. Isn't it beautiful?"

Max turned me toward him. "I can't believe you got all that from that picture of you and Ruby with your grandfather. I didn't notice all those things."

"I didn't either. I just remembered."

I know who I am. "I am a DiCamillo."

"You are one brave woman."

I shrugged and shook my head. I didn't think I was brave. It was Max and Susannah who had made me brave enough to go back to La Rosaleda. "It means a lot to have you here."

"I'm glad I could be here. But as much as I love being here with you, I'm thinking that when Kitty and Dr. Larimer get here, I should leave."

My face fell.

"Only if you think that's okay," he said quickly. "I just think it might be more comfortable for Kitty if she doesn't have an audience of nonfamily observing her every move, because if you can get her to Frances-DiCamillo, it's going to be something very private."

I nodded, feeling disappointment but knowing that he was right. This was something Kitty and I needed to do on our own.

I leaned over and gave him a peck on the cheek.

"When the semester is over, maybe we'll all be out here to see my grandfather." I gestured toward the gates. "Maybe he'll cut off that chain and toss away the sign."

Max looked in the distance, at the house. "He's been waiting, Lucy, and I don't think those will be the only chains tossed away today."

Thirsty and a little tired from our brisk walk, Max and I fell into a comfortable silence again. I couldn't stop thinking about all the possibilities, doubts, and fears.

I recalled the prayer Freda had whispered to Kitty and wondered, Could everything that has happened lately be an answer to my great-grandmother's prayers? That was such a long time ago.

I thought of the prayer I'd said with Ruby every night. The one Kitty had tried to say with me but hadn't known how. It had been our secret prayer, something special Ruby and I took turns praying each night. First me, then Ruby. Now I knew that Ruby had shared Max's faith.

"Okay?" Max asked.

I opened my eyes and nodded.

I thought about Kitty's words on the phone. *Your heritage.*

Max squeezed my shoulders, lending his strength to the power of my memory. I didn't feel like saying anything at all for a while, and I knew he didn't expect me to. I would tell him my thoughts in time.

34

We stood outside the place my grandfather had scrimped and saved to rent, and eventually bought for his beloved Kitty. But Matt and Kitty weren't there. I was anxious to see inside this place where it all started, so I called Matt's cell phone to see how close they were.

"They'll be in La Rosaleda in ten minutes!" I snapped shut my cell phone.

Max gave me a quick hug. "This is more than exciting, Lucy. This is a miracle."

"I know!"

I felt disappointment run through me when he reached into his pocket and pulled out his keys.

"I really better go."

I groaned.

"Will you be okay?" He grasped my hand.

"I will. I'll just sit here for a few minutes and collect my thoughts."

"Call me if they don't show up or something."

"With Kitty, that could be a possibility."

He laughed with me. "Well, bye," he said, fumbling with his keys, dropping them on the ground between us.

He bent down to get them and as he rose, I was in his arms again. This time the kiss was filled with purpose.

He stared at me when we separated, a serious look in his eyes.

"I want to be with you. Just you." His words came in a nervous rush, and I had to focus to make them out.

"I understand if you aren't ready," he said. "So just think about it."

I laughed softly, remembering the night before.

"Your manners have greatly improved," I teased. He attempted a laugh, but I could see the nervousness blanketing his face. "I don't need to think about it," I said, my words a whisper.

He gently shushed me.

"Don't rush this. So think about it, talk it over with Kitty and Susannah if you want, and we'll talk more this week."

I smiled inwardly as he pulled me into his arms one more time.

After Max left, I sat back down on the porch and closed my eyes as I let the memories of visiting La Rosaleda with Ruby wash over me. I felt Ruby's love like I hadn't felt since the day she died. It poured around me, and I felt her hands on mine. I felt her arms wrapping around me, I heard her laughter, and I felt her soft cheek pressing up against mine. I heard her call me mija, I smelled the scent of roses as we played hide-and-seek around the Rose House, and I remembered her chastising me when I stole some grapes out of the vineyards.

My mouth still watered thinking of how sweet the grapes were. I hadn't realized that grape juice was dribbling down my chin, and my full cheeks with puckered lips gave me away. I remembered being confused because even though I seemed to be getting in trouble, Ruby was laughing.

Memories of my grandfather were surfacing too. I couldn't recall everything, but I remembered sitting on his lap on the front porch and watching Ruby and someone—had it been Matt?— walking hand in hand down the driveway toward the gate.

In my mind I was a little girl hiding from my grandfather

among the huge barrels and tanks. And when he caught me, he'd tickled me for so long that my glad shrieks had sent one of the workers into the building to see if I was okay. He'd been so delighted by my uncontrollable laughter that he'd gone to fetch some of the other workers to come see. I remembered that as my laughter continued to erupt, everyone laughed with me. It had made it even harder to stop laughing.

There had been a lot of laughing when Ruby was in La Rosaleda, I remembered.

As memories flooded around me, I recalled how sometimes Kitty and Ruby argued.

"We're mother and daughter," Ruby would say, as if that explained everything.

"Dear, why the tears for your Kitty?"

I looked up and quickly brushed the tears away. Kitty was moving toward me, and I'd been so lost in my memories that I hadn't realized she and Matt would be walking up any minute.

"Come here, dear." I walked quickly to her and held her as tightly as I could without crushing her. I was reminded again of how thin she'd grown in the last few months from all the worry. At least she was thin for Kitty, who could never be described as skinny.

She looked radiant, and she didn't seem to be leaning on her cane as heavily as usual. I hadn't seen her in two days, but it was the longest I'd ever been away from her in my life, and the sight of her buoyed my grin.

"Oh, my Lucy, Kitty is here. Don't you cry anymore."

I stood back, and that's when I remembered Matt. He was standing a few feet away, as if he didn't want to be in the way.

"Thank you for bringing her."

"Anything for you."

I walked toward him. He pulled me into a bear hug and tousled my hair.

"What about your family?"

"My family is fine. In fact, they're looking forward to meeting you."

The idea made me smile. Otherwise I would be a secret from them, and I was tired of secrets.

When I turned back toward Kitty, she was staring up at the balcony.

"Your grandfather kept the flowers up."

"He did more than that. Wait until you see the vineyard."

She quickly turned around to face me. "Have you been?"

"Only to the front gate, twice."

"Well," said Kitty in her matter-of-fact voice, "let's see the loft."

I helped her up to the first step, but before she did anything she paused and looked pointedly at me.

"Dear," Kitty said, "Matthew told me about your tests."

I glanced at him, shocked. *He told her?* "I'm sorry, Kitty," I started to explain.

She jiggled the doorknob, and I remembered the key. Digging it out of my pocket and handing it to her, I tried to decide how to explain my dishonesty.

"You are a grown woman, Lucy. You can do what you want. But," she said, turning to face both of us, "I wish I'd been more honest with you. I could have told you the truth long ago. I guess I was just being very selfish and afraid."

She was looking at Matt, who looked confused.

"I was afraid you'd try to take her from me, and she was all I had."

I watched Matt's face, and a flash of what looked like pain darkened his face but left as he watched her speak in the straightforward tone I'd come to depend on with Kitty.

"I'm sorry, but I should have told you years ago." She looked from me to Matt.

I stood gaping, suspended in the moment, as if the rest of the world was moving around me but we were all frozen in place. Any minute Kitty would say something, and whatever bound me in place at that moment would melt when she opened her mouth—and I knew I would crash down. I had no thought yet where I might land.

Matt and I both watched Kitty jam the key into the lock. She glanced back at me and smiled; then she turned the key. She lifted her proud chin. She sniffed, as if testing the air before proceeding.

"Matt is your father."

I gasped anyway.

"Ruby made me promise not to tell," Kitty said. "I think now that she's gone, it's my decision whether to continue keeping that secret, especially considering the situation we now find ourselves in." She turned back toward her present task.

The knob gave way easily, and she pushed open the door. A firm grip on her cane with one hand and the railing with the other, she tapped up the stairs, one step at a time.

After a long moment, I felt his hand on my arm, but I still didn't budge. When he walked around in front and tipped my chin up with his fingers, I recognized him somehow. He was my father. He'd always been there, in the gardens at La Rosaleda, at my grandfather's house at Frances-DiCamillo, in the hospital when I wanted to kiss Ruby good-bye, when I'd nearly suffocated from tossing away my inhaler. He'd been posing as my friend all those years, but secretly he was being the only kind of father he'd been allowed to be to me.

He leaned down and kissed the top of my head.

I wondered if he would take me into his arms, but he seemed

to be tentative, like he thought I might run away if he dared touch me more.

I wasn't sure what to do, but I leaned closer to him and pressed my cheek into his chest. That's when he finally wrapped his arms around me. As the realization hit that his tears were for me, the moisture of my own gathered in the corner of my lips, and if I hadn't tasted the salt of them in my mouth, I might have believed my imagination was only toying with my heart. And when I felt my father's tears dampening my cheek, I let my arms reach up, joining him in a long-awaited embrace of more than just flesh and blood.

It was a moment I never wanted to leave, but after a while he held me out and his eyes scanned mine.

"I have been waiting for you to know the truth for so long."

I clung to him as he pulled me close.

"You've always known, haven't you?"

"I knew. No matter what anyone said, I knew it."

Matt and I were interrupted by a sound, unmistakably coming from Kitty, floating down to us through the fire escape window.

We froze, and both our faces mirrored heartrending expressions as the cry turned into weeping.

35

We opened the door to the scent of roses, a huge cluster of them in ruby shades arranged in a vase on a wicker coffee table. I picked up a card sitting beside the freshly filled vase that read:

> Kitty Cat,
>   Welcome home.
>   Blake

I handed the card to Matt. Blake had been expecting her, and I wasn't sure how to feel—or how Kitty was feeling.

Her crumpled figure at the window seemed to be filled with grief, happiness, and something I couldn't really identify, perhaps regret. She hugged a crumpled quilt to her chest and cried deep sobs into it.

I walked across a shining oak floor toward her, noticing fresh roses all through the loft. The place was spotless: immaculately cared-for houseplants, a shiny wood floor, a fireplace mantel sprinkled with black-and-white photos—one of Blake sitting on a tractor, one of Kitty in an old-fashioned striped swimsuit at the beach, the one of their wedding day, and one of Ruby at about age four with impossibly curly hair tousled over her shoulders.

Matt left us and walked into the kitchen area, taking note of more flowers and a small basket of tea next to a teapot that looked ready to be used.

I sat down tentatively beside Kitty, who handed me the quilt. We spread it in the small space between us.

"Exquisite," Matt whispered, returning.

Exquisite barely covered the handwork of the intricate design. I recognized the house from Frances-DiCamillo, surrounded by layer upon layer of hills, each decorated with winding vines and the tiniest stitching in the shape of grapes and leaves. Above the house was embroidered the date of Kitty's birth, and below the house were the words WELCOME HOME, DAUGHTER, and in the corner was embroidered I KNEW YOU WOULD COME. MOTHER.

I tried to hug Kitty, but she turned away, staring out the window. Matt and I left her and walked down the stairs. Hand in hand, we sat on the stoop and talked until she was ready to come down.

Matt whistled teasingly when nearly two hours later Kitty left the loft and met us on the stoop. She'd pulled her hair back into one of the many scarves I knew she carried in her purse. I stared at a locket hanging from her neck I'd never noticed before; it looked new.

She dismissed Matt's whistle with a wave. "Don't be silly. I'm an old woman." She saw my eyes fixed on the locket and opened it for us. A miniature picture of Ruby as a child smiled at us, and it was like looking at a reflection of me.

"I'm ready," she said.

"Ready to see Frances-DiCamillo?" Matt asked.

"Ready to see Blake. And ready to see the roses he planted for all his girls." She winked at me, and I felt a swell in my throat.

"Would you like to get something to eat first?" Matt offered. "Maybe take a few minutes to collect yourself?" I noticed his effort to keep a straight face, and I covered my own mouth with my hand.

She chided him. "Matt Larimer, I've been collecting myself for more than thirty years. I think I've had long enough."

During the short drive, I tried to prepare Kitty about the chain and sign, careful not to let on about rumors that Blake had somehow murdered Ruby—but Matt filled in those details.

I politely said nothing, musing at how he was falling into the whole parent thing quite easily with me.

Kitty scoffed, "My husband no more murdered my daughter than you did, Lucy."

I was caught off guard and didn't respond to her. She twisted around in her seat and jabbed her finger toward my face.

"You didn't kill your mother, so stop thinking it's your fault. Ask your doctor, or I guess I mean your *father*…whichever one you'll believe the most."

I said nothing. How was it that Kitty could pick my brain so easily, as if I knew nothing? And how was it that she was so often right?

"It's true," Matt said softly. "It wasn't your fault, Lucy. Ruby's air passages had been closing up more often than normal for several weeks." He stopped, struggling, and took a deep breath.

I breathed in with him.

"I'd seen her in my office twice the week before, and we'd been discussing a change in treatment. Maybe a stronger medicine. Maybe wearing a face mask when she gardened. Maybe weekly treatments at the hospital. We never got to try them."

I wasn't responsible for Ruby's death. How many times would I need to tell myself that before my mind really accepted that it wasn't my fault? I leaned back and closed my eyes, feeling the familiar place in my chest tighten from the power of this idea and reached into my pocket for my own inhaler.

I stared out the window at the grapes we passed and the tangle of vines. I wasn't surprised when I heard Kitty's sharp intake of breath. We had turned the bend to see the Frances-DiCamillo estate, but at the entrance I had to gasp too. The KEEP OUT sign was gone, and the gate was swung wide open. How could that be?

Matt stopped the car in front of the gate and said nothing.

"Did you call ahead or something?"

He nodded. "Yes, but Blake already knew. Some friends from town saw you and Max at breakfast this morning."

I didn't respond. I wasn't sure if I should have felt thankful or betrayed.

"It really wouldn't have mattered anyway," Matt said. "He's been preparing for this since the day Kitty left."

Kitty struggled for the door handle. "I want to walk."

Matt put the van in park. and we jumped out at the same time, both rushing around to open Kitty's door.

"I only need one of you to help," she fussed. "Matt, go turn off your car."

"Shouldn't I move it out of the entrance?" he asked.

"No. I don't think we want company. Leave it where it is, blocking the gate."

Matt smiled as he shut and locked the door. We both tried to hold Kitty's elbow for the long walk down the driveway, but she shrugged us away.

"I'm not that old," she said. "It's bad enough that I have this stupid cane. I don't want him to think I'm an invalid, and I've walked this driveway so many times you wouldn't believe it."

I patted Matt's arm. *He must see Ruby everywhere,* I thought. I did.

"Ruby is among us." It was as if Matt had read my thoughts.

"I remember walking to the gate with her." I smiled at the new memory. "It was something we did sometimes in the morning. To the gate and back…"

"I feel her in these hills," Matt said. "We used to walk them, me and your mother. She loved the vines."

I remembered walking them with Ruby too. "She's in them, don't you think?"

"Yes," he said, slowing his pace. "Even though she's gone, her life makes a difference for us every day." He paused, looking out over the vineyard hills. "I used to think her time here had been so senseless, so short. She smiled on us for a while, and then her death was so fast."

"How could you think that?"

He shook his head. "I don't know. I guess I just had so many regrets about my time with her that I forgot about her smile."

"But that's why you can't forget her," I said.

He smiled. "Yes, that's why. She left an imprint on my life. And here you are."

My father, Matt, was right. Ruby was among us.

"She has come back to me just since I've come back to La Rosaleda," I said.

"My Lucy," Kitty said, turning back to us. "Ruby has always been with you, even when you couldn't remember." Kitty tapped her chest. "She was in here all along." She tapped her temple. "You were focusing too much on up here, trying to figure it all out for yourself."

I looked at Kitty, her smile intense despite the nervousness I knew filled her about encountering Blake again. Her eyes were bright, and in them I saw my mother. The likeness between the two was so similar, and I knew Ruby would have looked like Kitty as she aged. I ached to collect my paints and fill in my portraits of both of them but, most intensely, of myself.

I looked at the house before me, and I wanted to paint all three of us, standing on the porch together.

I watched as Kitty turned and walked more deliberately toward the house.

I could tell by her limp that she was starting to get tired, and we were only halfway down the driveway. But she wouldn't accept help.

"I have to go to him on my own," she said. "You can't do it for me."

We got closer, and Kitty started walking faster.

"I see him," she said. "He's waiting for me!"

She quickened her pace, digging her cane into the ground more strongly with each step. I watched her and she seemed so young, even with her limp. Her favorite red dress, woven with white roses, flowed loosely around her knees; the red made her sparkling brown eyes and hair, streaked with silver now, seem richer.

Suddenly I caught the slightest movement on the porch from within the shadows of one of the columns.

Grandfather.

"Blake!" Kitty cried.

Blake Birkirt sat up straight, looking around as if just roused from a nap in his white rocking chair all these years. His eyes fixed on Kitty, and he froze for an instant, then stood slowly and leaned on the banister next to him. I saw the recognition flash across his face as he rushed down the porch steps. His beloved Kitty waved a handkerchief and called his name. She looked as she had so long ago, beautiful in that red dress that reminded him of when they were younger. Only now Kitty leaned on a cane. Compassion washed over Blake, and he made his way down the stairs to meet her so she wouldn't have to walk another step alone.

Later he would tell us how he had almost given up after so many years. But today his friend Carlos from the café had handed him back hope when he called after meeting a girl in his diner. The girl was named Maria, and she looked just like Ruby.

When Blake saw Max and me staring through the gate of La Rosaleda, he knew, but it was Matt's phone call that confirmed it. Kitty was on her way back.

Kitty stopped walking when she saw him coming toward her. She threw aside her cane and held her hands out to him. Blake swept his wife up and swung her in circles.

I knew Matt and I had faded into the background, but it didn't even matter. I was holding my father's hand, and my family was complete. I could wait.

Only those who have experienced a reunion of some kind, a for-giveness, a redemption, can picture the visage of relief, pain, youth, age, sadness, and joy unleashed all at once. It was a reawakening, a gulp of life, new life, like the breeze sweeping through the valley across Frances-DiCamillo in the spring, rippling the vines as if to renew the promise of treasured fruits previously thought lost.

Blake had led Kitty slowly to the Rose House, and they disap-peared behind the canopy of red petals and blooms, thorny stems, and leaves. It was there that Kitty confessed her biggest secret to Blake.

When Blake's face clouded, Kitty saw his grief. It matched her own, and she felt that all her fears had been realized. Her dreams withered around her. She had lost her dignity, her mother and father, Ruby, and now she would lose him too. She should have lis-tened to her own voice, which had whispered warnings despite her longing to go home.

She turned to leave through the canopy of roses she had just entered; they were so misleadingly fragrant around her. She had tried and had feared the worst, but Lucy's optimism, as bright as the roses twining around her, had buoyed her spirits to hope.

Her reunion was marred more with thorns than wrapped with the rich velvety blooms behind her. She knew she hadn't deserved any sort of welcome, but she hadn't expected it would end like this.

36

Kitty reached for the banister to guide herself down the porch steps, and Blake put his hand over hers. She stared down at it, roughened and worn, and saw the lost years in every line and callus mapped across his skin. She didn't want to lose more.

She stood still, unsure of the possibility that his presence behind her spoke, uncertain if she could trust him. She had taken Ruby from him, taken his life in so many ways, and she knew deeply that she didn't deserve to be at La Rosaleda—or with him—anymore. Now maybe he knew it too.

"How could you have carried that ache with you all these years, Kitty? Have you forgotten about grace?" Blake's hand wrapped around her waist, and his breath touched her cheek. She felt young again, ready to receive what she'd so longed for on the dreadful day he'd found her arguing with Mike in the vines.

"For a long time," she replied, "I did."

"It wasn't your fault."

Her breath caught in her throat.

Then Blake's deep voice, stronger than before, said, "I could never blame you for something someone did to hurt you. I am so sorry, Kitty, so sorry I didn't believe you when you said it wasn't like I thought. I should have known. I did try to find you, knowing there had to be another explanation, but, well… I wanted to tell you I was sorry. I am sorry, Kitty, for not protecting you."

In that moment she realized she had been angry at him all

those years. She'd needed to hear him say he was sorry, not only for not protecting her, but for not being on her side. Now that he'd said it, all she could think about were their choices—how he'd been as much a victim as she and how their choices had unfairly decided things for Ruby. Through desperate choices, everyone had in some way become prisoners to the past.

One terrible act had shaped her family's estrangement; Kitty would give anything to go back and change it. A sob escaped her throat.

"No," she whispered in reply. "I'm the one who's sorry. I'm sorry for leaving and not allowing time to run its course. I should have trusted you and told you the truth then."

"Has it run its course?" he asked quietly.

Kitty turned slowly to face Blake. His eyes were the same as before, more tired, but they still held a light. She desperately wanted to have that light illuminate her life again.

So when he pulled her into his arms, she knew she wouldn't sacrifice another day. "I love you," she whispered.

"I would like to say the same," he said. "But love all by itself doesn't even begin to cover it."

When Blake and Kitty stepped from the house of roses, it was my turn to embrace my grandfather, and I felt suddenly shy and unsure. Kitty stood with her arm through Matt's, and they both smiled encouragement at me.

I could tell Kitty wanted to rush over and save me from my insecurities, but instead she gripped Matt tighter…or was it that he was gripping her firmly, holding her back so I could do it alone?

Was I all he'd hoped for? Would he be proud of me? This must have been how Kitty felt too.

"Lucy girl," my grandfather said, holding me at arm's reach. He stared into my eyes, making me feel like he was searching for something recognizable in my soul.

What was he looking for? I watched the corner of his mouth twitch and was amazed as he blinked away tears too. My soul reached out to him.

He embraced me then. "My Lucy, you're finally home."

We walked to the great house and through corridors that twisted and turned until we stood in the bell tower.

"The bell house," Kitty announced.

"This bell has not rung since the day you left." Blake nodded to Matt and then to a long rope hanging from above.

Matt clasped the rope and pulled as the clang of the bell filled the room and echoed out over the hills. Ruby's hills.

Even then I imagined that folks from miles around stopped picking in the fields, memories of Frances-DiCamillo rich in their minds. Maybe people stepped onto their porches and remembered the wedding between Blake and his beloved Kitty. Those in La Rosaleda might have remembered the night the bell rang during and after an earthquake when a baby named Ruby was born.

Matt pulled the rope now with a force I wasn't sure was from joy or grief. Perhaps both. I leaned forward to help him and was surprised by the tug upward of the rope, by the sound now resonating through the tower and echoing across the vineyard. The weight of it was heavy, and I don't think I could have rung it myself, save for the help of my father and the presence of my grandparents—and the knowledge of another who was ever present with me.

As I pulled I felt an unraveling around me, a breaking free from the past. With it came the memory of Ruby's smile, her laughter ringing through me, filling my mind.

"Welcome," I whispered, my words lost in the ringing all around us.

There had been a homecoming at Frances-DiCamillo.

READERS GROUP
GUIDE

Readers Group
Guide

1. Chapter 1 begins, "The first person to hold Ruby was the
   last person to let her go. That was her mother, Kitty."
   What do you think Lucy meant by this statement?

2. Lucy, by no choice of her own, has never lived in a
   traditional family, but she has been sheltered first by
   Ruby and then by Kitty. Do you think Lucy calling her
   mother and grandmother by their first names indicates
   a healthy adaptation of family for her? a confused sense
   of family? What is the relationship of Lucy to her
   mother, Ruby? to her grandmother, Kitty? How are
   these different or the same?

3. What is the significance of the names Lucy and Ruby—
   in general and specifically to each of them?

4. What do you think of Kitty's question upon Ruby's
   death? How can God allow terrible things to happen?
   Why doesn't he protect children from horrible things?

5. What questions and issues does Lucy tuck away when
   Ruby dies? Do you think Kitty's efforts to keep so many
   secrets were to shield Lucy from pain or to protect herself? Were her intentions noble or selfish?

6. Could Lucy have become whole without learning the
   truth about Ruby? about Kitty? Why or why not? Did
   Kitty ever become whole?

7. Each woman in the novel has artistic talents and interests—piano, art, quilting, literature. What parallels do
   you see between Lucy's artistic pursuits and those of

Ruby and Kitty? And what parallels do you see in other aspects of the story?

8. Why do you think Lucy and Kitty keep so many of Ruby's things?

9. How might the references to air and breath and to Ruby's and Lucy's asthma inhalers be symbolic?

10. When Lucy, with Max, first sees the fountain in La Rosaleda, how might its streams be meaningful to her?

11. What does the scenery in the novel—gardens, vineyards, La Rosaleda—evoke? Do the roses and vines bear any significance to the rest of the story? What parallels do you see?

12. In the end, what did Lucy mean by "a homecoming"?

TINA ANN FORKNER writes contemporary fiction that challenges and inspires. Raised in northeastern Oklahoma, she graduated with honors in English from California State University, Sacramento, ultimately settling in the wide-open spaces around Cheyenne, Wyoming, where she now resides with her husband and their three children. Tina spends her time working on novels, writing articles, and serving on the Laramie County Library Foundation Board of Directors. *Ruby Among Us* is her debut novel.

Visit her online at www.tinaannforkner.com.